A WISH AT THE DAFFODIL CAFE

A MRS WISHMORE NOVEL

ALIX KELSO

LAKE FALLS PUBLISHING

A WISH AT THE DAFFODIL CAFE

Cover design by dmeacham design

ISBN (paperback): 978-1-913098-08-7

Published by Lake Falls Publishing

PROLOGUE

Mrs Wishmore gazed out at the scenery passing by beyond the windows as the bus trundled along the narrow roads and country lanes. The morning was bright and sunny, the temperature was already high, and it was set to be a beautiful summer's day. The Hampshire countryside rolling by outside was vibrant with green grass and old trees in full leaf, and Mrs Wishmore had lost count of how many pretty chocolate-box towns and villages she'd passed through already on this journey.

She sensed it would soon be time to get off the bus and that her destination was drawing near.

After navigating a long stretch of country lane lined with high hedges, the bus slowed down as little cottages began appearing alongside the road. A sign appeared outside the window, announcing that the town in which they'd arrived was called Willowbridge and that visitors would find a very warm welcome should they decide to stop.

The bus rounded a corner and a pretty village green came into view, dappled with sunlight falling through tall trees. An ancient church stood to one side of the green, its spire reaching up into the blue skies. The town's high street rose along an incline, lined with quaint shops and cafes and cosy pubs. Flower-filled baskets hung from every lamppost along the street, and people meandered here and there, a mix of townsfolk and tourists who were visiting this attractive little hideaway on the edge of the glorious Hampshire New Forest.

Mrs Wishmore smiled and understood that this little town was where she was supposed to be and that this was where she was needed.

Clutching her large blue handbag to her side as she rose from her seat, Mrs Wishmore pressed the button to request a stop. The bus driver pulled over to the side of the road, stopping at the bus shelter at the top of the high street. Mrs Wishmore thanked him and climbed out, taking in a deep breath of the fresh air and enjoying the sunshine on her face. She unbuttoned her red jacket on account of the warm morning and loosened the light scarf draped at her neck, her soft cloud of silvery hair catching the edges of the material as she pulled it free.

Mrs Wishmore glanced around at her new surroundings. Willowbridge was a pretty place. There was no doubt about that. It would be lovely to spend some time here, she decided, doing whatever it was that she'd come here to do.

Further along the high street, there was a small garden tucked beside the pavement, comprising a few flower tubs and a scrap of lawn beside an old wooden bench. Mrs Wishmore bustled towards the bench and sat down and watched the world around her. People came and went from the shops and cafes. Passers-by smiled and nodded hello as they strolled by on the pavement. Two confused American tourists wandered towards her and unfolded a map, asking if she might help them find their way to the nearby walking trail they wanted to explore. Although Mrs Wishmore had never been to Willowbridge before and knew nothing of the local area or the location of the walking trail, she helped them just the same and soon pointed them in the right direction.

But she knew only too well that she hadn't come here just to help a couple of lost tourists. There was a far bigger job for her here somewhere. Quite what that job was, though, she didn't yet know.

On the pavement that ran alongside the little stretch of public garden where Mrs Wishmore sat, a woman pushing a buggy passed by. A toddler lay sleeping inside the buggy and a small boy of maybe three or four was skipping beside his mother as they walked. When the woman's phone rang, she came to a halt while she dug the phone from her bag and answered it, gesturing to her son to stand still while she spoke to whoever had called her.

The little boy spun around a few times on the pavement, making Mrs Wishmore laugh softly at his attempt to entertain himself. When the little boy spied her on the bench, he gave her a curious look as he contemplated her.

Then, inevitably, his eyes grew wide. Throwing a glance up at his mother, still engrossed in her phone call, the little boy turned and stepped closer to Mrs Wishmore.

"Hello there, young man," Mrs Wishmore said as he stared at her.

"Hello." His eyes narrowed in concentrated study before a surprised smile lit up his expression. "Are you Mrs Santa Claus?" he whispered, awestruck.

Mrs Wishmore laughed. "No, I'm not Mrs Santa Claus."

"You look like her."

"Well, that's a lovely compliment, thank you."

The boy peered at her some more. After looking back over his shoulder to where his mother stood a few steps away, still talking on the phone, he reached out and pressed his chubby fingers against Mrs Wishmore's arm, as if testing something. "Are you a fairy?"

Mrs Wishmore laughed again. "No, I'm not a fairy, either."

A warm breeze tumbled through the flower beds in the little garden, making the roses that grew there nod their heads.

"Are you an *angel?*" the little boy asked, his voice filled with wonder as he gazed up into Mrs Wishmore's face.

Mrs Wishmore smiled. Children always seemed to understand, or at least understand some of it, and that knowledge always brought warmth to her heart. Children saw things that grown-ups could no longer see, things that grown-ups no longer *wanted* to see.

"Why don't you run along back to your mother?" she told the boy, still smiling as she ruffled his hair.

The child beamed up at her before hurrying off to catch up with his mother, who'd finished her phone call and was already gesturing at him to come back over and telling him not to annoy the nice lady sitting on the bench minding her own business. The boy waved at Mrs Wishmore as he followed his mother on their journey along the high street, and Mrs Wishmore waved back.

Pleasant though the interaction had been, it wasn't what had brought her here. For now, she had to be patient and wait for the sign that would signal the start of her work. Sometimes that sign came in the rustle of a breeze moving through the trees. Sometimes it came from the laughter in a dog's bark. Sometimes it came through the uncertain smile of a stranger, or a burst of song, or the tinkling of bells, or any number of other ways.

Mrs Wishmore's gaze settled on a pretty little café across the road with a soft yellow painted façade and cheerful tubs of flowers standing beside the bevelled glass windows. The sign above the old-fashioned glass-and-wood door read

Daffodil Café and in smaller lettering below it announced, *Tea – Coffee – Home Baking*. Friendliness and welcome and comfort rolled off the little café in waves.

Along with something else, too. Something darker. Mrs Wishmore closed her eyes and let her mind listen. She soon heard the truth that lay beneath the surface of the café's good cheer.

There was heartbreak there. Heartbreak and confusion and fear.

Mrs Wishmore wondered if this was why she'd come here. Perhaps someone in the Daffodil Café needed her help.

If so, then they only had to ask. But as Mrs Wishmore knew only too well, people weren't very good at asking for help when they needed it most.

But she was sure she'd found herself sitting on this bench across from the Daffodil Café for a reason. She would understand the sign when the time was right.

All she had to do was listen for the sound of a wish being sent out into the world, a wish that seemed utterly hopeless, at least to the person who was making it. Only then would her work begin.

Mrs Wishmore sat back on the bench and waited.

CHAPTER ONE

Lisa Morgan slid the freshly baked carrot cake into the café display case and felt a punch of satisfaction at how good it looked. The sweet buttercream icing swirling across the domed surface of the sponge was dreamy and delicious, and the cute icing-sugar carrots decorated on top were fun and whimsical. Beneath the icing, the sponge was warmly spiced and as light as a feather, even if she said so herself. Baking always made everything feel just a little bit better, which was why Lisa loved doing it and why she'd done quite so much of it today.

As she positioned the cake amongst the other treats that she'd already baked and set out in the display case, two wrinkled faces appeared on the other side of the counter and grinned at her through the glass. Mildred Marsden and Jean Compton were regular customers at the Daffodil Café on Willowbridge high street, and were probably her most cheerful customers, too. Today, of all days, Lisa was happy to see their friendly smiles.

"Hello, ladies," Lisa said, moving to the counter beside the display case to avoid squinting at her customers around piles of muffins and teacakes. "How are you both today?"

"We're just fine, dear, aren't we, Jean?" Mildred said, and glanced at her friend for confirmation.

"That's right, we're both quite fine," Jean agreed. "And having just spied those cherry scones in the display case, we're now very happy indeed."

"We love your cherry scones, Lisa," Mildred said. "So light and fluffy."

"Thank you, Mildred," Lisa smiled. "I appreciate that."

"We'd like one scone each," Jean said, unwinding the silk scarf around her neck and unbuttoning her anorak. "With butter and jam. And a pot of tea. We're gasping for tea, aren't we, Mildred?"

"Always."

Lisa smiled at the elderly women and plated their scones. She'd long since given up reminding them that they didn't have to place their order at the counter and that she'd come and serve them at their table. The two old ladies liked to inspect the daily offerings in the café display case, sometimes lingering for several minutes as they debated their choices, and once they'd made up their minds they simply informed whoever was working behind the counter what they wanted before shuffling off to a table. During the four years she'd owned the Daffodil Café, Lisa had learned the habits and idiosyncrasies of her regular customers, and happily accommodated them. Keeping her customers content and feeling valued was what kept her in business.

"Grab a seat, ladies, and I'll bring over your order right away," Lisa said with a smile.

Usually, the two women would do just that. But today, they remained on the other side of the glass display case, exchanging concerned looks with one another as Mildred patted the big leather handbag clasped at her side and Jean fidgeted with her scarf.

"We hope you don't mind us saying this, Lisa," Mildred finally said, her expression anxious. "But we want you to know we are thinking of you today."

"We can't imagine how difficult this day is for you," Jean said, folding and refolding her scarf. "But you are in our thoughts and our prayers."

The sight of the two concerned faces across the counter made Lisa's throat squeeze with emotion. She'd hoped to get through today without anyone mentioning that this was the one-year anniversary of Peter's death, because she wasn't sure if she'd be able to hold herself together if anyone brought it up. But the occasion going unnoticed was highly unlikely in the little Hampshire town of Willowbridge, where most of the locals knew one another and where Lisa was a well-known face thanks to the high esteem in which people held her lovely Daffodil Café.

Peter had naturally been on her mind since the moment she'd opened her eyes that morning—very early that morning—but the busy work of the café had so far kept her raw feelings at bay. Now, an image of Peter flashed in her head, with his dark good looks and irresistible smile, and Lisa felt her heart ache with loss.

The two old ladies across the café counter were looking increasingly alarmed at her continued silence. Lisa pulled herself together and offered them a smile.

"That's very kind of you, ladies," Lisa said. "Thank you."

"It was such a terrible thing that happened," Mildred said, shaking her head sadly. "Just terrible."

"Indeed it was," Jean nodded. Her gaze stayed on Lisa's for a moment, and Lisa wondered if she realised she was struggling against rising emotion, because Jean quickly added, "But let's not keep the girl from her work any longer,

Mildred. There's a free table by the window. We should grab it before someone else does."

Lisa watched the two old ladies make a beeline towards the front of the café, where they deftly intercepted another customer who'd been about to claim one of the prized window tables that boasted a view of the pretty village high street. The comedy of the moment cut through the thick grief that had engulfed her, and she was grateful for it. Although this couldn't be anything other than a day filled with poignant memories and deep sorrow at the loss of the fiancé she'd adored, she refused to spend it as a sobbing wreck.

Peter wouldn't have wanted that.

She tucked a stray strand of her auburn hair back into the clip from which it had sprung free, and busied herself with preparing the scones and tea things for Mildred and Jean. The cherry scones stacked inside the display case did look lovely today, Lisa thought with a smile, and she doubted the batch she'd baked would last much beyond lunchtime.

As it was late June, tourists and visitors were already finding their way into the sweet little town nestled on the edge of the New Forest, eager to enjoy coffee and cake and the quaint village setting before exploring the many attractions of the national park. There was fierce competition throughout the summer months between the Willowbridge locals and the tourists in order to bag the best tables in the Daffodil Café and indulge in Lisa's baked goods before they sold out. As she spied a clutch of folk disembarking from a minibus across the road and ambling towards the café windows to peer inside, while adjusting the cameras strapped around their necks and the rucksacks on their backs, Lisa decided it was just as well she'd been up even earlier than usual this morning, adding to the café's baking stock. She had a feeling this would be a busy day.

Seeing the cake display case filled with tasty treats always made Lisa feel content and accomplished. She liked knowing she was putting good things out into the world for people to enjoy.

"Shall I write the lunch specials on the board, or do you want to do it, Lisa?"

Turning, Lisa saw the café's cook, Fiona, hurry through from the kitchen with a scrap of paper clutched in her hands on which she'd written the daily specials. While Lisa was the Daffodil Café's baker, she happily delegated the cooking to her capable chef and friend who'd been with her since she'd first opened the café. Fiona kept the menu simple but delicious, and the soups, sandwiches, and pasta salads that comprised the Daffodil Café's offerings kept the customers satisfied and coming back for more. Lisa appreciated Fiona's skill and speed in the kitchen, because it meant she could spend more time baking and serving, both tasks that she loved.

"Go ahead write up the specials," Lisa replied. "I'm busy finishing this order for Mildred and Jean, and there are already new customers sitting at tables and waiting to be served."

With a nod, Fiona uncapped the blackboard pen and began printing out the specials she'd chosen for the menu. "Are you okay today?"

"I'm fine," Lisa said, grabbing cups and saucers for the old ladies.

Fiona turned from the blackboard and gave her a concerned look. "If you need to take time off today, I can cover for you once it's quieter later and Vicki's here," she said, referring to the café's lunchtime waitress who was due to start her shift shortly.

"I'm okay, really," Lisa said.

And then proved the exact opposite of what she'd just

claimed by dropping a teacup to the floor, where it smashed against the tiles with a noisy crack that had the café's customers turning towards the counter to see what all the fuss was about.

"For goodness' sake," Lisa muttered, grabbing the dustpan and brush. "I've got butter fingers today."

As she swept up the broken teacup, Lisa felt Fiona's gaze on her, and when she turned to dump the smashed cup into the bin, her friend's face was etched with worry.

"You don't have to pretend to be brave today, Lisa," she said quietly. "It's okay to feel sad. Losing Peter was a terrible thing, and it's okay to need some time by yourself."

"I know." Lisa tucked the dustpan away and let out a breath. "But I just want to stay busy and get through today and then put this anniversary behind me."

Fiona didn't look convinced by the logic of this explanation, but she turned back to the specials board anyway and started writing again. Lisa was glad to have side-stepped the issue for a second time in as many minutes. She wished she had better control over her emotions when it came to thinking about Peter. And she wished, too, that the emotions she felt today weren't so confusing.

Her heart hurt for the man she'd loved, and she knew she ought to talk about him and the accident that had claimed his life, because talking would help her deal with the anniversary and the loss she'd suffered.

But talking might also force her to think about the confusing emotions that had crept into her heart lately and which only made her feel worse than she already did.

"Listen, I know this might not be the best day to bring this up," Fiona said, stepping back from the menu board, which she'd now filled with the daily specials. "But do you remember a few weeks ago I mentioned an old friend of mine, Tim? Well, I bumped into him last night at the pub and he asked again if you might be interested in going for a drink with him sometime?"

Lisa froze at the coffee machine where she was filling a teapot with hot water. She remembered the photograph Fiona had shown her on her phone of this friend of hers, Tim, when she'd first mentioned him. He looked like a nice guy—attractive and fun, judging by his laughing face in the photo, and she knew he must be a decent person if he was a friend of Fiona's.

In the same instant as she remembered the photo Fiona had shown her of Tim, she thought of Peter and felt that stab of loss all over again.

"I wasn't going to say anything today," Fiona continued, now looking awkward as she fidgeted with the blackboard pen. "But Tim's really keen, and if you're as okay with today's anniversary as you say you are, then I saw no harm in bringing it up, and—"

"Uh, I don't think so, Fiona." Lisa set the teapot on the tray and added a little jug of milk. "I'm not interested in dating or seeing men or anything like that."

Fiona nodded, and Lisa couldn't help but notice the mixture of sadness and doubt on her friend's face.

"I shouldn't have mentioned it. I'm sorry," Fiona said. "I just thought—"

"It's fine." Lisa smiled and picked up the tray. "I'd better get this order over to Mildred and Jean before they expire from lack of tea."

With a forced laugh, Lisa hurried from the counter to deliver the old ladies' order, then jotted down new orders from the customers who'd arrived in the last few minutes and made themselves comfortable at empty tables. Busy, busy, busy, that's how Lisa liked it, and that's how she wanted it today. Staying busy would stop her mind from wandering, and once the lunchtime rush began later, she hoped it would stop Fiona quizzing her any further about things she simply didn't want to talk about.

As Lisa returned to the counter to start work on the new orders, she glanced at her watch and saw it was already past eleven o'clock, which meant that Vicki, the lunchtime waitress, was now officially late for work.

Frowning as she cut two thick slices of Victoria sponge, Lisa wondered where Vicki could have got to. She was a reliable member of staff and hard-working, and Lisa could count on the fingers of one hand how many times Vicki had been late in the three years she'd worked at the café. The young waitress, who at twenty-one was Lisa's junior by a decade, was saving for a flat deposit so she could move out of her mother's house, and had even volunteered to cover shifts for the other Daffodil Café waitress, Helen, who was currently staying with her elderly father in Cornwall for a couple of weeks while he recovered from an operation. Running a small café and keeping it properly staffed was no simple matter, as Lisa had learned since starting the business, and she relied on her small team of hard-working women to turn up on time and pitch in and make sure that the customers were happy.

After tragedy had struck last year when Peter died, Lisa's staff at the café had been her rock. The doors would have stayed closed for far longer than they had but for Fiona, Vicki, and Helen mucking in. Which was why Lisa couldn't help but wonder why Vicki was so late for work today. It was completely out of character.

As Lisa set plates of cake onto a tray and eyed yet another set of customers walking through the café door, she only hoped Vicki would arrive soon before they found themselves overrun.

Just then, Lisa's phone rang. Grabbing it from her apron

pocket, she felt a rush of relief as Vicki's name flashed up on the screen.

"Vicki, thank goodness it's you," Lisa said when she answered. "We're filling up fast here and I need help feeding these hungry customers."

"Oh, Lisa!" Vicki said on the other end of the line, her anxious voice causing Lisa to stop slicing the fruitcake she'd been cutting for a customer. "I can't come in today!"

"What's happened? Are you all right?"

"No, I'm not," Vicki said with a sob. "I had an accident and fell down the stairs at my mother's house."

"Oh, no!" Lisa gasped, startled by this news. "Are you badly hurt?"

There was another muffled sob down the line before Vicki answered. "I thought I'd broken my ankle, but I'm at accident and emergency and they say it's just a very bad sprain, although it feels much worse. I'm covered in bruises and still waiting for the painkillers to kick in, but I'm more shaken up from the fright I got when I tumbled down the stairs. I'm sorry, Lisa, but I can't come in to work. They're bandaging me up and I have to keep off my feet for a couple of weeks to let my ankle heal. I can't put any weight on it at all."

"You poor thing," Lisa said, feeling terrible for her unlucky waitress. "You're not at the hospital by yourself, are you?"

"My mum drove me here. Lisa, I'm really sorry about this."

"Don't be silly. You've had a nasty accident and you have to concentrate on getting better."

"But the café must be filling up by now," Vicki said. "How are you even coping by yourself?"

"I'm fine," Lisa insisted, and allowed herself a wry smile. How many times had she said *I'm fine* today? Too many.

Especially considering she wasn't fine at all, and was simply too stubborn to admit it to anyone. "All that matters is that you're okay."

"But now you don't have any waitresses. I'm laid up and Helen's off in Cornwall visiting her dad. What'll you do?"

Lisa frowned in concentration as she attempted to organise her scattered thoughts and come up with a plan to deal with the staffing emergency. "I'll ring the temping agency and see if they can send someone. And I still have the number of that girl who worked here in the spring while you were on holiday. I'll phone and see if she's interested in covering your shifts. And if we can't find an extra pair of hands today, Fiona and I will just have to make the best of it."

Even as she said it, she felt panic rise as yet another set of customers walked through the café doors. The place was close to capacity already, and once the lunch orders started pouring in, they'd be swamped.

"The doctor's here to talk to me," Vicki said. "I'd better get off the phone."

"Take care Vicki, and just concentrate on getting better!" Lisa said and hung up.

Glancing over the counter, Lisa saw new customers slide into the last empty table in the café. Other customers who'd already been waiting were throwing impatient looks in her direction. Although the Daffodil Café was small, with just ten tables in the place, it wouldn't be easy to serve everyone by herself. She had to find someone else to lend a hand and help her through the next couple of hours.

Lisa had hoped today would be busy. But perhaps not quite as busy as this.

Grabbing her phone again, she scrolled through her contacts until she found the number for the waitress who'd worked holiday cover during the spring. But when the young woman answered the call, she told Lisa she was already working at another job and wouldn't be able to help. Disappointed, but not surprised, Lisa was about to phone the temping agency she'd used in the past, but before she could find the number, a scowling customer at a nearby table waved her hand in the air and clicked her fingers.

"Yoo-hoo!" the woman called out. "I've been waiting for ages. Are you coming to take my order, or shall I just leave?"

Other customers turned to look at the woman, and Lisa could tell by their expressions that they were wondering the same thing.

"What's going on?" Fiona said, emerging from the kitchen with cheese toastie orders she'd prepared and looking around in confusion at the unhappy customers. "Hasn't Vicki turned up yet?"

"She had an accident and hurt her ankle," Lisa said, stuffing her order pad and pen into her apron pocket and grabbing the tray laden with plates of cake and cappuccinos. "She's at the hospital, and although she's fine, she won't be coming in. So, until I can find a moment to phone the temping agency and get some help, it's just you and me."

Fiona's face paled as she peered out at the waiting customers. "Right. Well, we'd better get stuck in."

"That's the spirit," Lisa said, hoping she sounded more certain than she felt. "This is nothing we can't tackle with some hard work."

But as she hurried off to deliver her order of coffee and cake, and apologise to the customers who were waiting, before returning to the counter to cut more cake and prepare more hot drinks, Lisa couldn't help but think that she'd need more than hard work to get through today.

She'd need a miracle.

CHAPTER TWO

Jake Reid only realised there were splashes of red paint all over the front of his white shirt when two of his students began sniggering and pointing with their paintbrushes across the table on which they were decorating a banner for the forthcoming Willowbridge School summer fair. Glancing down at the red splodges on the white shirt fabric, Jake sighed and grabbed a rag to dab at the splatter, which only made the smudges worse.

"Oops, Mr Reid, you've made a right mess of yourself," laughed one of the pupils, Bradley, a cheeky lad of thirteen who liked to tread a fine line between charming ruffian and irritating nuisance.

"Looks like it," Jake grinned, scrubbing pointlessly at the smudges before tossing the rag back onto the table. Looking around at the teachers who were supervising other student projects, he noticed that none of them had got covered in paint, which sounded about right. Jake had always been clumsy, and it stood to reason that he'd be the only one who'd have to change his shirt. "Are you two nearly finished with that banner?"

The two pupils sniggered again and gestured to the last section of painting still to be done. The banner would hang above the coconut shy that the boys and a few of their classmates were organising for the summer fair. The annual event was a staple of the Willowbridge secondary school calendar. Besides raising much needed funds for the school, it was also fun for the students to help put on the show and work together on the many preparations that were involved. Jake, too, liked being involved in the organisation of the stalls and activities. He enjoyed helping his students discover their skills and talents outside of the classroom, and seeing the less academically gifted kids find other ways to grow and thrive.

On a sunny June morning like this one, being outdoors in the playground was much more fun than being stuck in the staff room marking student assignments, of which Jake had a towering stack to get through. Getting covered in red paint wasn't part of the plan, but he only had himself to blame. Just because he was in his mid-thirties didn't mean he was too old to get carried away with a spot of fun painting.

After helping the boys finish the final flourishes on their banner, Jake checked his watch and saw it was time to clear up before the lunch bell rang. The other teachers were already corralling their students and carting folded tables and craft supplies back into the main building.

"Okay boys, I think this banner is officially done," Jake said.

"It looks good, sir," Bradley grinned. "Especially where you leaned on the edge and smudged the coconut I spent ages painting."

"Well, now you can call yourself a post-impressionist," Jake said, and hid a smile when the boy looked non-plussed. "Get this lot cleared up and don't forget to leave the banner lying flat on the floor when you take it into the gym hall to dry."

Bradley and his friend cleared up their paint things and negotiated the task of carrying their completed banner into the gym hall. As they walked off sideways like a couple of awkward crabs, Jake saw his colleague and friend, Marie Hanlon, crossing the playground towards him. They taught together in the history department, and had also lived at opposite ends of the same street in Willowbridge for the past six months since Marie and her husband, Scott, bought a house there not long after they got married.

"You're messier than the kids, Jake," Marie laughed as she took in his paint-streaked shirt. "What are we going to do with you?"

"Nothing, I'm beyond all help," he shrugged. "Good thing I keep a spare shirt in the boot of my car."

Marie shook her head, still laughing softly. "My lot have already taken their stuff back inside, so I'll give you a hand with this table."

Together, they folded the trestle table and carried it towards the doors and the school annex storage cupboards beyond.

"Got any plans tonight?" Marie asked as they walked.

"No, why?"

"Scott's asked a couple of friends over for dinner. I thought you might like to join us."

Jake glanced over his shoulder and saw the all-too-innocent smile on Marie's face. "One or more of these friends wouldn't happen to be single women, would they?"

"Actually, now that you mention it, I think Scott might have said that Emily wasn't seeing anyone right now, and... what? Why are you shaking your head?"

"Stop trying to set me up with random women, Marie. I'm not interested."

"Not interested? What are you talking about? You haven't

even met Emily yet. She's perfectly nice. And gorgeous, too, just for the record."

"I'm sure she is. But I'm still not interested. So, if the only reason you were inviting me over was to pair me off with someone, then I'll pass, thanks."

"Jake, for god's sake, you're not even going to give her a chance?"

They'd reached the annex doors. Jake nabbed a passing pupil and got him to hold the door open while they shuffled the heavy table inside.

"Marie, I don't want to get involved with anyone right now," he said as they walked along the corridor, his voice quieter now to avoid being overheard by any nosy pupils who'd be thrilled to hear all about his love life—or lack of it—so they could broadcast it all over social media. "I'm happy by myself. Is that so hard to understand?"

"Are you happy, though?" Marie's tone was now more concerned than jokey. "You spend too much time by yourself, if you ask me."

"I spend half my life in this school, dealing with hormonal teenagers and insane educational bureaucracy, so I wouldn't exactly say I was a hermit, Marie."

"You know what I mean."

He did know. He just wasn't about to admit it.

"Just because you've had a run of bad luck in the girlfriend department doesn't mean you should give up," Marie continued.

Jake couldn't help but laugh. A run of bad luck was putting it mildly. In his entire life, he'd never kept a girlfriend for longer than six months. They always seemed to get fed up with him eventually, or find someone else more interesting to be with, which wasn't surprising. After all, wasn't he a man who'd just got himself covered in paint because he was too easily distracted by the fun of colouring-in letters on a coconut shy banner? What kind of woman wanted to be in a relationship with a man like that?

No woman he knew, that was for sure. He was clumsy and unfashionable and a bit of a dork, if the truth be told. And at thirty-four, Jake knew it was too late now to change who he was, even if he'd wanted to. Which he didn't, come to think of it.

Well, maybe he'd change the clumsy part, given the chance, if it meant he didn't have to traipse around splattered with paint and enduring the giggling and snorting of his teenage students. He could probably do without that.

"I'm not giving up on anything," Jake said to Marie. "But I'm also not looking for someone either."

"You're discouraged," Marie said.

"No, I'm a realist," he replied with a grin.

Once they reached the storage cupboard, they hauled the folded table into place beside the others and headed back along the corridor.

"Are you sure you won't come to dinner?" Marie asked.

"Thanks, but no. I've got a tonne of marking to finish tonight, and if I get through it all, my reward is a nice long walk in the park with Ruby to enjoy the summer's evening."

Marie sniffed. "And I'm making my famous lasagne, too. Are you sure you don't want to come over?"

"I'm sure."

She let out another annoyed sniff. "I can't believe you're turning down my lasagne in order to mark homework and walk your dog."

"Save me some, and I'll have it for dinner tomorrow."

"If there's any left," Marie said, pretending to be in a sulk. "I'm on canteen supervision duty this lunch time, so I'd better get over there and keep the barbarians in line while they queue for their chips. Let me know if you change your mind about tonight."

Jake waved her off and turned for the exits that led to the staff car park in order to fetch a clean shirt from his car. He wouldn't change his mind about Marie's dinner offer, even it meant missing out on her freshly baked lasagne. He wasn't in the mood to sit through polite conversation with yet another new female who'd be interested in him only for as long as it took her to decide they'd be better 'just as friends'. Jake had heard that phrase enough to last him a lifetime.

Being single was the right move. Sensible. Safe.

The more he thought about it, he realised he was lucky to be alone. Romance was more trouble than it was worth when Jake knew it only ever ended in him being politely but firmly dumped.

In fact, it would take some kind of miracle to convince him to get involved with another woman ever again.

CHAPTER THREE

For a while, Lisa thought they might keep ahead of the chaos threatening to engulf the Daffodil Café.

In a flurry of non-stop activity, customers were served and fed and watered and kept happy. The café regulars offered kind smiles of encouragement as Lisa dashed around the tables, and Mildred and Jean gave her hand a friendly squeeze as they left after paying for their tea and cherry scones, telling her to keep her head up. The unfamiliar faces of the tourists looked a little on the grumpy side because of the slow service, but soon softened once they were tucking into their cakes and toasted sandwiches.

But as noon approached and the lunch orders piled up, Lisa realised she'd been kidding herself. Even with Fiona working flat-out in the kitchen and helping to clear tables when she had a spare second, it was impossible to stay on top of the work. It took three people to run the café during the busy lunchtime service. Two just wasn't enough.

As orders piled up, and tables remained uncleared, and customers scowled and checked their watches, Lisa felt it all unravel. No matter how fast she worked, it wasn't fast enough. When she finally grabbed a few minutes to call the temping agency and ask about finding an emergency waitress, they told her it would be several hours before they could get someone to the café, by which point, Lisa knew, the lunch rush would be over.

She'd wanted today to be busy. Instead, it had descended into disaster. The chaotic café, combined with the anniversary of Peter's death, crashed together in a sudden rush of emotion that caused hot tears to brim in her eyes. For one silly moment, Lisa imagined asking the customers to leave and locking the doors behind them, before retreating to her tiny flat upstairs and spending the rest of the day there, crying and feeling sorry for herself. It was a stupid idea, granted, but an attractive one just the same.

Standing beside the hissing coffee machine, Lisa closed her eyes and whispered, *I wish I knew how to get through this day. And I wish I was strong enough to cope.*

Behind her, the café door opened, the little bell tinkling as someone made their way inside. Lisa turned at the sound of the bell, which seemed much sweeter and melodic than usual, its bright and cheerful tones taking her by surprise. An older lady stood in the open door, glancing around the busy café with a smile on her face. She wore a cheerful red jacket, with a big blue handbag hooked over her arm. The midday sun outside framed her in the doorway, making it look like her soft cloud of silvery blonde hair was glowing.

The woman took in the occupied tables and the waiting customers and then looked over at Lisa. For reasons Lisa couldn't explain, seeing the smile on the woman's face made her feel just a little less wretched and overwhelmed.

"Hello!" the woman said, still smiling as she made her way towards the café counter. "It's certainly busy in here."

Lisa watched the older lady amble further into the café. After a moment, Lisa realised she was staring at the woman, as if transfixed, although she couldn't understand why. She was just another customer, after all.

"The table by the door will be available soon," Lisa said as she finished the order of lattes she was preparing and slid them onto a tray. "Just grab a seat when it's free and I'll be right with you."

The woman glanced at the table Lisa had indicated, where a couple were draining their coffee cups and pushing back their chairs. While the woman in the red anorak hovered near the table, Lisa hurried off to serve the lattes and apologise to the customers for their delayed soup orders. But when she spun back to the counter to start work on the next set of hot drinks, she stopped in astonishment at the sight of the older woman in the red anorak stacking dirty dishes at the newly empty table near the door.

"Oh my goodness, let me do that." Lisa hurried over, embarrassed that things had got so bad in her café that the customers now felt obliged to lend a hand.

"It's no trouble, dear," the woman said with a chuckle. "After all, that's why I'm here."

Lisa frowned. "What do you mean?"

The woman gave a bright smile. "Well, I'm here to help in the café. You're short-staffed, aren't you, and in need of a waitress?"

Lisa stared at the older lady standing before her, piling empty cups onto a tray. "Are you from the temping agency? But they said it'd be a couple of hours before anyone could get here."

"And yet, here I am." The woman laughed and carried the tray of dirty cups and plates behind the counter. "Now, where shall I hang my jacket and handbag? And where do you keep your clean aprons?"

Lisa looked again at the bustling woman with the silvery blonde hair. She had to be somewhere in her mid-sixties at least, Lisa guessed, and although she never judged a book by its cover, she wondered if the slightly rotund older lady was up to the challenge of rushing around in a busy café during the hectic lunch service. Both Vicki and Helen, her current waitresses, were in their early twenties, and the staff sent to her by the agency in the past had all been young, too. When Lisa had advertised for waiting staff in the past, she'd never received applications from anyone over the age of thirty-five.

As if the older woman had read her thoughts, she waved a hand in the air and let out a soft chuckle. "Now, I know what you're thinking. I'm not exactly what you were expecting. But let me assure you, I have plenty of experience and know what I'm doing. And I'm far more sprightly on my feet than might seem at first glance." She laughed again, the sound warm and somehow musical.

"Oh, I wasn't thinking that at all… I mean…" Lisa blushed as the words died in her throat. "I'm just surprised the agency found someone to come here so quickly. Willowbridge is out of the way and they said it'd take time for a temporary waitress to get here."

It had only been thirty minutes since she'd phoned the agency. What if they'd sensed her desperation and fobbed her off with someone who wasn't up to the work, while still charging her an arm and a leg for their services? The last thing she needed today was yet more mayhem in her café.

"When I learned you were in a difficult position on account of your usual waitress suffering an unfortunate injury, I was keen to lend in a hand in any way I could," the woman said, her expression kind. "But I understand that you want to be certain about anyone who works here in your lovely café. So perhaps I can help for the next couple of hours to get you through this busy spell, and if you aren't happy with my work, I'll be on my way with no hard feelings. What do you say?"

The woman held out her hand. Lisa knew she'd be crazy to turn her away, even if her lingering doubts about the woman's waitressing skills remained.

"That sounds fair," Lisa said.

Reaching out, Lisa shook the woman's outstretched hand. Relief rolled through her, warm and welcome.

"In that case, I'll get started," the woman said, hanging her jacket and bag in the cupboard Lisa pointed out near the kitchen. "As you're too busy to show me the ropes behind the counter and on the cash till, I'll stay out front with the customers, taking orders and delivering food and clearing tables. How does that sound?"

"It sounds perfect."

Just then, the coffee machine began making the beeping sound that indicated the coffee beans were running low, and an annoyed-looking customer at a table near the window waved his hand in the air and demanded to know when his ham and tomato sandwich would be ready.

"My first customer of the day needs a few soothing words," the older woman said as she tied a fresh apron behind her back. "Let's see what we can do to keep him happy."

Lisa watched the woman bustle out into the lunchtime fray. She was about to deal with the beeping coffee machine when something occurred to her.

"Oh, wait!" Lisa called out to the woman. "I don't even know your name!"

The woman turned and let out a soft laugh. "I'm Mrs Wishmore, dear. Doris Wishmore."

"Nice to meet you, Mrs Wishmore. I'm—"

"—you're Lisa Morgan, owner of this lovely Daffodil Café," Mrs Wishmore interrupted with a smile. "I already know that, dear."

Of course, the agency would've explained to the woman

who she'd be working for. Lisa wondered why she hadn't already realised that. Still, something about the older lady and her sudden appearance in the café left her feeling just a little discombobulated. She wasn't sure why. After all, what she needed most of all right now was a spare waitress to save the lunch service from disaster.

If Mrs Wishmore detected her puzzlement, she showed no sign of it, only giving an easy smile before walking off to deal with the lunch crowd. Lisa watched her go and thanked her lucky stars that the temp agency had sent someone to help. Only time would tell if this Mrs Wishmore knew what she was doing when it came to the hectic world of waitressing.

Watching as the older lady expertly handled the customer who was complaining about having to wait so long for his sandwich, Lisa decided that for now, at least, Mrs Wishmore was exactly the help she needed.

The coffee machine beeped again, louder this time.

"All right, keep your screws on," Lisa grinned at the machine, and got back to work, feeling a little lighter in her heart than she had before.

WITH HER NEW waitress holding her own amongst the customers of the Daffodil Café, Lisa got through the lunchtime service with surprising ease.

Mrs Wishmore served the hot drinks Lisa prepared behind the counter, ferried food orders from the kitchen, cleared tables, and took orders from newcomers as they arrived. With the customers well cared for, Lisa focused on working the coffee machine and plating cakes, dealing with bills and payments, and helping Fiona in the kitchen during the peak hot food pinch point. Once the lunch rush was over,

Mrs Wishmore dealt with the afternoon coffee-and-cake crowd with ease, leaving Lisa free to help Fiona load the dishwashers before the cook's shift ended at three o'clock, and sort out the many other jobs that came her way during her busy shift as café owner.

By the time four-thirty arrived, and Lisa was wiping down surfaces and preparing to close for the day, she was more than a little shocked at how well everything had turned out, considering the tight spot she'd been in just a few hours earlier.

"I think we ought to congratulate ourselves on getting through this busy day," Mrs Wishmore said cheerfully as she collected the last of the dirty dishes. "We did rather well, considering this is the first time we've worked together."

"You saved the day, Mrs Wishmore," Lisa smiled. "I would've been lost without you."

"I'm sure you would've found some other solution to your staffing crisis. You strike me as a very resourceful young lady."

"I didn't feel resourceful this morning when I discovered I was short-staffed," Lisa admitted. "I even considered closing the café for the day. I couldn't see how we'd get through the lunch period without disappointing our customers."

The older lady's gaze held hers for a moment and then flicked down to where Lisa was twirling the diamond ring that hung on her necklace. Lisa hadn't even realised she'd been fidgeting with it until Mrs Wishmore glanced there.

"That's a beautiful ring you have there on that necklace," Mrs Wishmore smiled, carrying her tray of crockery to the counter. "I can't help noticing how that sweet diamond catches the light and sparkles."

Lisa lifted the ring between her fingers and looked at the diamond set in the white gold band. A memory pushed into her mind of Peter, down on one knee and opening a velvet jewellery box and offering the ring to her like a prayer.

"I imagine you prefer to keep the ring on a necklace while you work," Mrs Wishmore said. "I can only imagine how upset you'd be if it slipped off your finger in the rush of loading dishwashers and cleaning tables, not to mention all the endless handwashing involved to comply with hygiene regulations."

Lisa stared at Mrs Wishmore for a long second, realising that the older woman of course knew nothing about Peter or the accident. It was tempting to keep things that way. But she found herself shaking her head.

"The reason I don't wear it is that it's an engagement ring," Lisa said softly. "At least it *was* an engagement ring. My fiancé passed away."

Mrs Wishmore's smile dissolved. "I'm so sorry to hear that. My goodness, what a tragedy." The older lady reached across the counter and gave Lisa's arm a gentle squeeze. The tender gesture brought an odd sense of comfort that Lisa wasn't expecting.

"It happened a year ago," Lisa said, even although she hadn't planned to keep talking about it. "He was in a road accident. A lorry driver crashed into the back of his car on the motorway. The driver hadn't been paying attention and didn't realise the traffic had slowed. Peter died instantly. I've been dreading today for weeks, because it's the anniversary of Peter's death. It's hard to believe he's been gone so long already. Sometimes it feels like it just happened yesterday."

Lisa realised she was still toying with the diamond ring on her necklace, and let it fall back beneath her shirt. She offered Mrs Wishmore an apologetic smile.

"Sorry, I'm sure you don't want to hear any of that," she said with forced cheerfulness and picked up the tray of dirty dishes Mrs Wishmore had set on the counter.

But the older lady shook her head. "You suffered a dreadful loss. And on the anniversary of losing someone you loved, it would be strange if he wasn't on your mind. If you'd like to talk about him, I'd be happy to listen."

As Lisa looked into the older lady's bright blue eyes, she almost wanted to talk to her about Peter. Almost. But if she started talking about the man she'd loved with all her heart, the man she'd agreed to spend the rest of her life with, she'd turn into a sobbing wreck.

"You're very kind," Lisa said and smiled. "But I'm visiting Peter's mother this afternoon once I've closed the café, and I ought to get moving. She lives by herself and has no other family nearby, and I don't like thinking of her alone on the anniversary of Peter's death."

Mrs Wishmore gave a nod of understanding. "That's very thoughtful of you. I'm sure she'll appreciate seeing you on this difficult day." She glanced around the café and pointed to the brush she'd fetched from the store cupboard and propped against the wall. "Let's get this place ship-shape so you can get on your way."

It wasn't long before everything was cleaned and tidied. Lisa was glad Mrs Wishmore didn't need much hand-holding when it came clearing up. Lisa remembered her earlier worries that the woman might not be up to the challenge of busy café work and scolded herself. Mrs Wishmore could run rings around any of the other temporary staff Lisa had hired to work in the café over the years.

As they grabbed their jackets and bags from the cupboard in the corridor, Mrs Wishmore gave Lisa a serious look. "Did I pass the Daffodil Café test? Shall I come back to work tomorrow?"

"Mrs Wishmore, of course you should come back tomorrow," Lisa grinned. "If you don't come back, I'm not opening up."

Mrs Wishmore laughed. "I think we'll make a good team, you and I, while your regular waitress recovers from her injuries. And as your excellent cook, Fiona, handles the kitchen so beautifully, things were far less hectic than I imagined."

"You saved me from disaster today. You're an angel."

At this, Mrs Wishmore let out a warm laugh, her eyes sparkling, and turned for the café doors. They stepped outside together, where Lisa found the high street quiet now that most of the shops and cafes had closed for the day. A warm breeze moved through the trees on the village green further up the street, and the sky was a deep cloudless blue. Summer had arrived in all its glory, and Lisa was glad of it on this day that might otherwise feel much too dark.

"Can I give you a lift somewhere, Mrs Wishmore?" Lisa asked as she locked the café doors and pulled down the shutters.

"Thank you, dear, but my bus is due and it takes me straight home."

"In that case, I'll see you tomorrow. Can you come in for eleven o'clock?"

"Of course." Mrs Wishmore's smile dimmed a little. "I hope your visit with your fiancé's mother goes well this evening. I'll be thinking of you both."

"Thank you, Mrs Wishmore."

"Goodbye, dear."

With a wave, Lisa turned towards the lane further along the street that led to the rear of the building where her car was parked. She'd already made it past the hair salon three units down from the café when it occurred to her that she hadn't even taken a note of Mrs Wishmore's phone number, or any other details for that matter. It was a silly oversight, no doubt caused by the upheavals of the day, but one that would annoy her all evening if she didn't correct it.

Turning on her heel, Lisa glanced along the high street in the direction she'd just come from, but saw no sign of Mrs Wishmore walking along the pavement. The older lady was far more sprightly on her feet than she'd given her credit for. Lisa hurried past the café towards the bus stop at the other end of the high street, keen to catch up with her new waitress.

But when she rounded the corner, the bus stop was empty. A bus was disappearing up the road, and as Lisa caught her breath, she wondered how on earth Mrs Wishmore could have made it up the high street so quickly and already boarded a bus.

It seemed impossible.

Shaking her head in bewilderment, Lisa retraced her steps down the hill, her mind already turning to the sombre visit that lay ahead with Peter's mother.

CHAPTER FOUR

Jake was sitting at his kitchen table, approaching the halfway point in the pile of marking he was tackling, when his little dog, Ruby, trotted through the open back door from the garden and deposited a saliva-covered tennis ball on the tiles at his feet. The scruffy terrier looked up at him in expectation, her tail wagging.

"Ruby, let me mark one more of these homework assignments and then I'll throw your ball," Jake said.

In response, Ruby nosed the grubby tennis ball closer to his feet and sat down, turning her big brown eyes up to him and letting out a little whimper.

"You really know how to wrap a man around your finger, Ruby. Or around your paw." Jake grinned and rose from the table, grabbing the damp tennis ball from the floor. "Okay, let's have a break and play."

The dog dashed outside to the garden with an excited yap and began spinning around on the grass, waiting for Jake to toss the ball. The back garden was small, but that never dimmed Ruby's enjoyment of the chase. Jake knew she liked it when he lobbed the ball into the bushes so she could scurry around in the shrubbery after her quarry. Although he paid a dog-walker to come every weekday and exercise Ruby while he was at work, Ruby still looked forward to time off lead, running around and playing. Jake looked forward to it, too. There was nothing quite like seeing the excitement on a dog's face at the prospect of chasing after a smelly ball to remind you to take pleasure in the small things in life.

Jake tossed the ball across the lawn and laughed as Ruby barked and raced after it, her little legs flying and turning her into a black-and-white furry blur.

It was a gorgeous evening outside, the midsummer sun still high and warm. The air smelled sweet thanks to the roses his neighbour grew on the other side of the fence, and Jake could hear kids kicking a football around in one of the gardens further down. Ruby trotted back with her tennis ball clamped in her mouth, and Jake threw it again. Hearing the little dog's excited barks as she scampered off, Jake lost all enthusiasm for going back inside and completing his marking chores. He glanced up at the periwinkle blue sky and drew in a lungful of warm evening air.

"Ruby, let's have a walk to the park while it's still nice and light," he said. "The marking can wait until later."

As if understanding every word, Ruby dropped the tennis ball on the lawn and hurried back inside the house. Jake found her in the hallway, staring at the front door and waiting for her lead to be attached to her collar.

"You really are a comic, Ruby," he said, grabbing his keys and phone. "And I probably shouldn't talk to you quite so much as I do. It's not like you're going to answer, are you?"

Ruby barked, making Jake laugh. For such a tiny dog, she had a huge personality. His last girlfriend had been more upset about parting ways with Ruby than she had about ditching Jake. Quite what that said about him Jake chose not to think about.

The park was a ten-minute walk across Willowbridge from his house, and when they got there Ruby sped along the path that wound around the flower beds, eager to say hello to the other dogs she knew and who were also enjoying an evening stroll with their owners. Once they got closer to the stretch of woodland near the eastern edge of the park, Jake unclipped Ruby's lead so she could run around. She was a well-behaved mutt, and Jake had taught her recall not long after adopting her from the local rescue centre two years ago so that she could explore the world under her own steam.

As Ruby trotted off to sniff at a tree trunk further off the path, Jake's phone beeped. When he checked the screen, he saw a message from his friend, Marie.

This is what you're missing, Marie had written and attached a photograph of a glorious lasagne she'd obviously just pulled from the oven. Jake grinned at the photo, and couldn't deny that his mouth watered at the sight of the delicious food. Marie knew her stuff when it came to homemade lasagne.

It looks amazing, enjoy! Jake texted back.

It's not too late to come over, Marie replied. *Emily is here and I think you'd like her.*

Shaking his head, Jake sighed. *I'm at the park with Ruby and enjoying a walk. Talk to you tomorrow.*

He pressed send on the message and was about to slip the phone back into his pocket when he heard Ruby barking. When he glanced up, he saw no sign of the dog anywhere. She'd run off during the fifteen seconds he'd spent looking at his phone and had disappeared amongst the trees.

"Ruby, come here girl!" he called out, trying to determine which direction the barking had come from. "Ruby, come here!"

Another bark rolled through the evening air, but there was still no sign of Ruby reappearing. She rarely failed to come when he used her recall command. Jake hoped she hadn't found a pile of dirt, or worse, in amongst the trees and was now rolling around in it in ecstasy. It wouldn't be the first time she'd done something along those lines.

"Ruby! Come here, girl!"

He heard another cheerful bark, and this time homed in on where it came from. Jogging off the path and into the trees beyond, he saw a flash of movement in a clearing and spied Ruby jumping around and wagging her tail as someone leaned down beside her.

Jake hurried over, hoping Ruby wasn't pestering some poor woodland rambler who'd much rather be left alone. When he stepped into the clearing, he found the dog prancing around the feet of an older lady in a red anorak and with a big blue handbag clutched to her shoulder. The woman was laughing as she ruffled Ruby's ears.

"Sorry, is my dog being a pest?" Jake said, preparing to clip the lead back onto Ruby's collar.

The older lady straightened and laughed again, waving him off when he moved in with Ruby's lead. "Not at all, dear. I think she must have sniffed out the treats in my pocket."

The woman held up a bag of dog biscuits and Ruby planted her bottom on the ground and raised a paw, making the older lady laugh again.

"She's quite a character," she said, offering a biscuit to the little dog. "And very polite, too, knowing how to beg like this." As Ruby crunched the biscuit treat, the woman patted the dog's head again.

"I can't believe she ran all the way in here to chase down someone with a bag of dog biscuits," Jake frowned. "That's not like her at all. I'm sorry."

"My goodness, there's nothing to apologise for. Many of my friends have dogs and I always carry a bag of biscuits in my pocket. And anyway, I don't think that's the reason she ran over. A rabbit hopped past just before your dog appeared and I think she must have been hot on the chase."

"That's very naughty, Ruby," Jake told the dog, struggling to conceal his smile as Ruby begged for more biscuits from the stranger.

"She was just having fun, I'm sure. In fact, she may have saved me from getting lost. This is my first visit to the park, and I may have got turned around when I stepped off the path towards the woodland. Can you tell me, dear, which direction should I take to return to the park gates?"

Jake pointed over his shoulder. "Back that way. If you go any further into the woods, you'll reach the stream and only have to come back out again."

"Silly me," the woman said. "Thank you for keeping me right. And thank you, Ruby, for your help, too." Holding out another biscuit for the dog, the woman smiled as Ruby snaffled it from her fingers.

"Are you new to the town, then?" Jake said as they began walking through the trees and towards the path.

"I'm helping a new friend who lives here in Willowbridge and thought it would be nice to get to the know the place a little better while I'm here." They stepped out beyond the trees and the woman paused and held out her hand. "I'm Mrs Wishmore. Doris Wishmore."

"Please to meet you, Mrs Wishmore," Jake said, offering his own hand. "I'm Jake Reid. And you've already met Ruby."

His phone trilled in his pocket and he frowned when he saw another message from Marie.

Emily is disappointed you haven't joined us! Want to arrange another dinner and you can come along this time?

"Everything all right, dear?" Mrs Wishmore asked, eyeing him carefully. "You look a little annoyed suddenly."

Jake shook his head and shoved his phone back in his

pocket. "No, everything's fine. My friend keeps trying to pair me off with random women she thinks I'll like."

A slow smile crept across Mrs Wishmore's face. Now that they were no longer beneath the trees and had the evening sunshine above them, Jake saw how bright blue the older lady's eyes were and how much they sparkled. Her face was oddly charismatic and her expression somehow enchanting as they strolled together side-by-side.

"I take it you aren't interested in meeting any of these women your friend has lined up for you?" Mrs Wishmore said, her tone amused.

"Not really."

"What's stopping you? Perhaps it would be fun."

Jake laughed. "Not in my experience."

Mrs Wishmore threw him a look as they stepped off the grass and onto the pathway. Jake couldn't help but feel that she was scrutinising him, her gaze scouring his face. As if the older lady had picked up on his thoughts, she smiled and nodded at Ruby who was darting around Jake's feet.

"Dogs certainly are good company, aren't they?" she said.

"Better than people, more often than not," Jake said, and they both laughed when Ruby barked in agreement and trundled off to sniff at a patch of overgrown grass along the edge of the path.

"Well, thank you for pointing me in the right direction for the park gates," Mrs Wishmore said. "Perhaps we'll bump into each other again."

With a warm smile, the older lady turned in the opposite direction and made her way along the path. Jake waved goodbye and continued towards the pond further along, where Ruby liked to sniff at the edges of the water and bark at the ducks.

"Shall we get a move on?" Jake asked Ruby as she fell into

a trot beside him and looked up with an unmistakable smile on her face.

Jake's phone buzzed again, but this time he didn't check it. He knew it would only be Marie, harassing him about this Emily person she was so desperate for him to meet. Why couldn't Marie listen when he said he wasn't interested?

Ruby bumped against his leg and gave a little snort, her sweet way of showing affection during their walks. Jake ruffled her ears and she bumped against him again.

"You're all the female company I need, aren't you Ruby?" Jake asked the little dog, scratching her head and laughing as she raced off towards the pond to yap at the ducks.

Jake hurried after her, his mind already turning to the pile of marking still waiting for him back home.

CHAPTER FIVE

Joan King had lost weight since Lisa had last seen her six weeks ago, and the sight of the thin woman standing at the front door was enough to make Lisa's breath catch as she locked her car out on the street. Peter's mother hadn't been quite right since her son's death, and over the course of the past year the once fashionable elegant lady had turned into a ghost of her former self. Now she looked almost painfully frail, her eyes dull even as she offered Lisa a smile of welcome. The anniversary of her son's death was taking its toll on the poor woman.

Joan King lived a half-hour drive away from Willowbridge on the outskirts of Winchester, in a rambling red brick town house that had been Peter's childhood home. Joan's husband, and Peter's father, Declan, had passed away many years before. When Lisa first met Peter, Joan was living an active life filled with many friends and social commitments. But all that had changed with Peter's sudden death, and grief had turned Joan into a near recluse. Lisa thought she actually looked worse now than she had in those terrible days and weeks following Peter's accident.

"Hello, Lisa," Joan said and greeted her at the door with a weak hug. "It's good to see you."

"You too." Lisa embraced the woman who would have been her mother-in-law had things turned out differently, feeling nothing but skin and bone beneath Joan's baggy blouse. "Joan, you've lost weight again. I'm worried about you."

Joan sighed and closed the door behind them. "I don't have much of an appetite. As this one-year anniversary got closer, I just lost all interest in food."

Her voice was toneless as she beckoned Lisa through to the living room, where she pointed to a tray sitting on the coffee table. "I made tea and sandwiches. I thought you'd be hungry, coming here straight after closing the café."

"That's kind, but you didn't have to go to any trouble."

"It was no trouble."

Joan poured tea and passed a cup to Lisa, then held out the plate of sandwiches and insisted she load some onto a plate. Having skipped lunch on account of her hectic day, Lisa realised she was famished. But when Joan took no food for herself and merely sank into the armchair by the fireplace with a cup of tea in her hands, Lisa's appetite vanished, too.

"You should try to eat something, Joan," Lisa said. "Maybe I could rustle up a hot dinner for you while I'm here?"

But Joan only grimaced. "If I'm hungry later, I'll eat something. But right now..." She sighed and sipped her tea, the matter apparently closed. Lisa thought of the bright, energetic woman Joan had been, back when Peter was still alive. Grief had hollowed her out and left behind nothing but a husk.

The house was eerily quiet and dust motes danced in the air, caught in the sunlight streaming through the windows that overlooked the back garden. Framed photographs lined the mantlepiece and the sideboard, most of them depicting Peter at various stages of his life—as a young child grinning on the beach while he played with a bucket and spade, or hoisted up on his father's shoulders in a sun-drenched swimming pool at some sunny resort, or laughing as he opened Christmas presents beneath the tree while his mother watched on and smiled. In other photos, he was older—performing on stage in a school play, and later graduating from university, and then proudly sitting behind the wheel of his first car.

And then, in amongst a clutch of more recent photographs given a prominent position on the mantelpiece, there was a framed shot of Peter beaming as he stood with Lisa at his side, holding her hand up to show off the diamond engagement ring he'd placed on her finger. Peter's mother had been beside herself with joy when they'd visited her to share their happy news and had insisted on opening a bottle of champagne to celebrate. Lisa could still remember the lovely afternoon the three of them had spent in the sunny garden, talking about the wedding they were about to plan together and how much fun it would all be.

Lisa stared at herself and Peter in that framed photograph. Within a week of the picture being taken, Peter had been dead. Even now, the loss still seemed absurdly impossible. How could someone be getting engaged one week and then be dead the next? It was incomprehensible.

"Thank you for coming to see me today," Joan said quietly, interrupting Lisa's thoughts. "I appreciate it."

"Today is tough." Lisa set aside the plate of sandwiches she no longer had any interest in eating. "I didn't want you to be by yourself all day."

"You're a good girl, Lisa. And it's sweet of you to be so kind to an old woman."

"You're not old, Joan."

"I feel old. I've felt old ever since Peter died." She waved a bony hand and shook her head. "Ignore me, I'm feeling sorry for myself. And the truth is, I haven't been alone all day. A couple of friends stopped by this morning to pay their respects on Peter's anniversary. It was nice of them to do that, considering I hardly keep in contact with people much these days."

"You mustn't let your friendships drift, Joan. Friends are important."

"I know. And I'm sure once this anniversary is past, I'll feel a little differently about things." Joan's gaze settled on Lisa. "Today must be very hard for you, dear. How have you been?"

"All right, mostly. It helped to be busy at the café, and I had a major staffing crisis that kept me on my toes, too."

Joan's brow furrowed in concern. "Is everything okay?"

"It is now, thank goodness. But there was a moment when..." Lisa stopped herself and smiled. "Never mind, ignore me."

"I certainly won't ignore you. Tell me what you were about to say." When Lisa stayed quiet, Joan smiled kindly. "You don't have to worry about upsetting me. If you and I of all people can't be honest about how we feel today, then there's no hope."

Lisa laughed. "It wasn't a big deal, really. When you run a busy café, there's always some mishap or mistake to deal with. It's just part of having your own business and managing employees and customers and suppliers. I'm used to things going wrong and having to think on my feet to sort them out. But when I found myself unexpectedly short-staffed today, all I wanted to do was close the café doors and go back to bed and hide there for the rest of the day."

Joan let out a quiet laugh. "I don't blame you in the slightest. I'm only surprised you opened the café at all."

"When I found myself short-staffed, I wished I hadn't. Even when I reopened the café after Peter died, I never felt overwhelmed the way I did today. It was strange to feel all these emotions suddenly rush through me."

Joan nodded. "I've had plenty of moments like that during these past days and weeks. After my husband died, I felt the same way as the first anniversary of his passing approached, but this time it's been much worse. A parent shouldn't have to bury their child." Her gaze steadied on Lisa and she smiled. "But you're doing just fine, Lisa. I'm proud of you and how you've coped. And Peter would've been proud of you, too. He would've been appalled at how I've fallen apart, and I try to remind myself that I need to pull myself together and keep going because that's what he would've wanted. Peter was always about living life to the fullest."

Lisa smiled, remembering Peter's infectious enthusiasm. He hadn't been perfect, because no one was perfect. But he'd always approached life with joy, and Lisa missed that part of him most of all—his great love for life.

"I can't believe it's been a year since we lost him," Joan said. "Sometimes it feels like it was only yesterday that he died. It's as if time is playing a cruel trick."

Joan's eyes filled with tears, and Lisa got up from the sofa and hurried over to comfort her. For a moment, they hugged each other, their tears falling in remembrance.

"You said yourself that once this one-year anniversary is behind us, you might feel a little differently about things," Lisa said. "Perhaps you'll want to get out more? You must miss seeing your friends as much as you used to and spending time with all those social clubs you belonged to. I'm sure they must all miss seeing you, Joan. You were the life and soul of things."

Joan only nodded and wiped the tears from her eyes with

a tissue. "I didn't mean to cry. Today must be hard enough for you without having to put up with a mad old lady, too."

"Don't say things like. I'm not 'putting up with you'. I'm here because you're important to me, Joan."

Joan smiled as she blew her nose. "I would have loved to have you as a daughter-in-law, Lisa. You're so very kind and caring. Although you and Peter were never married, I still think of you as a member of my family."

"Same here," Lisa said and squeezed Joan's hand.

"You two would've had a beautiful wedding day," Joan said. "I remember when you both came over to visit just after you got engaged, and we talked out in the garden about the sort of wedding you wanted. You probably would've been married by now if Peter had lived, and I find myself thinking about what your wedding would've been like. I imagine a quaint church ceremony on a sunny May afternoon, followed by a lovely reception at one of those pretty hotels in the New Forest. I would've been the doting mother-of-the-groom, as proud as punch. I like to imagine Peter in his smart suit, watching you walk down the aisle in a beautiful white dress, and... oh, Lisa! Are you okay?"

Lisa wasn't okay. Listening to Joan talk had brought the tears that she'd been fighting against all day and now they fell freely down her cheeks as a choking sob gathered in her throat.

"I'm so sorry, Lisa, what was I thinking?" Joan frowned and handed her a tissue from the box on the coffee table. "I shouldn't have said any of that. Of course it was only going to upset you."

"It's okay, really." Lisa blew her nose and wiped her cheeks. "I imagine those things too. It's hard not to."

"Still, the last thing I want is to make you cry, for goodness' sake." Joan sighed and shook her head. "Look at the pair of us. We're a couple of wrecks."

Lisa laughed and wiped away the last of her tears. "Maybe we both needed a good cry today after all."

"Maybe we did. Sometimes it feels like everyone else has moved on and we're the only two people left who really loved Peter and who will miss him always."

Lisa nodded sadly, knowing it was true. Peter's friends and work colleagues had moved on in life, because that's what people did. He'd had no siblings or other close family to remember him. His memory now lived in the hearts of his mother and the woman he'd planned on marrying.

The weight of that memory suddenly felt far too heavy inside Lisa's soul. She rose from the edge of the sofa and offered Joan a smile to hide the confusing thoughts and feelings racing through her mind.

"I'll brew some fresh tea," Lisa said. "Tea makes everything feel a little better."

LATER THAT NIGHT, Lisa washed dishes at the sink in her little flat above the Daffodil Café and thought about her visit with Joan King. The poor woman's deep sadness had left a mark on her, and it was hard seeing Joan struggling to get her life back on track.

Lisa wished she hadn't got upset when Joan had talked about the wedding plans they'd begun making in the days before Peter died. She'd wanted to be strong for Joan and be a shoulder to cry on, and yet she'd let herself fall to pieces at the mere mention of the wedding day that had never happened.

As she dried dishes, she thought of what that day might have been like. She imagined the dress she might have worn, the bouquet she might have held, the first dance she might have had in the arms of her new husband.

Who might she have become, if Peter had lived? She would've been a wife by now, that much she knew. Perhaps they might even have talked about having children together and building a family of their own. For a moment, she imagined herself in that alternate universe, with a wedding band on her finger and Peter at her side, the two of them dreaming of the little ones they couldn't wait to welcome into their lives.

Instead, Lisa was alone in her small flat with only the radio for company. Although she had friends in the village, and company all day in the café, and her parents at the end of the phone should she ever need to talk to them, the fact remained that she was deeply lonely.

She missed Peter and always would miss him. But lately a new and difficult thought had pushed its way to the front of her mind—that it was time to move on.

Lisa dropped the tea towel to the counter and closed her eyes. The idea of moving on both troubled her and excited her, and the two conflicting emotions only confused her further. It hurt to think about moving on and leaving Peter even further behind in the past. Yet she also knew it was what she now needed. What she now *wanted.*

She didn't want to spend her life alone. As much as she'd loved Peter, she couldn't live the rest of her life in the shadow of his memory. But admitting it openly was far from easy.

When Joan had talked about how they were the only two people left who'd really loved Peter and who would always remember him, it had made Lisa feel guilty. How could she think about moving on when poor Joan was in such misery? And how could she ever move on from the man she'd been ready to spend the rest of her life with?

She was also troubled about what moving on would actually look like in practice. Although Lisa hated feeling lonely, she also couldn't imagine becoming involved romantically with someone new. She'd been with Peter for over two years before his death, the longest relationship she'd ever had, and feared that being with someone else would feel too strange after all this time. It was this fear that had her refusing Fiona's offers to set her up with her friend from the pub, even although she knew that Fiona meant well and only wanted to help her find her feet again out there in the world.

Lisa wanted to move on, but hated leaving Peter behind in the past. She didn't want to be lonely anymore, but couldn't imagine spending time with someone new. It was a vicious circle that simply couldn't be squared.

And even if it could, how would she navigate the world of dating after all this time? She'd been out of practice for much too long. Dating wasn't for the faint hearted at the best of times. How would it feel going back out there again to meet men when she was now a bereaved fiancé?

She wondered if she ought to take Fiona up on her offer to set her up with this friend of hers from the pub, Tim something-or-other. But even the thought of it made her anxious. Even something as straightforward as a casual drink with a friend of a friend seemed crass and surreal after the shock of losing Peter.

There was one thing she knew for sure, though—she wouldn't meet anyone while hiding away in her flat.

With a sigh, Lisa finished her chores at the sink and turned out the kitchen light. This wasn't the right time to think about dating. No matter how lonely she felt, all she wanted to do tonight was have an early night and be glad she'd made it through this day without completely falling apart.

On her way to the bedroom, she paused in the hallway in front of a photograph of herself and Peter, snapped on holiday in Cornwall a month before he died. In the photo they were smiling beneath the sunshine, the golden beach and towering cliffs stretching out behind them into the distance, their hair wet from swimming in the sea. Peter's smile was brilliant, just like it always had been.

"Am I ready to let you go, Peter?" Lisa said as she gazed at the photograph and ran a finger over the glass frame. "Can I finally think about moving on?"

Behind the glass picture frame, Peter only smiled.

Lisa turned for the bedroom, wishing she knew the answers to the questions she'd asked.

CHAPTER SIX

Jake laid the pile of marking he'd brought with him onto the table near the window in the Daffodil Café and sank into the chair. It was Saturday morning, and he badly needed caffeine. The coffee machine at home in his kitchen had chosen today to give up the ghost, which was too bad, because the only way he'd make it through another twelve short answer assignments written by his students about the industrial revolution was if he could drink as much coffee as possible.

Which was why he found himself in the Daffodil Café. Not being the sort of person to spend his spare time in cafes, he'd never visited the place before, but it had the benefit of being on the end of the high street that was closest to his house, and so there he was. The café was bright and welcoming, with framed prints of cheerful daffodils hanging on the soft yellow-painted walls, and colourful mismatched vintage teacups and plates stacked on the counter and waiting to be put into service. Once refuelled with coffee and with the marking process once more underway, he'd work through the final assignments and then the rest of the weekend would be his own to do with as he pleased.

The café was busy, with most of the tables occupied. The two women working behind the counter were absorbed in the business of running the coffee machine and slicing the cakes on display in the glass case. The cakes looked delicious and Jake's gaze lingered on an especially tempting chocolate sponge cake. He ought to treat himself to a slice, he decided. It was Saturday morning, after all, and he was still working on his never-ending pile of marking. After the long walk he'd enjoyed with Ruby earlier that morning around the meadows to the north of the town, he was feeling peckish.

While he waited to be served, Jake opened the first assignment in the marking pile and began reading, his red pen poised to scribble encouragement and corrections in the margins. As he delved into the short essay answers in the paper, he didn't notice the waitress making her way across the café towards his table.

"Well, hello again!"

Jake looked up from his marking and saw a familiar face beaming down at him. It took him a second to place the woman.

"Mrs Wishmore," he finally said, taking in the apron she wore and the order pad clasped in her hands. "How are you?"

"I'm just fine, Jake. And how is Ruby this morning?"

"She's great. She's curled up at home fast asleep after a long walk."

"Good for her," Mrs Wishmore laughed and clicked her pen. "Now, what can I get you, dear?"

Jake ordered a large coffee and a slice of the chocolate cake he'd spied.

"Perfect choice," Mrs Wishmore smiled. "I'll be right back."

He watched the older lady trundle off towards the

counter. It struck him as odd that he'd bumped into the woman twice in as many hours, having never set eyes on her before. But Willowbridge was a small town, and he supposed coincidences like that happened from time to time.

Mrs Wishmore returned with his order a few minutes later, setting a steaming mug of coffee down beside his stack of marking.

"It looks like you're a teacher?" she said, glancing at the assignments. "You must be very committed to your students if you're spending your Saturday morning marking their work."

"Very committed or just very disorganised," he smiled.

"I'm sure you must be keen to finish all this work so you can enjoy your weekend. Didn't you mention last night that you had plans with the young lady that your friend wanted you to meet?"

It took a moment for Jake to understand what she was talking about. "Oh, you mean my friend who texted me while we were chatting in the park? No, there's nothing happening there. You must have got mixed up."

"Ah, that must be it," Mrs Wishmore said with an easy shrug. She set the slice of chocolate cake he'd ordered down beside the coffee mug. "I hope you enjoy your cake. Lisa baked it herself this morning."

"Lisa?"

"Yes, Lisa," Mrs Wishmore replied, turning to point at the young woman working at the coffee machine behind the counter. "She's the owner of the Daffodil Café and is also the most wonderful baker."

Jake looked at the woman Mrs Wishmore was pointing to, but as she was operating the coffee machine, all he saw was the back of her head and the swish of her long auburn ponytail.

"Well, I'll leave you to enjoy your coffee," Mrs Wishmore said. "If you need anything else, just shout."

Jake nodded his thanks as Mrs Wishmore shuffled off. He drank some coffee and then dug into the chocolate cake. It tasted even better than it looked, and it already looked amazing. His gaze returned to the busy baker behind the counter, thinking that Mrs Wishmore was right when she'd described her as a wonderful baker. He watched the young woman pick up a tray loaded with plates of muffins and hot drinks and carry it to a nearby table, her ponytail bouncing as she crossed the floor.

Jake realised that while he was watching the Daffodil Café's talented baker going about her work, Mrs Wishmore was watching *him*, a smile tugging at her lips as she cleared dishes at a nearby table. Blushing, although not really knowing why, Jake glanced back at the assignment he was marking.

He'd barely begun reading the next answer on the paper when the café door flew open and a gust of wind blasted into the café, wafting Jake's pile of assignments up into the air and scattering them like confetti across the floor.

Horrified at the sight of his students' papers flying around the place, Jake leapt to his feet to grab them back up. But as he reached for the stray papers, he accidentally knocked his plate of chocolate cake off the table, sending it tumbling down the front of his jeans before it splattered on the floor and the plate smashed in two.

Every customer in the café turned towards the disturbance, their eyes wide at the banging door and the fluttering papers and the man now standing in shock with chocolate cake stuck to his jeans. As quickly as the wind had appeared and almost blown the door off its hinges, it died down again and the calm June morning was restored. The little bell above the door tinkled sweetly as the door slowly swung closed.

"Oh my, are you all right, dear?" Mrs Wishmore said, hurrying towards Jake.

"Uh..." Jake stared at the chocolate sponge smeared down the front of his jeans and eyed the student essays scattered all over the floor. "Um, I'm fine. I don't know how on earth that even happened."

"That was quite a summer breeze!" Mrs Wishmore said with a laugh. "It's almost like it came out of nowhere!"

She laughed again and Jake saw a baffling but unmistakably mischievous glint in the older lady's eyes as she grabbed a stack of napkins from a nearby table and handed them to him. Dabbing ineffectually at the chocolate frosting on his jeans with one of the napkins, he wondered when his bad luck with spillages and splashes would end. Yesterday at school he'd got red paint all over his shirt. Today, it was chocolate cake all over his jeans. Yet again, he found himself wishing he wasn't quite so clumsy all the time.

From the corner of his eye, Jake saw the café owner, Lisa, hurry over.

"Are you okay?" she asked, taking in his chocolate-covered jeans and the cake on the floor and the scattered student essays.

"Sorry about the mess," Jake said. "The wind blew my paperwork off the table and then I stupidly knocked cake all over myself. Sorry."

"Don't apologise. These things happen." Lisa frowned at the café door. "I've never seen the door blow open like that before, not even in the winter. I'll get this cake cleaned up and bring you another slice."

"No, I should probably go home and change out of these jeans."

"Oh, there's no need to do that," Mrs Wishmore said. "I'm sure a damp cloth will get rid of the chocolate stains."

Jake looked doubtfully at the sticky icing smeared across his jeans, feeling sure that only a spin in the washing machine would do the trick.

"I'll grab a cloth," Lisa said. "And I insist on bringing you more cake. It's on the house to apologise for all your paperwork getting blown around." Lisa turned to Mrs Wishmore. "Would you mind grabbing the mop and cleaning up this spillage while I slice more chocolate cake?"

"Of course not, dear," Mrs Wishmore said and hurried off.

Jake gathered the scattered essays from the floor and bundled them into a pile on the table. By the time he'd finished, Mrs Wishmore had already worked wonders with the mop and Lisa had reappeared with a fresh slice of cake and a warm damp cloth.

"This should get the worst of the chocolate off your clothes," she said, handing him the cloth.

Grateful, Jake sponged his jeans with the cloth, although he doubted it would make much difference given how much chocolate icing he'd got all over himself. And so, when the gooey mess miraculously disappeared as he rubbed the cloth over his jeans, he was astonished.

"What kind of cleaning products do you use here?" he joked, staring at his now perfectly clean jeans.

"Gosh, I didn't expect the chocolate to come off quite so easily," Lisa said, clearly as amazed as he was.

"What a nice stroke of luck," Mrs Wishmore grinned.

Jake glanced up at the older lady and couldn't help but think she looked rather pleased with herself. The sparkle in her bright blue eyes was distinctly crafty.

"Now that you're all cleaned up, you won't have to hurry home, Jake," Mrs Wishmore continued, her smile wide. "I'll pop this mop and bucket back into the cupboard. Lisa, perhaps you could find out if Jake would like more coffee?"

"Thanks for your help, Mrs Wishmore," Jake said.

"You're quite welcome, dear."

Jake watched the older lady walk off with the cleaning things, feeling like something rather odd had just happened in the last few minutes—besides getting covered in chocolate cake—although quite what that odd thing was exactly, he couldn't say.

"Are you a friend of Mrs Wishmore's?" Lisa asked, picking up the tray containing the broken plate and chunks of chocolate sponge that Mrs Wishmore had scooped up from the floor.

"We only met for the first time yesterday evening when we bumped into each other at the park. Although she became good friends with my dog, Ruby, by feeding her endless biscuits. Any friend of Ruby's is naturally a friend of mine."

Lisa let out a laugh and Jake smiled.

"So, can I get you another coffee?" she asked.

"My coffee miraculously survived my flailing arms, but I'll probably need another cup soon to help me through the last of my marking."

Lisa smiled again and turned to the counter. "I'll bring it over when you're ready."

He watched her get back to work, once more running the coffee machine and plating up bakery treats for customers. Then he realised he was staring again, just like he'd been staring before.

That was never a good thing to do, Jake told himself. Women generally didn't like it when clumsy, idiotic men stared at them as they went about their business. Still, something about the way she moved around the café, and always had a ready smile for her customers, left him a little breathless.

Or maybe it was just the embarrassment of spilling cake all over himself in the middle of a busy café that had done that.

With a sigh, Jake drank some coffee and turned his attention to his pile of marking.

CHAPTER SEVEN

Later that afternoon, once the lunch rush was over and the café was quiet, Lisa rose from her desk in the office off the corridor where she'd been making calls and sorting invoices, and wandered into the kitchen where Fiona was tending to a pot of soup bubbling on the hob in preparation for reopening on Monday. After loitering in the door, Lisa cleared her throat.

"I'm glad we're almost ready to close," Fiona said. "Today's lunch service was even busier than yesterday's."

"The nice weather is bringing everyone out of the house," Lisa said, stepping further into the kitchen and fidgeting with a tea towel.

"The new waitress, Doris, is working out well."

"We'd be lost without her."

"Can she cover all the lunch shifts until Vicki is back on her feet?"

Lisa nodded. "Which means I don't have to wrangle with the temping agency to find someone else who's up to scratch. I doubt they could send a better waitress than Mrs Wishmore. She's out there right now, scrubbing the shelves behind the counter. Even Vicki doesn't do that."

Fiona laughed and stirred the soup. "I like Doris. She's got a way about her. I'm glad she's staying on with us."

"Me too. But listen, I came through to ask you something."

Fiona set down the soup spoon and turned. When Lisa only stood there saying nothing, she gave an uncertain smile. "Okay, what did you want to ask?"

"Um..." Lisa sighed and shuffled her feet. She wasn't sure if she was ready to say what she was about to say. But there was only one way to find out. "That friend of yours, Tim. The one you said was interested in having a drink with me. Well, I was wondering..."

Before she could say another word, Fiona's eyes flew wide. "You want to go out with him? That's fantastic! But when I brought it up yesterday, you weren't interested."

"I know. Just thinking about going out with someone is still strange. But I have to start moving on." Sighing, she tossed aside the tea towel and shook her head, feeling the truth of the matter—and all its infuriating contradictions—hit home. "I miss Peter. But I'm lonely, too. I thought about things a lot last night and I've decided it's time to take the first step."

Fiona's eyes were damp as she pulled Lisa into a fierce hug. "I'm so proud of you, Lisa."

Mrs Wishmore appeared in the kitchen, carrying a tray of dirty dishes. "Well, what's all this?" she said, smiling as she took in the two friends embracing one another.

"Lisa's just agreed to go out on a date with my friend, Tim," Fiona said, already pulling her phone from her pocket. "I'll text him right now."

"Isn't that nice," Mrs Wishmore said, her gaze softening as

she looked at Lisa. "You're a lovely young woman, Lisa. It's only right that you should get out and have some fun."

Now that she'd set things in motion, Lisa felt a troubling mixture of doubt and excitement about what might happen next. "I haven't been on a date with someone new in years. What if I make a fool of myself?"

"Impossible," Fiona said, her fingers flying across her phone. "You two will have a great time. And you'll only be having a drink with him. I've told him to take things slowly."

"Don't make it sound like I need to be handled with kid gloves."

"But you do," Fiona said simply. Her phone pinged, and she looked up at Lisa with a grin. "Tim says he can't wait to take you out and wants to know if you're free on Tuesday evening."

"*Tuesday?* I didn't think it would happen so fast."

"It's days away, Lisa. Today's only Saturday."

"Which gives you plenty of time to prepare and get comfortable with the idea," Mrs Wishmore said kindly.

Or time to fret about it, Lisa thought.

"A nice weekday evening drink at the pub is perfect," Fiona said, once more typing into her phone. "No pressure, just nice and casual. I'll tell him you'll meet him in the Peacock Inn at seven o'clock."

Lisa felt lightheaded. "Gosh, I can't believe I'm actually going to do this."

"If you enjoy having a drink with Tim, maybe you'll go somewhere for a quick bite afterwards," Fiona said, finishing her text. "But if that's too much all at once, then no problem, because all you agreed to was a casual drink." She tucked her phone away and grinned. "I'm so excited! And so pleased!"

"It's just a drink," Lisa said, more to reassure herself than anyone else. "Just a friendly drink, that's all."

"Exactly," Fiona said with an easy shrug.

"I'm sure you'll have a lovely time, dear," Mrs Wishmore said. "You certainly deserve it."

"Thank you, Mrs Wish..." Lisa laughed. "I really should call you Doris."

"Of course you should," the older lady smiled. "Now, while you were in your office, a lady who works at the secondary school came into the café and dropped off this leaflet." Mrs Wishmore reached into her apron pocket and pulled out the piece of paper. "The school is holding a summer fair and the organising committee are looking for donations from local businesses. I heard you talking on the phone when I came to your office door and didn't want to disturb you, but promised to pass the information along."

Lisa glanced at the leaflet Mrs Wishmore handed to her. The Willowbridge School summer fair was a popular event in the town, enjoying the support of residents, parents, and businesses alike. In the past, Lisa had always baked a few extra cakes and several batches of muffins and donated them to the summer fair home-baking stall. It occurred to her that the event had passed her by last year, coming as it had just a few weeks after Peter's sudden death. With the café closed and Lisa left stunned by bereavement, the last thing anyone in Willowbridge would have dreamt of doing was knocking on her door and asking for cake donations for a school fundraiser. As she studied the leaflet, Lisa resolved to send extra cakes to the school this year, her small way of thanking the community for the support she'd had over these last tough months.

"I'll ring the head teacher on Monday and find out what the donation arrangements are," Lisa said, making a mental note of the task. "The fair is only a couple of weeks away, so I'll have to carve out time to whip up a few extra baked treats for the cake stall."

"That's very kind of you, dear," Mrs Wishmore said. "I'm sure the school will appreciate it."

After stacking the dirty dishes she'd brought through into the dishwasher, Mrs Wishmore shuffled off at the sound of the bell above the café door, announcing the arrival of a new customer.

"I can lend a hand with the extra baking," Fiona said, turning off the heat beneath the soup.

"You do enough around here as it is," Lisa smiled. "But thanks for the offer. And anyway, you know me. Any excuse to bake and I'm happy. I might even use it as an opportunity to try out some new cake recipes."

Fiona nodded as a smile spread across her face. "I'm so excited that you're going for a drink with Tim! You'll have a brilliant time, I just know it."

Laughing at her friend's enthusiasm, Lisa left the kitchen to help with the final customers of the afternoon before she closed up for the day. Her stomach was already churning with nerves as the prospect of the imminent date she'd just agreed to, and she only hoped that Fiona was right when she assured her she'd have a brilliant time.

"EVERYTHING'S TIDIED AWAY in the café, so I'm heading home now, dear," Mrs Wishmore called out, her head bobbing around the kitchen door.

Lisa glanced up from her inventory paperwork and smiled. "Thanks Doris. And thanks for all your help today. We had a busy Saturday, but you handled it like you've been working here forever."

Mrs Wishmore waved this away. "All part of the job I'm here to do." Her gaze travelled to the papers spread out on the counter. "I hope you won't be working too late."

"I don't mind the distraction. Keeping busy will stop my mind wandering to this date I've agreed to go on with Fiona's friend."

After giving her a careful look, Mrs Wishmore stepped into the kitchen. She'd already pulled on her red jacket in preparation for leaving, and now she set her blue handbag down on the counter. "You're taking a big step, going out with someone new. It's only natural to feel nervous. How long were you together with your late fiancé?"

"Two years."

Mrs Wishmore nodded. "Then it stands to reason that you'll have conflicting feelings about your first date with a man since Peter passed away."

"I know it's only a drink with a friend of a friend, nothing more. But…" Lisa sighed and pushed away the inventory paperwork. "I want to move on in life, but I can't help feeling that I'm betraying Peter's memory, even although I know that's silly."

"Of course it's not silly. It's simply how you feel. Perhaps once this first step is out of the way, things will seem different."

"That's what I keep telling myself. When I visited Peter's mother last night, it was hard to see her so torn up about the anniversary of his death. She hasn't been the same since the accident. Knowing how much she's struggling makes me feel worse for wanting to move on."

Mrs Wishmore smiled kindly. "Any mother would feel terrible grief on the anniversary of her child's passing. It's a dreadful thing to bear. But you mustn't make yourself feel guilty."

"Peter's mother is a good woman and I hate seeing her in so much pain. And I hate knowing I'd be adding to that pain if I ever met someone else who I wanted to be with and I have to tell her and—"

"Now you're jumping much too far ahead," Mrs Wishmore interrupted with a soft laugh. "You said yourself that you're only having a quick drink with this friend of Fiona's. Perhaps you and this young man will hit it off, or perhaps you'll decide that one drink together was the beginning and end of things for the both of you. But don't tie yourself up in knots worrying about what Joan will say about you becoming romantically involved with someone new, when that hasn't even happened yet."

"I know you're right, but…" Lisa gave Mrs Wishmore a puzzled look. "I don't remember telling you that Peter's mother's name is Joan."

Mrs Wishmore stared for a moment and then let out another laugh. "Of course you did, dear. You mentioned it yesterday when you explained that you were going to visit her."

Lisa frowned. She couldn't remember getting into those kinds of details during their conversation. But there had been a lot going on, so perhaps she'd forgotten. Her thoughts had been so scattered lately.

Mrs Wishmore reached across the counter and squeezed Lisa's hand. "You mustn't overthink things, Lisa. And you mustn't worry so much about the future that you forget to live in the present."

Lisa nodded, appreciating Mrs Wishmore's kindness. The gentle squeeze of the older lady's hand on hers made things seem less muddled.

"Good night, dear," Mrs Wishmore said and turned for the kitchen door. "Don't work too late."

Lisa listened to the older lady's footsteps disappearing out into the café and heard the tinkle of the bell above the door as she left. After tidying away her inventory paperwork and pulling the shutters on the front door, Lisa headed upstairs to her little flat above the café, already thinking about the accounts she'd work on for the rest of the evening.

Working would stop her from worrying about the date that was now looming on the horizon. Mrs Wishmore may have advised her not to overthink things, but Lisa knew that was far easier said than done.

CHAPTER EIGHT

After losing track of time during his Monday morning free period while working on a lesson plan in the school library, Jake hurried through the reception lobby towards the staff room, where he hoped to grab a quick coffee before the bell rang. Next period he was teaching a class of Year Nines, and thanks to a handful of regular troublemakers in the group, he liked to arrive fully caffeinated and ready for anything.

Not for the first time, it occurred to Jake that he probably drank far too much coffee for his own good.

He was pushing through the swing doors when he saw a familiar face crossing the other side of the lobby, her auburn ponytail swinging as she walked beside the school head-teacher. His stomach twisted when he realised it was Lisa, the woman from the café on the high street.

After shaking the headteacher's hand and saying goodbye, Lisa turned in Jake's direction. Her gaze found his as she drew near, and Jake saw her eyes narrow as she tried to place him.

"You might not recognise me when I'm not covered in chocolate cake," Jake grinned.

Lisa laughed as recognition dawned. "It's a look not every man could pull off."

He liked her sense of humour and the easy way she carried herself as she paused beside him at the swing doors.

"What brings you here?" he asked.

"I'm donating some baked goods for your school summer fair," she explained. "Since I was passing on my way back from a visit to the wholesaler, I thought I'd drop in and find out what the arrangements are for the event. Your head-teacher had a spare moment and filled me in on the details."

"We appreciate all the help we can get. And if you're donating cakes to the baking stall, I'll be at the front of the queue with my wallet open."

"That's very kind," Lisa said, a pretty blush colouring her cheeks.

"Will you need a hand transporting the cakes here? I'm one of the organisers of the summer fair, so it's in my wheel-house if you need help."

"I should be fine loading everything into my car, but if I'm stuck, I'll let you know." She gave him a curious look. "I donated cakes to the summer fair a couple of years ago, but I don't remember seeing you then."

"This is my first year on the organising committee."

She nodded at his explanation. "Well, good luck. It must be a lot of work."

"I'm having fun helping the kids put it together. It raises a lot of money for school funds, but the kids get a lot out of it too and that's what matters most."

Lisa's gaze stayed on him for a long moment as a smile tugged at her mouth. Jake thought she was about to say something more, but the school bell rang just then, signalling the end of second period.

"The marauding hordes will swarm through here any second," Jake said as the scraping of chairs and the chatter of voices erupted in the classrooms above them. "If you want to get out of here without being caught up in the chaos, now's a good time to make a run for the exit."

Laughing, Lisa glanced along the corridor beyond the swing doors where pupils were already pouring out of the adjoining rooms.

"Thanks for the safety tip," she laughed. "Bye."

"Bye."

Throwing a wave in his direction, she hurried for the main exit on the other side of the lobby. As Jake watched her leave, he saw Marie Hanlon emerge from the school office and stride towards him with an enormous grin on her face.

"What's got you looking so cheerful?" he asked.

"Oh, nothing," Marie said. "I just happened to glance through the reception window while I was in the school office and saw you practically drooling over that very pretty lady you were speaking to. So, who is she?"

"I wasn't *drooling*, for god's sake," Jake frowned as the lobby filled with noisy students hurrying to their next class. "I was just chatting to a member of the public who is donating some home-baking to sell at the summer fair."

Marie's eyebrows bunched together in thought. "Wait, *now* I recognise her. She's the woman who runs that café on the main street. They sell amazing cakes in there."

"Which is why we're so lucky she's agreed to help us."

An amused grin spread across Marie's face. "You like her."

"I like her generosity," Jake corrected.

From the corner of his eye, he saw two boys laughing and shoving each other, their boisterousness causing them to knock into the other kids who were moving along the corridor.

"Okay, you two, calm down," Jake called out. "No pushing. You know the rules."

The boys snorted laughter at each other, then cut their eyes in his direction in a half-apology before going their separate ways. When he looked around again, Marie was supervising the students heading up and down the stairs across from the reception lobby.

Grateful that the change-over mayhem had saved him from further interrogation, Jake headed to his next class on the second floor.

He was halfway through the lesson before it occurred to him that he hadn't got his morning coffee after all.

CHAPTER NINE

Tuesday evening arrived much too quickly for Lisa, bringing with it the date she'd agreed to have with Tim.

Despite second-guessing the wisdom of the decision she'd made to meet the man for a drink, the busy café left her with little time to worry about it. Mrs Wishmore was right when she'd cautioned her against overthinking things, and with the café operating at full speed all day long, she focused her attention on filling orders and keeping the place running smoothly, which was where it belonged.

Since Mrs Wishmore's arrival, the café seemed to be running better than ever. The new waitress was a miracle worker, managing the lunch time busy spells with an ease that left Lisa quietly amazed. Even when food orders poured in and the place was packed, Mrs Wishmore never seemed fazed. Lisa couldn't have hoped for a better temporary waitress to replace Vicki while she recovered from her ankle injury. The older lady had even come in early the last two days, allowing Lisa to run important business errands, safe in the knowledge that Mrs Wishmore and Fiona could handle the café until she returned in time for the lunch rush.

Now, as she stood before her bedroom mirror deciding which top to wear with the smart jeans she'd selected for the date with Tim, Lisa was even happier that Mrs Wishmore was so effective in her waitressing job, because it meant she'd been able to leave the older lady to finish clearing up while she hurried upstairs to wash and style her hair.

It had been so long since she'd last used the styling tongs, she could barely remember how to create the big tumbling curls she'd once loved. Since Peter's death, she'd had no desire to spend time in front of the mirror making herself pretty. While working in the café, she opted for little more than rubbing some tinted moisturiser into her skin and scraping her hair up into a tidy ponytail.

Which meant she was out of practice in the beautification front. The work she'd done with the curling tongs had left her hair much too big and over-volumised. Dissatisfied with what she saw in the mirror, Lisa grabbed a scrunchie and wrangled her hair into it. It wasn't ideal, but the alternative was turning up for her date looking like a backing singer from a 1980s rock music video.

At least her make-up had turned out all right. She'd kept it basic with neutral eyeshadow, a sweep of mascara, a hint of blusher, and a soft pink lipstick. This was just a casual drink and she wanted to look relaxed and natural, even if she had spent the better part of an hour achieving the careless look she'd sought.

Lisa held up the two tops she'd yet to decide between. The choice was a soft pink t-shirt or a flowery floaty blouse. She settled for the t-shirt, deciding that the blouse was too dressy for a quick drink in the pub. But what if the pink t-shirt made it seem like she hadn't made much effort at all?

"Just pick one," Lisa muttered, and pulled the t-shirt over her head.

She glanced in the mirror, then sighed and pulled off the t-shirt and swapped it for the floaty blouse. As she tucked it into her jeans and adjusted her belt, her gaze settled on a framed photograph of Peter on the chest of drawers. He was smiling, his expression amused as he grinned for the camera.

"I'm out of practice with all this," Lisa told his photograph and gestured to the spread of discarded clothes on the bed, the abandoned curling tongs on the dressing table, the three pots of blusher she'd wavered between before opting for the palest pink. "I'm exhausted already and I haven't even been on the date yet."

As she selected earrings from the jewellery box and put them on, she studied the picture of Peter. His warm smile beaming out from the not-so-distant past gave her pause for a long moment as she realised what she was about to do—go out for a drink with a man.

She stared at Peter's photograph and wondered whether any man could ever make her feel the same way he had.

With a sigh, she slipped on her shoes, grabbed her bag, and headed for the door before she came to her senses and cancelled the whole thing.

"It's just a drink," she said, locking the flat door and turning for the pub at the top of the main street. "Just one drink. No more, no less."

Except it *was* more, a little voice whispered inside her head as she walked up the street, her heart hammering inside her chest.

The Peacock Inn enjoyed a prime position in an old stone building on the corner of Willowbridge high street.

Its tumbling flower baskets and pots added charm to the narrow beer garden that was packed with drinkers on the warm summer evening. When Lisa saw no sign of Tim at the outside tables, she went inside and scanned the bar. At a snug table near the unlit fireplace, she spied her date.

"Lisa, hi!" Tim said, smiling as he stood to greet her.

"It's nice to meet you," Lisa replied, awkwardly trying to shake Tim's hand as he settled for a friendly arm-squeeze that avoided invading her personal space while still acknowledging that they were, after all, on a date.

"I'm glad you could come tonight." Tim gestured to the seat across the table. "I've been looking forward to this ever since Fiona said you'd be interested in getting together. What would you like to drink?"

"White wine, please."

Tim walked to the bar. While he ordered her drink, Lisa watched him from the corner of her eye while tugging off her bag and getting comfortable in her seat. He'd looked attractive in the photograph Fiona had shown her, and he looked even better now. Tall and broad-shouldered, with an athletic build and fair hair, he wore a smart shirt and dark jeans, and Lisa had caught the spicy scent of his aftershave when he'd leaned in to squeeze her arm in welcome. He'd gone to some trouble to look good for tonight, and she was glad she'd chosen to wear the dressy blouse instead of the relaxed t-shirt.

When Tim returned to their table with her white wine, he raised the bottle of beer he'd already ordered for himself and clinked it against her glass.

"Cheers, and here's to new friends," he said.

"Cheers."

They sipped their drinks. When Lisa shuffled in her seat, Tim grinned.

"First dates can be a little weird," he said. "But let's just enjoy getting to know one another."

"Sounds good to me."

"I know you own that little café further down the high street, but that's all I know about you." Tim paused as an uncomfortable look crossed his face. "Well, I also know you lost your fiancé last year. That must've been hard. I'm sorry."

"Thank you. It was tough, but in the end you just have to keep going." She offered a smile, keen not to dwell on sad things tonight. After convincing herself to move on again in life, she wasn't about to spend this first date talking about the shattering bereavement that had brought her to her knees and kept her there for so long. "So, Tim, what do you do?"

She could tell from his expression that he, too, was glad to move the conversation on to safer terrain. As they enjoyed their drinks, they traded stories. Tim told her about his sales manager's job with a hotel chain, his love of football and rugby, his dream of one day travelling to Australia and visiting cousins who'd emigrated there. Lisa told him about her café and her love of baking, how she enjoyed walking in the New Forest but didn't get to do it often enough, and about the advanced pastry class she hoped to take some day at a respected cookery school in London. They talked about their favourite films and bands, books they'd read, places they'd visited.

An hour passed. It was all perfectly pleasant. And yet, when Tim asked if she'd like another glass of wine, Lisa shook her head.

"I need to get back and prepare cake batter for tomorrow in the café," she lied, picking up her bag. "But I've enjoyed getting together with you, Tim."

As his gaze searched hers, he didn't look convinced. "Maybe we can have another drink sometime."

"Sure." She blushed as she said it, knowing it would never happen and sensing that Tim understood that, too.

After a brief hug goodbye, Lisa left the pub, reminding herself that she'd only agreed to a quick drink with the man. Fiona had explained all that to him, and there'd been no expectation that they'd spend the entire evening together. Tim was a nice guy, and maybe under different circumstances she would've stayed for that second drink and agreed to meet him again some other time to see where things might go.

But despite their friendly conversation, she felt no real connection to the man, nor the potential for one. Although they'd spent a pleasant hour together, she'd run out of things to talk about by the time she was draining the last of her wine from the glass.

Worse, she'd found herself thinking about Peter. Not that he'd ever left her thoughts to begin with.

The high street was bathed in late sunshine as Lisa hurried past the Peacock Inn's beer garden towards home. She'd told a little white lie when she'd explained to Tim that she had baking preparations to deal with for the café, but it wouldn't be a bad way to spend the rest of the evening. She was edgy after the date with Tim, both wishing it had gone better and wishing she hadn't agreed to it at all, and knew she would only fret and worry without some task to keep herself busy.

As she considered what goodies she might like to whip up in the café kitchen, she heard someone calling her name from across the street. Glancing across the road, she saw Mrs Wishmore walking past the shuttered shops, her big blue handbag clutched at her shoulder and the light cardigan she wore over her summer dress billowing in the soft breeze.

"Lisa! Hello!" Mrs Wishmore smiled, waving her over.

"I'm surprised to see you here. I thought you were having a nice drink with Fiona's friend tonight?"

"I was. I did." Lisa joined Mrs Wishmore on the other side of the road and they fell into step beside each other. "I just left the pub a minute ago."

Mrs Wishmore glanced at her wristwatch, then back at Lisa. "That was a quick drink. You didn't want to stay longer?"

"Tim was lovely. But one drink was enough to realise that..."

When Lisa said nothing further, not liking how cold it might sound, Mrs Wishmore smiled and finished the sentence for her. "You didn't quite hit it off the way you'd hoped. And that's perfectly all right."

"I feel bad about rushing off so soon."

"I'm sure the young man will survive," Mrs Wishmore laughed.

"Hmm, still—"

"And I can tell you're about to overthink the whole thing."

Lisa let out a laugh, realising the older lady was right. "I tend to do that."

"Well, I have the perfect remedy. I was about to take a stroll through the park on my way home. Would you care to join me?"

Lisa thought of the baking she'd planned to do back at the café. Then she glanced up at the pretty blue sky and decided a summery evening walk in the park sounded much better.

"I'd like that, thanks Doris." Turning towards the park, Lisa glanced at Mrs Wishmore. "Listen, I can't thank you enough for all the hard work you've put in at the café these past few days."

"You're quite welcome, dear."

"When you first arrived at the café, things were so hectic I didn't have time to ask about your previous waitressing experience. Where have you worked in the past?"

"Oh, here and there. A few cafes, a few restaurants, although none around here, so I doubt you would've heard of them. Although I must confess that, much as I enjoy waitressing, I'm a jack-of-all-trades." Mrs Wishmore looked over and smiled. "Wherever someone needs a little help, I'm happy to lend a hand."

Lisa nodded at this and was about to ask Mrs Wishmore another question, but they'd arrived at the park gates and the older lady's eyes widened as she pointed to the tubs of flowers standing on either side of the wrought iron entrance. She clapped her hands together in obvious joy.

"Aren't these flowers just glorious?" Mrs Wishmore said. "Look at those blooms! The park gardeners certainly know their business."

Lisa admired the flowers, which did indeed look lovely tumbling down the sides of the large pots in a riot of deep pink and bright red and soft white.

"There's nothing quite like an evening walk through the park in the last of the day's summer sunshine to clear the mind, don't you think?" Mrs Wishmore said.

Drawing in a deep breath of air and already smelling the scents of the roses in the flower beds beyond the gates, Lisa nodded.

"I haven't walked in the park for ages," Lisa said.

"Well, that's a pity."

They'd only made it a few steps beyond the gates when a little dog came barrelling along the path and raced around Mrs Wishmore, its tail wagging.

"Well, hello there again!" Mrs Wishmore said, bending to pet the scruffy creature as it rolled onto its back and presented its belly for scratching. "Now, that's quite a display you're putting on for us."

"Who's this?" Lisa said with a laugh, unable to resist petting the dog as it wriggled on the ground.

"This is Ruby. We met last week when she discovered I keep a supply of dog biscuits in my pocket."

Mrs Wishmore removed a small plastic bag from her cardigan pocket and pulled out a bone-shaped biscuit. Ruby hauled herself into a sitting position and offered a paw. Clearly delighted, Mrs Wishmore fed the biscuit to the animal, who gobbled it down and then glanced hopefully at the plastic bag for more.

"Ruby! Come back here!"

Further along the path, Lisa saw a man hurrying in their direction. It only took a second to recognise him.

"Hello, Jake," Mrs Wishmore laughed when he reached them. "Ruby must have sensed our arrival the moment we walked through the park gates."

"She never usually runs off like this, and now that's twice in as many days," Jake said, shaking his head and attaching a lead to Ruby's collar. "It must be something about you, Mrs Wishmore. She's mad for you."

"I'm sure it's the biscuits in my pocket and nothing more." The older lady grinned and fed the dog another treat before tucking the plastic bag back into her pocket.

When Jake straightened up after reattaching the dog's lead, his gaze fell on Lisa. His eyes widened in surprise. "Oh, hi."

"Hi," Lisa smiled. "This is a sweet dog you have."

"She's trouble," he replied with an indulgent grin that suggested he thought the animal was anything but. After a moment's silence, Jake raked a hand through his hair and said, "So, have you decided what you'll bake for the school summer fair?"

"Not yet. Although chocolate crispy cake always goes down well with the children."

Mrs Wishmore looked at Lisa and then at Jake, and it seemed to Lisa that the older lady's eyes were dancing with humour. When Mrs Wishmore's phone pinged, she pulled it from her bag and glanced at the screen.

"That's a message from my friend, wondering where I've got to," Mrs Wishmore said, tucking the phone back inside her big blue bag. "I'm dropping by to visit her and must get on my way. Lisa, I hope you don't mind if I leave you to take that walk through the park by yourself."

"Oh, of course not," Lisa said.

"Perhaps Jake and Ruby can keep you company instead?" she said, glancing at Jake.

Jake looked a little stunned for a moment before nodding. "Sure. We were just about to take another loop around the path."

"Lovely. In that case I'll leave you both to it. See you tomorrow at the café, Lisa."

With a wave, Mrs Wishmore hurried back towards the gate. Lisa watched her disappear, wondering at her sudden departure. When the older lady had met her on the high street just a few minutes earlier, she hadn't said anything about going to a friend's house. In fact, Lisa was sure that Mrs Wishmore had said she was on her way home.

How odd, she thought.

"If you'd prefer to enjoy the rest of your walk by yourself, that's all right," Jake said, giving her an uncertain look.

"No, I'd be glad of the company," Lisa smiled. "Mrs Wishmore just took me by surprise, because I thought... actually, it doesn't matter." She shrugged off her confusion. "I'm looking forward to a stroll through the park and it will be even more fun with a sweet little dog in tow."

Ruby barked at this, as if confirming what she'd said, and Lisa laughed.

"Let's head towards the pond," Jake said, pointing across

the park. "Ruby enjoys chuntering at the ducks and making a fool of herself trying to catch them."

"The ducks are wise to her?"

"She makes such a racket, barking and yapping at the edge of the pond, that she doesn't have the slightest chance of ever catching one. And if she did catch one, I doubt she'd know what to do with it. She's a softie at heart."

Ruby beamed up at them both as they walked along. The cute little dog was irresistible.

"How long have you had Ruby?" Lisa asked, still smiling at the scruffy creature.

"Two years. I adopted her from a rescue centre. Or maybe she adopted me. You're a good pal, aren't you Ruby?"

Ruby glanced up and snorted.

"She has a big personality," Lisa said. "It's almost as if she knows everything you're saying."

"I wouldn't be surprised if she did. I probably chat away to her far more than is normal, and I'm sure she's figured out some words and voice inflections over the years. She's good company at home and it doesn't matter that she doesn't talk back. Company is company, whether it's a human or an animal." Jake laughed and then gave her an embarrassed look. "That probably sounds stupid."

Lisa shook her head. "It doesn't, not at all. You live by yourself?"

"I've had housemates in the past, but when I moved to Willowbridge and could afford my own place, I decided it would be nice not to have to share anymore. The last housemate I had was a disgusting slob, and I'd had enough of his dirty dishes abandoned in the sink for days on end, and cartons of leftover take-away food turning putrid in the fridge because he was too lazy to clear them out. I liked the idea of only having my own mess to worry about for a change. What about you? Do you have flatmates, or a partner, or…"

"I'm by myself, too," Lisa said, and left it at that. She didn't want to get into the upsetting reasons why she was alone, because it would only turn their conversation gloomy, which would be a shame considering they were enjoying this lovely peaceful walk in the late evening sunshine.

They arrived at the pond and Ruby strained on her lead in excitement at the ducks flapping their wings in the water. Jake unclipped her lead and the little dog ran off yapping and wagging her tail. After announcing her arrival to the ducks, who quacked in response, she detoured to some shrubs at the water's edge where she began sniffing with interest.

"We only walked around the pond five minutes ago," Jake laughed. "Ruby acts as if everything is brand new and she's seeing it for the first time."

"And yet she looks completely engrossed," Lisa said, charmed by Ruby's intense exploration of the shrubbery and its scents. "Dogs have a thing or two to teach us about living in the moment, if we'd pay attention."

"You're absolutely right." Jake gave Lisa a thoughtful look. "It's funny, but I've lived in this town for two years, and yet I'd never visited your café until Saturday when my coffee machine at home went on the blink. I've walked past the café more times than I can count, and if I'd known the cakes you sell there were half as good as they turned out to be, I might have found it hard to stay away."

Lisa blushed at the compliment. "That's very kind, thank you."

"Mrs Wishmore said you do all the baking yourself?"

"Guilty."

"I don't see how it's possible to bake all those cakes and treats I saw for sale in that display case in your café. There were so many choices. How do you do it?"

"I've been doing this for a long time and have a good system in place that means I can produce a lot of baking to keep the stock levels healthy. And it helps that I love what I do. When I'm mixing and baking and decorating, it doesn't feel like work." She glanced towards Jake and shrugged. "When you're passionate about something, you want to do it all the time."

Jake's gaze held hers for a long moment. "That makes perfect sense. I feel the same way about teaching."

"What subject do you teach?"

"History. I studied British and American history for my degree, and I love them both. It's fun getting paid to teach something I enjoy so much, and I love working with the kids and helping them thrive."

Lisa smiled. "I always thought that teaching was a high-pressured and difficult job. At least, that's what it sounds like when there are stories in the news about how tough things are in our schools."

"Don't get me wrong, there are lots of things about the job that annoy me. The endless paperwork and bureaucracy, I could do without those, no question. But I love the actual teaching. I love helping the kids to learn and understand and discover what they're capable of. I love knowing I'm playing some small part, no matter how tiny, in helping them get the most they can out of school and sending them off into the world with the confidence and skills they'll need out there. Our kids deserve the best we can give them, and..." He tailed off and looked embarrassed. "I'm getting carried away, sorry."

But Lisa shook her head. "I'm enjoying listening to what you're saying." It was true. Jake's eyes had lit up while he'd been talking about his work, and his animated smile and bright energy had drawn her in. It seemed to her that Jake felt about teaching the same way she felt about baking.

She paused, wondering if she ought to share that thought, or if it would sound crass considering the two jobs weren't at all similar. Glancing at Jake, she saw his open expression and found herself talking again.

"My job is completely different from yours," she said. "But I like to think I'm making a contribution, too. I love baking and I love making my little café into a haven from the world where people can take time out and relax and enjoy something delicious. I happen to believe we all need a slice of home-made cake from time to time. It's nourishing and comforting. When I bake my cakes, I imagine I'm sending good things out into the world for people to enjoy. It's a small contribution, but it gives me pride and a sense of purpose and..."

Now Lisa was the one to stop talking. She cast a shy glance towards Jake, realising she'd said far more than she intended. Given that this was only supposed to be a quick stroll around the park with a passing acquaintance who she'd only recently met, it surprised her how easy it had been to talk so freely with him.

And to talk about things that mattered to them both, too, and about which they were passionate.

Jake's gaze stayed on her as they stood beside the pond. "For what it's worth, the slice of chocolate cake I ate on Saturday was the highlight of my day."

Lisa saw the look in his eyes and felt the intensity of his gaze, and gave an embarrassed laugh. "In that case, you need more excitement in your life."

Too late, she realised her comment sounded mean. The man had already told her he lived alone, and what she'd said might be hurtful. Jake had complimented her baking, and she'd responded with a stupid remark, because of the way he'd been looking at her. She searched his face for signs that she'd insulted him, but Jake's expression was now hard to read.

"Although considering the highlight of my day is the moment I fill my café display case with all the cakes and treats I've baked, I probably need a bit more excitement in my own life, too," Lisa said, keen to make amends for her inconsiderate comment. "And I should get out and enjoy the fresh air more often than I do. This is the first decent walk I've had in ages. Working in the café all day and dealing with business admin in the evenings doesn't exactly make it easy to find time to get out and about."

"That's one excuse I don't have, thanks to Ruby," Jake said. "No matter how busy I am, she needs to go out for a walk. Even when I'm up to my eyeballs in marking in the evenings, I still need to set aside the work and take her out. It probably does me more good than Ruby. It helps clear my head and gets me refocused."

"I should make more of an effort. Especially now that it's summer."

They paused at the edge of the pond, and Lisa closed her eyes and tilted her head and breathed in the sweet evening air. When she opened her eyes, Jake was watching her, a shy smile at his mouth.

"Ruby and I usually drive into the New Forest during the weekend and enjoy a long walk," he said. "You'd be welcome to come with us."

Lisa turned in surprise at the invitation. "Oh, that's a nice offer, but I wouldn't want to intrude—"

"You wouldn't be," Jake said quickly, then gestured to his little dog who was now trotting ahead of them on the path. "Ruby would love it if you came along. She's always looking for someone new to show off around."

Lisa smiled and then laughed when Ruby spun around on

the path and barked. The scruffy animal had an amazing knack for knowing when she was being discussed.

"Well, in that case, how can I refuse?" Lisa said.

"Great!" Jake said.

Lisa saw the surprise in his face. Perhaps he hadn't thought she'd agree, and she hoped he wasn't having second thoughts about the invitation. When he spoke again, Lisa's doubts disappeared.

"We usually set off around eleven on Sundays," Jake said. "Does that work for you?"

As the Daffodil Café was closed on Sundays, it worked perfectly. "That's fine with me. Where in the New Forest shall I meet you?"

Jake looked like he was weighing something in his mind. "I can pick you up, if you like. No reason why we should both take our cars when we're going to the same place."

"Okay, thank you."

"I'll check out some trails, and later in the week I'll let you know where we're going. Is that all right?"

"It's perfect."

They were exchanging phone numbers when it struck Lisa that this now felt an awful lot like they were planning a date together. Her cheeks coloured and she suddenly felt awkward. One moment the two of them were enjoying relaxed conversation and a stroll around the park following an impromptu meeting. Now, they were arranging to get together again and exchanging contact details. Lisa wondered if that was such a good idea, especially considering how keen she'd been to escape her date with Tim earlier in the pub.

But as she put Jake's details into her phone, she felt no desire to get away from him. As they turned towards the park gates, she was sorry that their evening walk was over. She'd enjoyed his company and that of his sweet little dog.

"So, I'll see you on Sunday," Jake said as they prepared to part ways at the gates.

"I'll look forward to it." Leaning down, Lisa ruffled Ruby's ears. "Bye, Ruby."

The dog pushed its nose into her hand and Lisa laughed. With a wave, Jake and Ruby walked off in one direction and Lisa walked off in the other. When she reached the turn for the high street, she couldn't resist glancing back over her shoulder. She blushed when she realised Jake had looked back, too.

Lisa hurried home, feeling foolish and excited and also strangely unsettled. She'd enjoyed Jake's easy company and comfortable conversation, she told herself, and that was all. Perhaps they'd become good friends.

Or perhaps they'd become more than good friends, said a voice inside her head.

She shut the voice down before it could say anything else.

CHAPTER TEN

The following morning, Lisa was busy in the Daffodil Café preparing an order of toasted teacakes and cappuccinos when Fiona hurried through the door with an anxious frown on her face.

"Lisa, what happened last night with Tim?" Fiona asked, pulling off her jacket and dumping it in the staff closet. "He phoned and said the two of you barely lasted an hour together in the pub before you left. Didn't you like him?"

Lisa turned to her friend and made a calming gesture with her hands. "I liked him fine. He's a sweet guy. But I just didn't feel much of a connection."

Fiona's frowned deepened. "That's not surprising, considering you only stayed for an hour. The two of you hardly had time to get past the awkward first-date getting-to-know-you stuff."

"We had plenty of time and I enjoyed chatting with him. But I just wasn't attracted to him, Fiona. Not romantically, at least. I'm sorry, but I didn't see much point in hanging around for a second drink when I knew it wouldn't go anywhere." She glanced across the café to where customers were waiting for their order. "I'd better deliver these cappuccinos before they get cold."

Lisa picked up the tray she'd prepared and carried it to an elderly couple sitting by the window. The sun was shining outside and the high street looked especially quaint and pretty this morning. The gift shop across the road was already attracting passing tourist trade and it wasn't even ten o'clock yet. Half the tables in the café were filled, too, with customers enjoying morning coffee and cake. It was set to be another busy summer's day in Willowbridge, and Lisa wondered if she ought to pop an extra batch of clotted cream scones into the oven to make sure there would be enough baked goods to keep her customers happy.

When she returned to the counter, Fiona was still hovering there. Lisa set aside thoughts about her baking stock. She owed her friend more of an explanation than she'd given her about last night's date.

"Fiona, I'm really grateful that you set me up with Tim," Lisa smiled. "It was thoughtful and kind, and you gave me the kick up the backside I needed to get back out there again as far as men are concerned. But you don't want me to waste Tim's time, do you?"

An uncertain look crossed Fiona's face. "Well, no, of course not."

"And we said it would just be one quick drink together, right?"

"Sure, but..."

When Fiona said nothing further, Lisa squeezed her friend's arm. "I hope you're not angry with me. I'd hate for us to fall out because of this. If I'd known that might happen, I would never have agreed to the date in the first place."

Fiona's eyes widened in surprise. "No, of course we're not falling out. Don't be silly. All I wanted was to get you out of that flat of yours and spend time with a nice guy. It's not like I expected you to come in here this morning and tell me you'd fallen head-over-heels in love after one evening in the pub with an old mate of mine. But…"

Again, she trailed off, and Lisa saw Fiona biting back her words.

"What is it?" Lisa said. "Tell me what you were about to say."

Fiona huffed out a breath and shrugged. "I just hope you didn't cut things short last night with Tim because you were comparing him in your head to Peter. You'll only end up miserable if you do that with every man you spend time with."

Fiona's frank tone startled Lisa. It was true that she'd thought about Peter last night while she'd been in the pub with Tim, and she'd only be lying to herself if she denied having compared the two men. But she couldn't help it. Peter had been the love of her life.

"Last night was the first time I've been out with a guy since Peter died," Lisa said softly. "As much as I enjoyed Tim's company, I couldn't stop my mind straying and thinking about Peter. Maybe that was only to be expected. I can't turn off what I still feel for Peter and pretend like he never existed."

A pained look crossed Fiona's face. "I'm sorry if I rushed you into last night."

"You didn't. I was one who asked you to set it up. And the evening wasn't a total loss in the end."

Lisa couldn't help the smile curving at her lips. Seeing it, Fiona's unhappy look turned to one of curiosity.

"What happened?" Fiona asked.

"After I left the pub, I bumped into Mrs Wishmore and we took a stroll through the park together. We ran into a friend of hers, Jake. I met him for the first time at the weekend when he came into the café for coffee. The two of us got chatting and..."

"And?" Fiona demanded, her eyes wide with obvious excitement.

"And we had a quick stroll together around the park and Jake asked if I'd like to drive over to the New Forest this weekend. He has a little dog, Ruby, and we agreed to take her a walk there together."

For a moment, Fiona only stared. Then she grabbed Lisa's arms and let out a screeching whoop that had the café customers glancing over in alarm.

"That's amazing!" Fiona all but yelled as she shook Lisa like a rag doll. "I'm so pleased!"

"Calm down," Lisa laughed. "We're only going for a walk in the forest."

"But you're doing it under your own steam, not because someone steered you into it, the way I did with Tim."

Lisa thought about this. "I suppose that's true. Although, now that I think about it, I can't help but wonder if Mrs Wishmore might have had a hand in this somehow."

"What do you mean?"

"I was supposed to be walking with *her* in the park when we ran into Jake and his dog. And as soon as Jake appeared on the scene, Mrs Wishmore hurried off and left us alone."

Fiona only shrugged. "Maybe she had to go somewhere?"

Lisa thought back to the odd explanation Mrs Wishmore had given when she'd suddenly departed last evening. One minute, the older lady had been planning a relaxed walk in the park on her way home, and the next she'd been in a rush to visit her friend. It hadn't made much sense then, and it didn't make much sense now, either.

"So, tell me about this guy, Jake," Fiona said, interrupting Lisa's thoughts. "What does he look like? If you're ditching Tim for him, he'd better be completely gorgeous."

Lisa laughed, and was about to surprise herself by saying that Jake was indeed completely gorgeous, although not in the conventional sense Fiona meant, when the café door opened, the little bell above it tinkling sweetly, and Mrs Wishmore walked in.

"Good morning, ladies," Mrs Wishmore said. "I thought I'd start early today, Lisa. It's such a lovely day, and I guessed the café might be busy." She glanced around at the customers already enjoying coffee and cake, and chortled. "And I see I'm right. I'll get my apron."

While Mrs Wishmore stored her jacket and handbag in the cupboard, Fiona threw a wink at Lisa.

"Lisa was just telling me about this amazing new guy she met last night in the park," Fiona said. "His name is Jake. Apparently he's a friend of yours."

Mrs Wishmore tied on an apron and her smile widened. "That's right. I'm lucky to count Jake and his little dog, Ruby, amongst my friends." Her gaze turned to Lisa. "So the two of you had a nice walk in the park together after I left?"

"We did," Lisa said. "We were sorry you had to rush off, though."

"It couldn't be helped," Mrs Wishmore said cheerfully.

"And maybe it was for the best," Fiona said. "Because now Jake and Lisa are having a date together in the New Forest this weekend."

"It's not a date!" Lisa insisted, although she knew her objection sounded lame.

"He asked you out, and you said yes," Fiona said with a shrug. "That's a date."

"We're going for a walk with his dog, that's all. The fresh air will do me good. I was just thinking that I don't get out into the New Forest enough. It's right on our doorstep and I ought to make the most of it."

Fiona's eyes danced with amusement. "It's a date."

"It's two new friends getting together to enjoy the great outdoors," Lisa said.

"Oh, please." Fiona rolled her eyes and turned for the kitchen. "I'm off to start the lunch preparations. And while I'm working, I'll be thinking about how happy I am that you've got a *date* lined up. A *date* you organised all by yourself. And it's about time, too."

After Fiona left, Mrs Wishmore gave Lisa a kind smile. "I'm delighted to hear that you and Jake will be spending some time together. He really is a lovely young man."

"Do you know much about him Mrs Wishmore?" Lisa said as she stacked clean cups and saucers beside the coffee machine. "He said you'd only recently met, but it would be nice to have a bit more information about him before I see him again."

"Well, as it happens—"

Before Mrs Wishmore could say anything further, Lisa's phone rang in her pocket. When she glanced at the screen, she saw it was the recruitment agency calling. The company still hadn't sent over any paperwork for Mrs Wishmore's temporary waitressing position, and Lisa assumed they were phoning about the matter. She answered the call as she hurried to her office at the back in case she had to pull up any information on her computer screen. The woman on the phone introduced herself as Katie Armstrong, a senior recruitment consultant with the agency.

"Ms Morgan, I'm sorry it's taken so long to get back in touch with you," Katie said.

"That's all right," Lisa said. "I know how paperwork can get a little jammed up in the system."

"I appreciate you being so understanding about this. We can't apologise enough."

Lisa frowned, wondering why the agency would be so concerned about administrative paperwork being delayed for a few days. It hadn't seemed to trouble them when she'd used their services in the past. "There's nothing to apologise for. If you email the forms through today, I'll make sure they're filled out and returned by tomorrow."

There was a long pause on the other end. "What forms do you mean?"

"The forms I need to fill out for Mrs Wishmore."

"Who's Mrs Wishmore?"

Lisa sighed. She wished the staff at the agency would get their details straight before they called her up. Mrs Wishmore was *their* job-hunting client, and she shouldn't have to remind them of the woman's name.

"She's the temporary waitress you supplied me with on Friday," Lisa said. "She's doing an excellent job here, and I'm thrilled to have her help while my permanent waitress is recovering from an injury."

There was another long silence on the end of the phone. "Ms Morgan, perhaps there's been some confusion," Katie said. "I was phoning to apologise because we failed to fulfil your employment request."

Now it was Lisa who was silent, not to mention confused. "What are you talking about?"

"We had a major IT malfunction here at the agency office on Friday," Katie explained. "Unfortunately, many of the requests for staff we received that morning were lost as a result, and it took a while for us to pull everything from our back-up system. In the upheaval of getting our services back online, we mislaid your staff request. We only discovered the mistake today when we finished auditing the IT outage."

Lisa listened to what the recruitment consultant was saying, but it didn't make much sense. Or any sense, for that matter.

"Look, there must be some mistake," Lisa said. "Mrs

Wishmore arrived on Friday afternoon and has been working here ever since."

"That can't be right. Our records show that we never processed your staffing request. As I said, it was lost in the system until we discovered it in our audit. As soon as we realised our mistake, we wanted to phone immediately and apologise. We failed to meet our high standard of customer service and we know we let you down."

"But you didn't let me down!" Lisa almost shouted down the phone as bafflement and frustration mounted. "I'm looking through my office door at Mrs Wishmore who is out there in my café serving my customers as we speak!"

More silence filled the line. "Well, I'm not sure how to say this," Katie said. "But we didn't send a waitress to you on Friday, because the IT outage meant your staffing request wasn't processed into our system or assigned to any of our recruitment specialists."

Lisa peered through the glass pane in the office door, watching Mrs Wishmore bustling around and slicing cake at the counter. "So how can you explain the fact that I have a waitress out there right now, working in my café?"

"I'm afraid I can't explain it," Katie said after an awkward pause.

As Lisa stared through the office door at Mrs Wishmore, she felt her brows beetling together in sheer confusion.

"What did you say was the name of the woman who's working there in your café?" Katie asked. "Perhaps if I can access her records directly in our system, we might get to the bottom of this."

"Her name is Mrs Wishmore, Doris Wishmore," Lisa said, feeling sure this new approach to the recruitment agency's obviously disorganised record-keeping processes would solve the mystery.

But after listening to the recruitment consultant tapping

a keyboard on the other end of the phone, Lisa heard the woman let out a frustrated sigh.

"We don't have anyone on our books with that name," Katie said. "I'm sorry, but whoever is working in your café, she didn't come from us."

Lisa shook her head. "I don't understand this."

"Did you request help from another recruitment agency? Perhaps this employee was sent by another company?"

But Lisa knew that was impossible. During Friday's mayhem, she'd only found time to contact one agency. "You were the only one I called."

"I'm not sure what else to say, Ms Morgan," Katie said. "It sounds like you ought to chat with your temporary waitress and find out how your wires got crossed. In the meantime, please accept our sincere apologies for failing to fill your employment needs and letting you down."

As Lisa said goodbye and ended the call, she didn't know what to think. If the recruitment agency hadn't sent Mrs Wishmore, then where had she come from?

Lisa was still staring through the office door at the older lady, watching her serve customers and fill their coffee and cake orders. She was obviously a highly competent waitress. But a troubling mystery now surrounded the woman, and the fact that the recruitment agency knew nothing about her made Lisa deeply uneasy.

Was it possible that the older lady wasn't quite the cheerful waitress she presented herself as, and was instead up to no good? Had she discovered the café was short-staffed and insinuated herself into the middle of the crisis, pretending to be a much-needed helping hand in order to exploit Lisa's trouble for her own personal gain?

Lisa's stomach clenched with anxiety when she thought of how she'd shown Mrs Wishmore how to use the cash till and the credit card system. It would be all too easy to steal money from the café, either in hard cash or through electronic transfers, and for the theft to go unnoticed for at least a few days, maybe longer. Feeling clammy at the thought, and angry with herself for not checking Mrs Wishmore's employment credentials before now, Lisa left her office and went out into the café.

"Mrs Wishmore, can I speak to you in my office?" Lisa said.

The older lady turned from the table where she'd been jotting down a customer order. "Of course, dear. But I was just about to start work on this order for tea and cake."

"I'll ask Fiona to deal with it."

Lisa saw the concern on Mrs Wishmore's face as she left the café front of house and went into the office at the back. After asking Fiona to deal with the new customer order and hold the fort for a few minutes, Lisa joined Mrs Wishmore, closing the door behind her.

"I had a phone call just now from the recruitment agency I called on Friday when I was short-staffed," Lisa began. "Mrs Wishmore, the manager I spoke to says they didn't send you here. In fact, they've never heard of you."

Lisa gauged the reaction on the older woman's face. Mrs Wishmore stared at her for a long moment before smiling and shaking her head.

"There must be some mistake," Mrs Wishmore said. "How else would I have known to come here?"

"Well, that's what I want to know. The agency say they had IT problems on Friday and overlooked my request for a temporary waitress. They were phoning to apologise for not sending someone."

Mrs Wishmore's eyes widened. "But they did send someone. They sent me!"

"They insist they didn't send you. They don't even have a record of your name in their files."

"Goodness, that simply isn't correct. Someone from the agency called me on Friday afternoon and told me about the urgent vacancy here at the café. As I was available and it was an emergency, I came as quickly as I could."

Lisa searched the older lady's face for signs that she was lying. But all she saw was the woman's open expression and kind eyes.

"I really want to believe that this is just some horrible mix-up," Lisa said. "Who did you speak to at the agency when they called on Friday?"

Mrs Wishmore narrowed her eyes in thought. "I can't remember the young man's name. But I can show you the record of the call on my phone."

She rose from the chair and left the office, returning a moment later with her blue handbag which she'd fetched from the store cupboard. After pulling a phone from inside a zippered compartment and tapping at the screen for a few seconds, she nodded in satisfaction before turning the phone around so Lisa could see it.

Lisa looked at the screen. Sure enough, there was the log of an incoming call from the recruitment agency, received early on Friday afternoon. Lisa saw from the time stamp that the call had arrived only ten minutes after she'd contacted the agency for help.

Still, she wanted to be sure that the contact details listed on Mrs Wishmore's phone did belong to the recruitment agency.

"Do you mind if I dial this number?" she asked. "As the agency manager insisted they don't know who you are, I need to find out what's going on here."

Mrs Wishmore nodded and held out the phone. "I understand, dear. Please, go ahead."

Lisa took the phone and dialled the contact number that was listed there as belonging to the recruitment agency.

After a few rings, someone answered and said, "Zenith Recruitment Agency, how can I help you?"

She hadn't been sure what to expect after dialling the number. Part of her feared that if Mrs Wishmore was up to no good in her café, and exploiting Lisa's staffing emergency for personal gain, she might have rigged her phone to make it seem like someone had called her on Friday morning from the recruitment agency, when no one had phoned her at all. On the one hand, that all seemed incredibly convoluted. On the other hand, Lisa knew she'd been too trusting, allowing a stranger to work in her café without confirming the details with the agency, and Mrs Wishmore's cheerful friendliness and undeniable waitressing skills had convinced her she'd got lucky when the older lady appeared and saved her from disaster just when she needed it most.

But it now appeared that someone from the recruitment agency *had* phoned Mrs Wishmore on Friday, just like she'd said. Perhaps there was a simple explanation to this mystery after all.

"I had a call a few minutes ago from one of your managers, Katie Armstrong," Lisa told the person on the other end of the line at the agency. "Can I speak to her please?"

"I'll see if she's available." After a moment, Lisa heard the call being transferred, and then it was Katie Armstrong's voice on the line.

"Ms Morgan," Katie said. "I was just about to phone you again."

"Good, because I've been speaking to my temporary waitress, Doris Wishmore, and she insists you sent her here. What's more, there's a call from your office to her phone that seems to suggest you do know her, despite what you told me."

"I know, and she's entirely correct," Katie said quickly. "I am so sorry, but all this has been a huge mistake on our part. I'm still trying to understand how it happened, but perhaps I could explain what I've discovered since I talked to you a moment ago?"

"Yes, please," Lisa said, feeling relief flood through her. She liked Mrs Wishmore, and hated to imagine her as someone who might be out to trick her. There was something about the older lady that made it impossible to see her as anything other than good.

"After we spoke," Katie said, "I went back into our systems to see if I could understand what happened. I was upset to think of an employee working inside your business who you thought had come from us and who we knew nothing of. When I dug a little deeper, I realised we did send Mrs Wishmore to you after all."

Lisa blew out a breath. "Thank goodness. So how did all this confusion happen?"

"Well, it's all a little odd. After we spoke, I went back into our records to look for the name Doris Wishmore, just in case there had been a search error. As soon as I started looking, her name popped up right away. I have no idea why my earlier database search didn't return her record."

Lisa frowned, her alarm at the prospect of Mrs Wishmore being some sort of interloper now turning into annoyance at the recruitment agency's incompetence. "And what about the fact that you said your staff didn't process my request for a waitress?"

"Again, that's more than a little odd, too," Katie said, her voice now sheepish. "Once I had Mrs Wishmore's file on my screen, I was able to click through to her current job assignment, which is with yourself, of course. As soon as I did that, all the record entries appeared for your recruitment request and our deployment of Mrs Wishmore to your business. It seems our staff dealt with the request right before our IT problems started. Quite why I couldn't find any of this in the system earlier isn't clear. My best guess is that our IT outage affected our record logs, although..."

Lisa heard the agency manager's uncertain tone. "Although?"

"It's probably just a computer glitch, and I won't bore you with the details, but I don't know how these records could have disappeared and then reappeared without some trace of the error appearing on our system. And when I finally located the files, my computer screen kept flashing on and off before the records appeared in the folders, which is very strange and something I haven't seen before. Our computer system is new and reliable and we've never encountered problems like this before, either the IT outage on Friday or this silly mess this morning locating these employment records. Rest assured our IT engineers are looking into this incident as we speak."

"Well, I'm just glad we got to the bottom of this," Lisa said, and glanced at Mrs Wishmore who was still sitting in the chair across from her, the understanding smile on her face making Lisa feel guilty. "It wasn't pleasant having to interrogate my waitress about all this."

"I sincerely apologise," Katie said. "I'm so sorry for the confusion."

They spoke briefly about the employment paperwork that was still to be completed, and the agency manager promised to send it through right away. Based on this morning's fiasco, Lisa didn't hold out much hope of receiving it anytime soon. Once the call was over, she turned to Mrs Wishmore.

"Doris, I'm so sorry about this. It's all been a big mistake and the agency have made a mess of this whole thing. I feel awful for quizzing you about things."

Mrs Wishmore shook her head and smiled. "You mustn't

feel bad. This is your business and you must have complete confidence in your employees. If there's been a mix-up at the recruitment agency, that's not your fault."

"It all sounded very complicated," Lisa said, frowning as she thought about the agency manager's description of disappearing files inexplicably reappearing, and malfunctioning database searches, and computer monitors flashing. It really was rather odd, just as Katie Armstrong had said. "The agency had a major IT problem that has snarled up all your personnel records."

"Well, these things happen from time to time," Mrs Wishmore said with an easy shrug. "And all these new-fangled computers can't be trusted at the best of times. They're so glitchy!"

When the older lady laughed, Lisa joined her, although she was surprised by the humorous sparkle in Mrs Wishmore's eyes, given that only a few moments ago Lisa had been interrogating her rather rudely. The older lady really was easy going and quick to forgive.

"Anyway, I'm just glad it's all sorted now and I can get back to work." Mrs Wishmore rose from the chair and gave Lisa an uncertain look. "That is, if you're still comfortable with me working here after all this confusion."

"Of course I am. You're a wonderful waitress, Doris, and I love having you here. I'm just sorry for quizzing you like that." Lisa blushed as she recalled imagining the older woman as some sort of thieving confidence trickster, skimming the café's income. She tried to push the thought away, but that only made her blush harder still.

As if reading her mind, Mrs Wishmore reached out and squeezed Lisa's arm. "It's perfectly natural to be sceptical and wary. But you can trust me, Lisa, I promise."

Mrs Wishmore gave her arm another gentle squeeze, and as Lisa looked into the older lady's bright blue eyes and felt the warmth of her smile, she found herself feeling deeply comforted. The alarm and anxiety of the last fifteen minutes vanished in an instant, and Lisa knew beyond any shadow of a doubt that Mrs Wishmore could be trusted, just as she'd said. The weight of Mrs Wishmore's hand on her arm reassured her, and Lisa felt a warm glow spreading through her body in response to the kindly woman's touch.

"I'll get back to work, dear," Mrs Wishmore said and turned for the door. "And I'll brew a nice pot of tea for us, too. After all this confusion, we could certainly use it."

Mrs Wishmore shuffled from the office, her warm chuckle making Lisa smile. She was relieved the woman had been so understanding about this stupid mix-up caused by the agency, and had no hard feelings following Lisa's awkward questioning. Mrs Wishmore didn't strike her as the sort of person who would bear a grudge, but she'd been remarkably reasonable and level-headed about it all.

Lisa thought of the strange series of computer glitches the agency manager had described. It was all a bit odd, even if it had worked out in the end. Lisa's hand moved to her arm and to the spot where Mrs Wishmore had squeezed her gently.

You can trust me, Lisa, I promise, Mrs Wishmore had said.

She knew it was true. But as she rubbed at the spot on her arm, and found it tingly and warm, Lisa couldn't help but wonder about Mrs Wishmore.

Peering through the office door, she watched the older lady brewing tea behind the café counter, humming cheerfully to herself as she worked.

There was something about Mrs Wishmore, Lisa decided. Something she couldn't quite put her finger on.

CHAPTER ELEVEN

Jake rang the doorbell to Lisa's flat and tried to stop his heart racing inside his chest.

It was Sunday morning, and he'd agreed to pick Lisa up at eleven for their walk in the New Forest. After their meeting in the park, Jake had expected her to back out of today's plans. They hardly knew each other, and he wondered if his invitation had caught her off-guard and she just hadn't wanted to admit it to his face. So when he'd phoned to arrange a pickup time, he'd been surprised to hear her talking enthusiastically about the outing and how good it would be to get out into the fresh air.

Now that he was here to pick her up, though, he couldn't help but wonder if she'd find some last minute reason not to go. When he thought back to their evening walk in the park, he cringed at how much silly chatter he'd inflicted upon her, rabbiting on about his disgusting former flatmate, and boring her about the joys of dog ownership and so many other things. Jake wasn't usually an excessive talker, but something about being with Lisa had made him nervous and loosened his tongue far too much.

So, he expected her to answer the door with some excuse at the ready, and he'd end up walking Ruby by himself as usual. After so many dates and relationships that had gone nowhere, it was easy to imagine being ditched and to prepare accordingly.

Just last week, when his friend Marie had invited him to dinner in order to pair him off with someone, he'd assured himself that life was better spent by himself, or at least a lot easier. He wasn't looking to get involved with a woman, and he wasn't looking for romance.

Or so he'd thought until that evening when he'd met Lisa in the park and asked her to join him for his weekend walk with Ruby. Quite where those words had sprung from, Jake would never know. He'd expected Lisa to turn him down. And yet, she hadn't.

Over coffee in the school staff room, he'd told Marie about his plans with Lisa, and admitted his doubts about whether it would actually go ahead. Marie, in typically blunt fashion, and told him to stop being an idiot and focus on the positives.

It was good advice, and as Jake waited for Lisa to answer the door, he put that advice into practice. Lisa had agreed to go with him on a walk, hadn't she? And she hadn't backed out when they'd agreed on the meet-up time. Those were all good signs.

So why hadn't she answered the door yet?

Jake rang the bell a second time. The door was at the top of a small flight of external stairs at the back of the building in which Lisa's café was located, and he took in the potted plants clustered on the steps and the cheerful gnome standing guard beside the doormat. Admiring the outdoor decorations told him something about Lisa—that she took pride in her surroundings, which he already knew from the time he'd spend inside her pretty café—and had the added bonus of stopping him from rapping the door again.

If he had to knock on the door a third time, that wasn't a good sign, surely?

Jake was about to turn and leave when he heard locks clicking and the door opened. Lisa stood there smiling and looking breathless, as if she'd hurried to get there.

She was so pretty it made Jake's head spin. Her hair, which he'd only seen in a ponytail before, fell around her shoulders in a tumble of curls. Her eyes sparkled and her cheeks glowed, and he caught a faint whiff of her perfume, his nose filling with the soft scent of jasmine. She wore dark jeans and a pale green sweatshirt that matched the colour of her eyes. Even the well-worn hiking boots on her feet looked spectacular to him, even although that was obviously ridiculous.

Jake realised he was staring with his mouth gaping open like a goldfish. He quickly plopped it closed and offered her a smile by way of hello.

"Sorry I took a minute to answer the door," Lisa said, looking apologetic. "I was icing a cake and had to complete the piping to avoid ruining the pattern and making a mess of the decoration."

"No problem. Do you have more work to finish?"

She shook her head and locked the door behind her. "I'm all done and looking forward to getting out."

They walked down the steps and Jake gestured to his car parked on the narrow road that ran behind the building. When he opened the passenger door for Lisa, she gave him a smile that almost had him falling over his own feet as he walked around to the driver's side.

When he got behind the wheel, Ruby was scrambling around in the boot of the hatchback, excited about the new passenger.

"Hello Ruby," Lisa said, turning in her seat towards the little dog. "Are you looking forward to a walk in the New Forest?"

Ruby barked and looked out the window, ready to go.

"Thanks for inviting me along on your walk, Jake," Lisa said. "We've got such a lovely day for it, too."

She was right. The sky was a perfect summer blue and the sun was already warm. Jake started the car and drove towards the main road out of the town.

"The walk I chose isn't too difficult," Jake said. "It should take about an hour, and there's another path we can add if we want to keep going a little longer."

"Sounds good."

Jake turned his attention to the roads, which were already busy with Sunday day trippers out enjoying the Hampshire countryside. Concentrating on the traffic had the added benefit of stopping him from talking too much. With the radio playing and the summer breeze blowing through the open windows, the drive south into the New Forest was more relaxed than Jake had imagined. The conversation was also surprisingly simple and easy, especially with Lisa pointing out interesting sights as they drove and commenting on the beauty of the landscape as they made their way deeper into the rural idyll.

When they pulled into a parking area thirty minutes after setting off, the sun was high and the air was sweet with the scent of trees now in full leaf. Jake had chosen this location because the trail would take them through a mix of terrain, including woodland and heathland and along the edge of a pretty stream, and show off the forest at its summery best.

"Look!" Lisa said, pointing through the trees beyond the car park. "Ponies!"

Jake smiled at the obvious joy on Lisa's face at the sight of a group of five New Forest ponies making their way through the trees, their tails and manes swishing. There were three adults and two foals. Two of the ponies were chestnut and the other three were grey, their coats catching the dappled sunlight falling through the trees and making the scene look like a picture-perfect postcard image.

"Although there are ponies everywhere in the forest, I never tire of seeing them," Lisa said, gazing at the gentle ponies as they grazed on a lush patch of grass.

Jake clipped Ruby's lead to her collar and locked the car. "Ruby seems to think the ponies enjoy being chased, which is why she stays on the lead when we come here."

Ruby snorted, as if disputing the necessity of her restraints, and they both laughed. The group of ponies started walking again, and one of the chestnut adults veered in their direction, curious about the visitors. When the animal walked straight over to Lisa and allowed her to reach out and touch it, Jake was stunned.

"Wow, that's never happened before," Lisa whispered and stroked the pony's neck, her expression awestruck. "What a treat!"

The pony blew out a warm breath from its long nose before returning to its group and they all disappeared further into the woodland.

"Ruby managed not to ruin the moment by yapping in the poor pony's face and scaring the life out of it," Jake said, just as amazed by this as he had been by the proximity of the friendly pony. "That deserves a gravy bone."

After feeding the dog a treat, they set off along the winding trail that led through the woods. Birds flitted amongst the top branches of the trees and the sweetness of the air only deepened the further they walked into the woodland. At one point, they caught sight of a deer darting across the trail in the distance, which brought another bright smile of joy to Lisa's face.

Jake liked seeing that smile of hers. It lit up her entire face and made her eyes dance. After only twenty minutes of walking, and with their conversation a blend of relaxed chit-chat about the scenery and easy back-and-forth as they got to know one another better, Jake realised the pretty café owner was making his heart do things it hadn't done in a long time.

He wasn't sure how he felt about that. So much for his policy of steering clear of women. He'd only just met this girl, and he was already letting himself get carried away with stupid ideas about what might be going on between them. If Jake knew one thing, it was that he couldn't let his inevitable excitement get the better of him yet again. He'd been down that road too many times to count.

"So, what's it like running your own café?" Jake said, keen to focus the conversation on easy chit-chat. "The work must be non-stop."

"It's a busy life, but I love it," Lisa said. "I like being my own boss and running things the way I want them. Although with the café open six days a week, it makes it hard to find time to get away and do things like this. Which is why I'm so grateful you asked me along today." She tipped her head back and breathed in the sweet woodland air. "I need to make more of an effort to come to places like this on my day off."

"You're welcome to join Ruby and I anytime," Jake said. "Now that it's summer and the days are long, we sometimes come here on weekday evenings, too. I could drop you a message the next time we're setting off, if you're interested."

What happened to taking things easy? Jake scolded himself. They'd only got out of the car and started walking half an hour ago, and already he was badgering the poor woman about seeing him again.

When Lisa glanced his way and nodded, he felt nothing but relief.

"I'd like that, if you didn't mind me tagging along."

"You wouldn't be tagging along. I like your company, Lisa, in case you haven't realised that."

He'd been more forthright than he'd planned. But as soon as the words left his mouth, he knew he wanted Lisa to understand that he hoped this might turn into something more than just two friends taking a Sunday morning stroll together. He couldn't help himself and wondered if there was any point in even trying. He glanced in her direction to see how she'd taken his comment. A blush coloured her cheeks, and she gave him a shy look.

"I like your company, too, Jake."

Ruby barked and scurried closer to Lisa. "And I like your company, too, Ruby," she added with a laugh.

"Have you always lived in Willowbridge, or did you move there because it was a good place to set up your café business?" Jake asked, keen to learn more about Lisa's life.

"I grew up near Reading," she said. "My parents still live there. When I was thinking about running my own café, I looked at lots of locations, but I loved Willowbridge the best. It's a sweet place and it has a great character. Plus, the town is large enough to support a high street café outside of the tourist season. The locals have given me a lot of wonderful support."

"It's a great place. I taught in a big city school for a few years before I took the job at the high school in Willowbridge. There were thousands of students on the register back there, and I like the change of pace with smaller classes and the chance to get to know the kids a little better."

"Everyone is excited about the school summer fair," Lisa said. "Are your preparations almost finished?"

"Nowhere near finished, but we'll all have a mad panic and pull out the stops and get it all done, if previous years' experience is anything to go by."

Lisa laughed and Jake watched her for a moment as they crossed a small stone bridge over a gurgling stream. "I was speaking to the headteacher last week about the cakes you're donating to the home-baking stall from your café, and she says the last time you dropped off a load of baking for the fair, it sold out in minutes."

"I'm sure she was exaggerating," she said. "But I'm glad to help raise some money for a good cause."

A thought occurred to Jake. "I helped with the fair last year, even although I wasn't on the organising committee back then, but I don't remember seeing you there, or seeing any baking from your café."

For a long moment, Lisa didn't respond. When Jake looked over, she was walking with her head down, her hands fidgeting inside the pockets of her sweatshirt. He'd thought he was just making conversation when he'd mentioned not seeing her at last year's fair, but judging by the pained expression on her face, he'd touched a raw nerve. Quite how, or for what reason, he couldn't guess.

"I wasn't able to provide any baking for the fair last year," Lisa said. She looked up with a smile on her face that seemed forced, and pointed towards the clearing up ahead, where an old coaching inn stood. "Oh, that's a sweet building, isn't it?"

Jake understood she was changing the topic, although he didn't understand why. He wondered what he'd said wrong.

"This is a great pub with great food," Jake said. "When I picked this trail, I thought it would make a good place to stop off. Can I interest you in some lunch?"

Lisa nodded. "You read my mind."

Jake only wished that was true.

THE COSY PUB was already busy with customers when they strolled through the door, but they got lucky when the waiter showed them to a table beside the window with a view of a stretch of open heathland where ponies were roaming. As the inn was dog-friendly, Ruby received a biscuit from the glass jar kept at the bar before curling up on the carpet at Jake's feet and falling asleep. The little dog roused herself when their meals arrived, begging a few chips from their plates before curling up again and snoring her head off beneath the table, much to the amusement of other nearby diners.

"Your steak pie looks amazing," Lisa said, peering across the table at Jake's plate and the enormous serving of pie and chips heaped on it. "I have order envy."

"Me too. Your chicken curry smells fantastic."

"Want some?" Lisa said.

Before he could answer, she spooned up some curry and added it to the side of his plate. The intimacy of the gesture—sharing her food with him in this way—caught him by surprise. In response, he forked up a generous helping of his steak pie and set it on her plate.

"This is delicious," Lisa said after tasting the pie. "The pastry is perfect."

"I don't know what they've done with this curry mix, but I love it," Jake said, wolfing down the chicken and the warm, aromatic sauce in which it was coated.

"I haven't had a good curry in ages. It's a fiddly thing to put together when you're only cooking for one, and…"

When she trailed off, Jake glanced up from his food and found her frowning.

"Why are you on your own?" he said, only realising how blunt it sounded once the words were already out there. "What I mean is, you're smart and funny and beautiful, Lisa. Any man would be lucky to have you."

His cheeks burned hot with embarrassment. He was making a total mess of this and saying things he shouldn't be saying, considering they'd only just met each other. But he was curious about why Lisa wasn't already in a relationship with someone. In the short time they'd spent together, she'd seemed lonely, although he couldn't quite put his finger on why he thought this, only that he did. Jake was sure there was no reason why Lisa should be alone if she didn't want to be.

For a long moment, Lisa said nothing as she pushed food around her plate with her fork. When she looked up at last, her eyes were clouded with sadness, and Jake's stomach clenched, wondering what was wrong.

"My fiancé, Peter, died last year," Lisa said, her voice quiet.

Jake couldn't help the stunned gasp escaping from his mouth. "Lisa, I'm so sorry. That must have been terrible."

Still pushing food around her plate, she half-nodded, half-shrugged. "It was. It still is. We'd only just got engaged and were excited about planning our wedding. It felt like the start of a wonderful adventure together, and then in the blink of an eye he was gone." She looked up and gave him a sad smile. "He died in a road accident. There was a motorway crash and Peter got caught in the middle of it. He was killed instantly."

He saw her struggling with emotion and saw the pain etched across her face. "I don't know what to say. I can't imagine what you went through. I feel stupid for what I said about any man being lucky to have you. I'm sorry."

"You didn't know anything about it, so there's nothing to be sorry for." She smiled and sipped her drink before continuing. "The truth is, I was hoping none of this would come up and that I could avoid talking about it, at least for now. When we were walking earlier and you asked why I didn't provide any baking for the school summer fair last year, I avoided answering because I didn't want to talk about what happened. Whenever I talk about Peter's death, or whenever I think about it, I just get so sad, and I don't want to be sad. I came out with you today because I hoped it would be fun, and it definitely won't be fun if I'm talking about my dead fiancé."

She laughed softly as she said this, and the mixture of humour and grief in her voice struck Jake as both honest and brave.

"I can't imagine what you went through," he said, realising he was repeating himself, but the magnitude of what she'd told him seemed to call for it. "And we won't talk about it if you don't want to. But losing your fiancé was a terrible, tragic thing to happen, and if you want to talk about it, I'm here to listen."

"Thank you, I appreciate that. I hope you don't think I'm pretending it didn't happen, because obviously that's impossible. When the one-year anniversary of Peter's death came around last week, I felt sad and stunned and angry all over again that he was gone. But I also realised something else, too—that I had to start moving on with my life, even although I can hardly imagine what that will look like."

"It takes a lot of courage to move on after something so awful and tragic. It can't be easy."

Lisa's expression softened and she smiled. "Peter was a good man and I loved him with all my heart. He was funny and kind, and filled with dreams about all the things we'd do together. I couldn't wait to be married to him. But I know he'd want me to get on with living my life, instead of hiding away from the world, which is what I've been doing. Although it's painful and hard, the anniversary of his death made me realise that the best thing I can do to remember him, and what we had together, is to just keep going, and hope that one day everything will feel better than it does right now."

Jake watched her as she spoke, and when she dropped her gaze and shifted in her chair, he saw her cheeks colour.

"Sorry, that was a bit deep," she said, giving an awkward laugh and glancing down at her food.

"No, it wasn't. It's a hard thing to talk about. I'm glad you wanted to share some of it."

Her hand lifted to the neckline of her sweatshirt and Jake saw her run her fingers over the pendant on her necklace. A blush coloured her cheeks, and when she dropped her hand away, Jake saw that the pendant she'd been fidgeting with was in fact a diamond ring.

"This was my engagement ring," Lisa said, clearing her throat and tucking the ring back beneath her shirt. "It wasn't easy taking it off after Peter died, and so I put it on a necklace instead. I know that probably sounds weird."

"Of course it doesn't," he said, watching her fight against an obvious instinct to touch the engagement ring again. It clearly still meant a great deal to her, even after all this time.

Jake couldn't help but wonder if Lisa really was ready to move on again if she was still wearing her engagement ring around her neck. He had no idea what to make of that.

Perhaps she saw the question in his expression because she waved a hand towards her meal and offered a bright smile. "Anyway, I've talked enough about my sad story, and our food is getting cold. I really want to finish this curry. And also steal another one of your chips."

Ruby's furry head popped up from beneath the table just then, her nose high in the air as she sniffed out their food. Her hopeful expression made them both laugh, and Jake was glad the little dog had helped lighten the mood. He was still absorbing the grim horror of Lisa's bereavement, his head reeling at the agony she must have endured, and the last thing he wanted was to spend the rest of their meal looking stunned by what she'd told him. Ruby's funny face peering up at them in search of treats was just what he'd needed to see.

"Time for a post-nap snack, is it?" he said, and fed Ruby a chip from his plate. As the dog munched on the morsel, Lisa helped herself to another of his chips, dipping it in pie gravy before popping it in her mouth.

"Hey, you two, leave some for me," Jake laughed, pretending to horde the plate to himself.

"There's enough food on these plates to feed four people, never mind two," Lisa said. "Which is a shame, because I was hoping I'd have room for dessert."

"In that case, we'll take our leftovers home in doggy bags."

Ruby let out a little yap at this, once more making Lisa laugh. Jake liked seeing her eyes light up as she ruffled the dog's ears, and was happy that his mangy mutt could make her happy, especially after what she'd just told him.

How did you find happiness again after losing the person you loved most of all in the entire world? Jake couldn't imagine it was possible. As he watched Lisa across the table, petting Ruby before picking up her fork and once more digging into her curry, he wondered about the kind of person she was, and the strength she must have inside her, to haul herself up and somehow keep going after what she'd been through.

"I'm glad you came out with Ruby and me today, Lisa," Jake said. "After what you just told me, I'm guessing you haven't been out much recently with... uh, men. Or their dogs."

Lisa stared for a moment before giving a surprised laugh. "I suppose you could say that. Although when you and I bumped into each other in the park last week with Mrs Wishmore, I'd just been on a date with a friend of a friend."

"Oh, right," Jake said, feeling blindsided by this news. The way Lisa had talked a moment ago, she was only just finding her feet in the world after the shock of her bereavement. Realising she was already seeing other men sent a bolt of resignation straight through him, wondering if it meant that she saw him as no more than a new friend. He poked at the chips on his plate as he tried to get his thoughts in order. "And, um, how did that go?"

"Not so good," Lisa said quietly.

Jake's spirits lifted. Keeping his expression neutral, he risked finding out more. "What happened?"

"There just wasn't much of a connection. It was the first time I'd been out with a man since Peter died, and it wasn't easy. To be honest, I felt sorry for the bloke, having to put up with me fleeing the scene before he could so much as buy me a second glass of wine."

Jake felt even better now, childish though he knew it was. Lisa hadn't stayed beyond a first drink with this other man, whoever he was, but she was still here with him today, eating lunch and making conversation. That had to count for something.

"If I'm being honest, I just wanted to get out of my flat and meet someone new," Lisa continued. "The guy I had the date with was a friend of a friend, and I thought it couldn't hurt to have a drink with him and at least get the ball rolling in that part of my life again. I feel bad for not sticking around longer for a second drink, and think my friend might have been more ticked off about it than she let on."

"I have a friend who's always trying to set me up with her female friends," Jake said. "She thinks I'm a pathetic git who needs to be paired off with somebody as soon as possible before I turn into a grumpy old man."

Lisa grinned. "She sounds like a good friend."

"She's a pain, most of the time, but I love her." Jake grinned. "And I secretly think she might be right about the grumpy old man thing."

"I never thought I'd be back out on the dating scene again after Peter and I got together. It's all a bit terrifying."

"You'll get used to it soon enough," Jake said, and then wished he hadn't said that, because he didn't want Lisa to get used to dating again. What he wanted, he realised, was for her to get used to dating *him*. "Anyway," he said, clearing his throat and spearing the last chunk of steak pie, "I hope this trip out isn't too hard for you."

She shook her head. "It's not hard at all. I'm having fun."

"Good." He smiled and gestured outside the windows, where a herd of ponies were ambling across the heathland as the summer sun shone down, tossing their manes and flicking their tales. "Because if you're planning on fleeing this place, like you fled your last date, you've got a bit of a hike back to civilisation."

Lisa grinned. "I don't plan to run off this time."

They fell into an easy silence as they finished their meals. Inside the cosy pub, the chatter of the other diners was pleasantly comforting, and as Lisa ate a final forkful of her lunch before pushing her plate away and insisting she couldn't eat another bite, Jake felt more relaxed than he had in a long time.

"Shall we get some dessert?" he asked.

"I'm absolutely stuffed."

"The sticky toffee pudding looks too good to turn down," he said, nodding to a nearby table where a family was tucking into enormous bowls of pudding drenched in ice cream.

"I couldn't eat anything else," Lisa said.

"Maybe next time?" Jake said, trying and failing to keep the hope out of his voice. This was just supposed to be a relaxed Sunday trip to the New Forest with no expectations or strings attached. He didn't want to pressure her into agreeing to seeing him again when they hadn't even finished the rest of their woodland walk.

"Sure, next time," Lisa said, a warm smile on her lips.

It was the only polite response available. But Jake would take it.

LATER THAT AFTERNOON, Jake pulled his car to a stop on the lane behind Lisa's building and wished their time together wasn't ending so soon.

Their New Forest walk and pub lunch had been fun, and Lisa's revelations about the tragic death of her fiancé had touched him and only made him want to get to know her better. After what she'd said about how much she'd struggled to move on in the year since her fiancé died, Jake knew he ought to tread carefully before asking if she wanted to get together again soon. He didn't want to scare her off by being too eager.

"Thanks again for lunch," Lisa said, releasing her seat belt and opening the car door. "And thanks for a great trip out into the countryside. It was wonderful seeing the ponies and enjoying the woodland. I really enjoyed it."

"My pleasure. And I think Ruby enjoyed the extra company, too."

In the back of the car, Ruby yapped out a bark.

"She has a sweet personality," Lisa laughed.

"Don't tell her that. It'll only undermine me when I remind her she's a useless, no good mutt and that I'm sick of the sight of her."

Lisa laughed again. Jake could get used to hearing that laugh. For a long moment, they stared at each other. Jake wondered what it would feel like to lean closer and lay a kiss on her cheek.

As if she'd read his mind, Lisa blinked in surprise and then threw open the car door.

"I should go," she said and jumped out from the passenger seat. "I've got baking to prepare for the café tomorrow and... some other things to do."

"Uh, Lisa, wait—"

"Bye Jake!"

In a flash, Lisa hurried up the back stairs to her flat and pulled her keys from her pocket.

"Okay, see you soon," Jake called out through the open car window.

She responded with a wave before unlocking the door and disappearing into her flat. Jake stared up at the back door for a long moment, wondering at her hasty departure.

Over lunch, she'd mentioned fleeing from the date she'd had last week. Had she just done the same thing again? Considering they'd spend half the day together, and lingered over lunch in the cosy country pub, he wouldn't exactly say she'd been eager to get rid of him.

But maybe she'd seen the intention in his eyes as they'd sat in the car and legged it before he could do anything about it.

It wasn't the first time something like that had happened to him. Still, the afternoon had gone pretty well, in his opinion, all things considered.

"What do you think, Ruby?" Jake asked his dog as he drove home. "Was she glad to get rid of me? Or will she want to see me again sometime?"

Ruby panted in the back, but offered no opinion either way.

"You're no use," he told the dog.

As he steered along Willowbridge high street, Jake wondered about that long moment he'd shared with Lisa in the car when they'd stared into each other's eyes and he'd come so close to kissing her.

Kissing her would've been a mistake. He realised that only too clearly. It was too soon.

But he'd enjoyed the moment, just the same. It had felt charged and also tender, even although Lisa had leapt from the car and fled to her flat.

He hoped she'd want to see him again. He hoped the pain of her bereavement wouldn't stop her from moving on in life. It was what she said she wanted to do, after all. Perhaps it was something she'd want to do with him.

How did someone ever move on from losing a fiancé? Jake wondered again as he drove. He'd never loved a woman enough to ask her to marry him. In fact, he'd never even come close. None of his relationships had ever lasted that long. The women in his life all eventually decided they only wanted to be his friend, rather than his lover. But that didn't mean he couldn't imagine what it must feel like to love someone enough to want to marry them.

The idea of falling in love with someone and getting engaged, only to have them ripped away because of a tragic road accident, was the stuff of nightmares.

So how did a person move on after losing the love of their life?

Hot on the heels of this thought came another—how could someone ever compete with a dead fiancé?

Jake sighed. He didn't like that question. He wondered if that was what he was hoping to do here—compete with a dead man for Lisa's affections. When they'd talked in the pub, Lisa hadn't hidden her feelings for her fiancé and had been honest about just how much the man had meant to her. She still wore the engagement ring he'd given her on her necklace because she'd loved him so much and had planned to spend the rest of her life with him.

Now here she was, dipping her toes back into the dating waters, trying to find her feet again out there in the world of romance. And all Jake could think was that he was already halfway to being completely smitten with her, even if they had only spent one afternoon together.

And all he wanted to know was the answer to one question—how could he compete with the man who'd once claimed Lisa's heart?

Jake pushed the question from his mind. He already suspected he knew the answer—he couldn't compete, not in a million years.

Sighing, he thought instead of the school assignments waiting to be marked back at home. Those would keep him busy, he knew, and stop him from pondering horrible questions destined only to have horrible answers.

CHAPTER TWELVE

On Monday morning, Lisa was pulling a batch of chocolate chip muffins from the oven when Mrs Wishmore walked into the café kitchen, smiling as she unbuttoned her jacket.

"Good morning, dear," Mrs Wishmore said. "And what a morning it is, too. It must already be close to seventy degrees outside and it's not even eleven o'clock yet."

"We're set for a scorcher," Lisa said, transferring the muffins to a cooling tray. "Which means the day trippers will be out in force again. I've baked more goodies to make sure we can meet demand."

As Lisa slid a gingerbread traybake into the oven, which she'd whipped up while Fiona held the fort out at the counter, Mrs Wishmore threw an admiring glance at the cooling muffins which were perfuming the air with the aromas of milk chocolate and vanilla.

"Those look wonderful," she said. "I'm sure they'll fly out the door."

"Here, try some."

Lisa picked up a muffin which had turned out lop-sided

and wonky, and which she wouldn't feel happy putting out for sale, and cut it in two before handing Mrs Wishmore the bigger half. The older lady's eyes lit up.

"What a treat," she said, biting into the piece of muffin. "And it's absolutely delicious. You are such a talented baker, dear."

"Hey, save some for me!" Fiona said, hurrying into the kitchen with a tray of dirty dishes and eyeing the muffin that Lisa and Mrs Wishmore were eating. Lisa grinned and slid a plate towards her cook, containing the chunk of muffin she'd already cut for Fiona from her own piece.

"As if I'd ever eat freshly baked cake and not share it with you," Lisa said, before starting a new batch of sponge batter in the mixing machine.

Fiona chomped her piece of muffin and gave Lisa a thumbs-up. "Gorgeous, as usual. Anyway, all the customers out in the café are happy, and now that Mrs Wishmore is here, I'll finish my lunch preparations."

"Good idea," Mrs Wishmore said, turning for the kitchen door. "I'll make myself useful and clear some tables."

Once Lisa's sponge batter was mixed, she scraped it into a tin and slid it onto a free oven shelf. When she turned around again, she realised Fiona was staring at her. "What is it?"

"Are you going to make me beg for details?" Fiona said, rolling her eyes. "I've been working here for half an hour already this morning, and you still haven't told me how your date went with that guy, Jake, yesterday."

Lisa frowned. "We've been busy. I haven't had time."

"You've got time now. The cakes are baking and the customers are happy. So, hurry up and spit it out."

"It wasn't really a date," Lisa said.

"Please don't start with that nonsense again," Fiona said.

Mrs Wishmore reappeared in the kitchen carrying a tray of dishes for washing.

"Mrs Wishmore," Fiona said. "Tell Lisa to stop being silly. She says she wasn't on a date yesterday, which is utter nonsense."

Mrs Wishmore laughed. "Lisa, Fiona says you should stop being silly. And I must admit, it did rather sound like a date to me."

"Okay, fine," Lisa said. "It was a date. And it went fine."

Fiona's gaze stayed on her, and when Lisa said nothing else, Fiona threw a perplexed glance towards Mrs Wishmore, who was unloading her tray on the other side of the kitchen.

"It went fine?" Fiona said. "That's all you've got to say about it?"

"We had a nice walk and stopped off for some lunch. I enjoyed it. Jake seems like a great guy."

"I sense a 'but' coming," Fiona said.

Lisa sighed and thought back to the strange moment she'd shared with Jake in the car at the end of their date. "When Jake dropped me off back home, I think he might have been about to kiss me. But I ran away before he could do it."

Cringing with embarrassment and confusion at the memory, Lisa grabbed a tray of chilled rocky road from the fridge and carried it through to the café counter. Fiona abandoned the sandwich preparation she'd begun and followed hot on her heels, with Mrs Wishmore bustling along in their wake.

"You *ran away?*" Fiona hissed, her expression horrified. "Why on earth did you do that?"

"Look, I don't even know if he *had* been about to kiss me, or not," Lisa said, slicing the rocky road into squares and transferring the chunky pieces to a plate. "He just had this look in his eye, but maybe I misread things. I don't know. I'm out of practice with all of this."

"When you say you 'ran away', what exactly do you mean, dear?" Mrs Wishmore asked kindly.

Lisa slid the plate of rocky road into the glass display case and blew out a breath. "I jumped out of his car and bolted up the stairs to my flat."

"Oh no," Fiona muttered, her eyes wide with disbelief.

"Did you at least say goodbye to the young man first?" Mrs Wishmore asked.

"Yes, of course."

At least, Lisa thought she'd said goodbye, although she couldn't be entirely sure. She remembered throwing Jake a wave as she fled up the stairs to her flat door, and seemed to recollect having said something to him right before she leapt from the passenger seat of his car, which might or might not have been along the lines of 'goodbye'. In truth, however, it was all a bit murky.

"Have you spoken to him since?" Fiona asked.

"Of course not. We only saw one another yesterday afternoon. I don't want to look like I'm desperate, do I?" When Fiona only glared at her, Lisa shrugged and added, "Although he sent a message in the evening, saying he'd had a good time and hoped we could see each other again."

Fiona's expression lit up at this news. "Brilliant! Well, at least we know you didn't scare the poor guy off when you ran away from him for no good reason."

"It wasn't for no good reason. I thought he was going to kiss me!"

"And what would've been so wrong with that?" Fiona asked.

"Do I have to spell it out for you?" Lisa said, irritated now at her friend's lack of sensitivity.

"No, of course you don't," Fiona said. "But maybe you

need to spell it out for yourself. You agreed to go out on a date with this guy, Lisa. You can't be surprised that he'd want to kiss you at the end of it. I mean, come on, you're a knock-out."

Lisa couldn't help smiling. "You're a good friend, Fiona."

"She is, indeed," Mrs Wishmore said, giving Fiona a fond squeeze on the arm. "And what she says is true. You're a smart, interesting, and beautiful young woman, Lisa. Jake would have to be a fool not to want to end your lovely afternoon together with a friendly peck on the cheek. And one thing I know for certain about Jake Reid is that he is no fool."

"Somehow, I don't think it was a peck on the cheek he had in mind," Lisa said, remembering the way Jake's gaze had dropped to her mouth and lingered there. Even thinking about it now made her skin tingle, and what made it worse was not knowing if she found that tingling exciting or terrifying or both.

"The last man I kissed was Peter," Lisa continued, her voice quiet. "I thought he'd be the only man I'd ever kiss for the rest of my life. Yesterday, when I said goodbye to Jake and I realised he might be about to kiss me, it all just felt too strange suddenly. I know I'm being a pathetic wimp."

"You're not," Fiona said. "You're just in uncharted territory, and that means you need to be brave. Plus, having a good snog with this bloke will put a sparkle in your eye, if nothing else, and that can only be a good thing."

Lisa blurted out a laugh.

"I should get back to the kitchen and deal with my sandwich prep," Fiona said, then threw her a wink and added, "The next time you see him, just snog him. I'm sure it'll be worth it."

"Fiona has a good point about jumping in with both feet," Mrs Wishmore said once Fiona had gone. "But only you know when it will be the right time for you to take these next steps in your life."

"When I agreed to go out with Jake, I thought I was ready. Now I'm wondering if I'm not really there yet. I don't want to mess this guy around or give him mixed signals like I did yesterday."

Mrs Wishmore smiled, her eyes filled with warmth and compassion. "Be kind to yourself, Lisa. You've already taken an enormous leap with young Jake. Just trust your heart to tell you when it's time to take another."

Lisa looked at the older lady for a long moment, feeling comforted by her words and by their easy simplicity.

"You're a fount of wisdom, Mrs Wishmore. Thank you."

"My pleasure, dear. I'm here to help, after all."

"Listening to my personal issues wasn't what you signed up for when you came to work in the café."

"Like I said, I'm here to help, Lisa. In any way I can."

Mrs Wishmore smiled again, and Lisa once more found herself comforted by the older lady's presence and appreciative of her good advice.

Over by the window, two women who'd just finished their coffees and cakes waved towards the counter to catch their attention, no doubt wanting to settle their bill.

"I'd better serve these ladies," Mrs Wishmore said, hurrying out from behind the counter and already smiling for the café patrons.

The café door opened and Lisa saw her two favourite customers, Mildred and Jean, shuffling inside and making a beeline for the cake display case.

"Ooh, look, Jean!" Mildred said as soon as they reached the counter. "There's rocky road today!"

"Freshly sliced not two minutes ago, ladies," Lisa informed the old women.

"Wonderful!" Jean said. "On our way here, we were just

saying we hadn't had any rocky road in ages, weren't we, Mildred?"

"That's right," Mildred agreed. "It plays havoc with my dentures, but I don't let that stop me."

Lisa laughed as she plated two thick slices of rocky road for the women.

"You look lovely today, Lisa, if you don't mind us saying," Jean said.

"Thank you, Jean."

"There's a sparkle in your eyes that hasn't been there for a long time," Mildred said thoughtfully. "It's nice to see you looking brighter."

"Yes, it is," Jean said. "It's very nice indeed."

"Any particular reason for that bright smile of yours today?" Mildred asked.

Lisa thought about the question, and was surprised when an image of Jake popped into her head, walking beneath the sunshine in the dappled shade of the New Forest, his little dog, Ruby, scampering at his feet.

"No particular reason," Lisa said, even as that image of Jake swirled in her head. "It's a glorious summer's day and I'm looking forward to a busy day of keeping my customers happy, that's all."

"Good for you," Mildred said.

"Ladies, here's a table for you by the window," Mrs Wishmore called over, beckoning the older women across the café. "I know how much you both love a window view."

"Perfect," the two old ladies said at the same time and trundled off towards the table that Mrs Wishmore had cleared.

"We'll have a pot of tea with our rocky road, Lisa," Jean called over her shoulder.

"Good strong tea, please," Mildred added.

"I'll pop an extra bag in the pot as usual," Lisa assured them.

While the two old ladies settled themselves at their window table and shared some friendly chit-chat with Mrs Wishmore, Lisa looked around at her little café, taking in the satisfied customers, and the fully stocked cake display case, and the aroma of freshly brewed coffee, and the smell of the soup Fiona was cooking in the kitchen for the lunch service, and suddenly she felt surrounded by all the good things she had to be grateful for in life.

She thought again of Jake, too. Although she'd botched saying goodbye to him yesterday, she knew she wanted to see him again and spend more time with him. Kissing him might be a step too far, for now at least. But the idea of not going out with Jake again wasn't one she liked at all.

As soon as she'd set tea brewing for Mildred and Jean, Lisa pulled her phone from her pocket and sent Jake a message.

If you're planning on walking Ruby tonight in the park, maybe I could tag along? Lisa typed. Her finger hovered for a long moment over the send button.

At last, she pressed it and blew out a loud breath of relief.

When she looked up, Mrs Wishmore was smiling at her across the café as she cleared plates from a table. When the older lady winked, Lisa couldn't help but wonder if she'd somehow guessed who she'd been texting and what she'd written in the message she'd sent.

Lisa dismissed the silly idea with a laugh. Mrs Wishmore might be a little mysterious, but she wasn't a mind reader.

The café door opened and new customers walked in. Lisa grabbed her order pad and got back to work.

CHAPTER THIRTEEN

Jake was collecting his afternoon lesson plan from the school staff room when he saw Lisa's message on his phone, which he kept in his locker during the teaching day. As he read the text she'd sent, his stomach flipped in excitement.

If you're planning on walking Ruby tonight in the park, maybe I could tag along?

After their botched farewell in the car yesterday, he hadn't known whether he'd see her again, or whether she'd find some excuse to avoid another date. Despite the great afternoon they'd shared, he'd been stunned by the look of surprised horror on Lisa's face when he'd almost leaned across the car seat and kissed her. The more he thought about that look, the more he wondered if Lisa was as ready to move on in her life as she'd claimed to be.

While he'd been asking himself if he could compete with the man she'd loved and lost, it had occurred to him that Lisa might not even give him the chance to find out.

So, seeing the message she'd sent made Jake smile from ear to ear. He tapped out a quick reply.

We'd love to see you. We'll come by your flat on our way to the park. How does six-thirty sound?

He sent the message and watched the screen to see if she'd reply right away. Then he remembered it was lunch time, which he guessed was Lisa's busiest time at the café. Jake tucked the phone back into his locker, resigned to waiting until the end of the school day before hearing from her again.

"What are you smiling about?"

Jake looked up and saw his friend, Marie, walking into the staff room carrying a towering pile of marking in her arms.

"I'm seeing Lisa again tonight," Jake said.

Marie balanced the pile of marking against her hip as she opened her locker and pulled out a canvas tote bag. She slid the stack of paperwork inside and grinned at Jake.

"And there you were worrying she might not want to see you again," Marie said. "I told you not to be such a doom monger. So, where are you two going?"

"We're taking Ruby to the park."

Marie arched an eyebrow. "Another dog walk? Can't you come up with something more exciting than that?"

"It was Lisa's suggestion. I think she wants to keep things low key, which, given what she said yesterday, I completely understand."

Over early morning coffee before the first period bell rang, Jake had told Marie about how Lisa's fiancé had died and that she was only now, a year later, venturing out into the world of dating again. The revelation had moved Marie, but while his friend might have compassion for Lisa's situation, Jake knew she had none for him.

"Well, if you two decide to see each other again after tonight, you'd better come up with something better than walking Ruby," Marie said. "This woman might still be finding her feet after a terrible loss, but that doesn't mean she doesn't want to be wowed by someone new in her life."

"I don't want to scare her off."

"You don't want to bore her to death, either. Get your thinking cap on, Jake, so you're ready with a good idea for your third date."

"Assuming she wants to go on one."

"She will. Why else would she suggest seeing you again if she wasn't interested?"

Jake said nothing. Marie had a good point. But in his experience, women usually enjoyed his company, and spending time with him, right until it was time to move things out of the friend zone and into the romance zone, at which point, everything ground to a halt. Which is exactly what had happened yesterday in the car, when Lisa had fled just before Jake had been about to kiss her.

Maybe Lisa just liked talking to him as a friend. Maybe she saw him as no more than a friend, and never would. Which left him where, exactly?

Jake frowned at the selfish thought. Lisa had lost her fiancé and had her heart broken, and all he could think about was whether she was interested in more than friendship. But he'd never get to that point if they weren't friends first. And as much as he'd wanted to kiss Lisa yesterday, he wasn't some revolting lech who was only interested in drooling all over the poor woman. He had more respect for women, and for himself, than that.

When the school bell rang for the start of the first period after lunch, Jake walked Marie out of the staff room and headed to his next class over in the history annex. He was halfway along the first floor corridor, navigating the streams of students making their noisy way to their classrooms, when he spied Bradley, the kid who was in charge of the coconut shy at the upcoming school summer fair, pinning something to a notice board on the wall. Bradley's friend, whose name Jake kept forgetting, was loitering beside him.

"Come on you two," Jake said. "Get yourselves to your next class or you'll be late."

"Sorry, Mr Reid," Bradley said, favouring Jake with his trademark cheeky grin. "But we wanted to put up all our posters during our lunch break, and this is the last one."

Jake peered at the poster Bradley was pinning to the cork notice board. It advertised the boys' forthcoming coconut shy attraction at the summer fair in bright colours and eye-catching font, and announced that the grand prize would be a gift voucher worth twenty-five pounds to spend at the Willowbridge pizza restaurant on the high street.

"How did you get your hands on a twenty-five quid pizza voucher?" Jake asked, amazed at the boys' entrepreneurialism.

"My uncle Jason owns the pizza place," Bradley said. "When I told him that Trevor and me were running the coconut shy to raise money for school, he donated the vouchers."

"That's nice of him," Jake said. "Be sure to tell him thanks from me."

"Will do, Mr Reid. Me and Trevor made these posters on my computer at the weekend. What do you think?"

"I think they look pretty good. You're born salesmen, lads."

The boys grinned, pleased with the compliment.

"But if you don't get a move on, you'll get in trouble with your next teacher," Jake added with a smile. "Off you go."

To make sure they started walking to their class, Jake hovered while the boys packed the rest of their posters and box of tacks back into their bags, and watched them hurry off along the corridor. When they'd gone, Jake looked back at the poster they'd pinned on the board, impressed by what the boys had created under their own steam. With these eye-catching posters, not to mention the pizza gift voucher they were offering as a grand prize, they'd attract a lot of attention to their coconut shy at the summer fair, which was now less than a week away. He was pleased the boys had found a productive outlet for their endless energy.

Jake was about to walk off towards his next class when another poster further up on the notice board caught his attention. Printed on bright yellow paper, it announced that the Willowbridge Open Air Cinema Club were showing a special screening of *The Greatest Showman* on Wednesday in the community centre car park. According to the information, tickets were available from the club secretary, there would be a hot dog vendor and popcorn cart available on the evening, and everyone was welcome, although space was limited and people were advised to book early.

Jake stared at the poster for a long moment, remembering Marie's advice that he ought to come up with something more interesting to do with Lisa on their third date, assuming there would be one. The idea of an open air cinema event ticked all the right boxes as far as Jake was concerned, and with the hot summer weather set to continue for the rest of the week according to the forecasts, it sounded like just the thing to show Lisa he meant business. *The Greatest Showman* wasn't exactly his favourite film, but there was no denying it would make for a fun evening of entertainment.

Jake jotted down the contact details for the open air club secretary, hoping there were still tickets available, and hoping that, if there were, he'd have a reason to use them after tonight's second date with Lisa.

If, in fact, it was a date, and not just another friendly walk in the park.

A man could hope.

Joining the hordes of students hurrying to their classrooms, Jake turned his thoughts to the afternoon of teaching that lay ahead.

AFTER ONE OF the busiest Monday afternoons the café had ever had, Lisa was glad to be outside in the fresh air, enjoying the evening sunshine in the park and listening to the amusing sounds of Jake's little dog, Ruby, scurrying after the squirrels as they raced across the grass towards the safety of the trees. She was glad she'd suggested tagging along on Jake's evening dog walk, and as she glanced at the man walking beside her, it wasn't just the warm summer evening she found herself appreciating.

"How was your day in the café?" Jake asked as they strolled beside the pond, the ducks quacking as Ruby abandoned her squirrel chase and raced towards them.

"Hectic," Lisa said. "Two minibuses arrived in the village this afternoon filled with hungry day trippers in search of coffee and cake," Lisa said. "I don't know how we served everyone. It was some sort of miracle."

"You have good staff."

"No argument there."

Lisa thought back to the non-stop afternoon and the endless stream of customers who'd come through the café doors. From one o'clock until three-thirty, no table had been left empty for longer than the time needed to clear away the dirty plates left by the previous customers and seat the new ones who'd arrived. Between serving food and brewing hot drinks and whipping up extra baking stock in the kitchen while Fiona tried to keep up with the sandwich and soup orders, Lisa was well and truly wiped out.

Quite how Mrs Wishmore had kept up with the pace was a mystery, and yet by the end of the afternoon, the older woman had looked as fresh as a daisy, with her cloud of silvery hair looking just as perfectly styled as it had when she'd walked through the door earlier that morning. Lisa, in contrast, had been sweaty and sticky on account of the hot day, and after dealing with so many extra baking tasks in the kitchen, had no doubt looked like she'd been pulled through a hedge backwards. She was glad she'd had time to freshen up before meeting Jake for their walk.

"I don't know what I would've done today without Mrs Wishmore," Lisa continued. "She's the best waitress I've ever had. And although she's much older than my permanent waitresses, she could beat either of them hands-down when it comes to stamina, and that's saying something. I don't know how she does it."

"Mrs Wishmore strikes me as someone who's always on the go," Jake smiled.

"There were times today…"

Lisa tailed off, thinking back to the hectic afternoon service. Sometimes, it had seemed as if Mrs Wishmore had been clearing dirty dishes and serving coffee and cake far faster than was humanly possible. In fact, there had been one moment when Lisa had wondered if it was possible that the older lady was performing some kind of… magic?

She shook her head at the ridiculous notion. Clearly, the busy day at the café had left her more frazzled than she'd realised.

"What were you about to say?" Jake asked.

"Nothing important," Lisa said and laughed. "Only that there were times today when Mrs Wishmore seemed more like a magical fairy godmother than a waitress."

Jake smiled. "You must be happy that your café is doing so well. You've obviously built up a great reputation for the place."

"Great coffee, yummy cakes, tasty lunches, and a friendly

welcome for everyone who walks through the door. It's as simple as that."

"It's not simple at all. It takes hard work and a lot of persistence to do what you've done. Don't make it seem like it's easy or that anyone could do it."

"It's not so hard to bake a cake."

"Now you're talking yourself down. You're a smart and savvy businesswoman, running a café that attracts visitors from miles around. You should own that, not shrug it off."

He smiled and Lisa saw the kindness lighting up his eyes. "You must be a brilliant teacher, Jake. I bet you know just what to say to your students to make them believe in themselves."

"Teaching isn't so hard."

"Hang on, didn't you just tell me not to shrug off my accomplishments, and now you're the one who's..."

Jake's laughter stopped her talking, and when she glanced over he gave her a wry smile.

"Fine, point taken," Lisa grinned. "Do you trick your students with those kinds of tactics too, when you want them to understand something?"

"All the time."

She laughed at his casual reply and shoulder shrug, and realised she could get used to this easy conversation and back-and-forth with Jake. She realised, too, that she liked just walking along beside him, liked just strolling through the park on a warm summer's evening as they chatted about their day. Being with Jake was simple and comforting, which she hadn't expected after their awkward farewell yesterday afternoon.

Remembering how she'd fled from his car the day before now made her blush. Had he been about to kiss her yesterday, or had it been no more than a figment of her imagination?

And if he *had* been about to kiss her, what kind of kiss would it have been?

This thought made Lisa's cheeks flush all the harder. Only this morning, she'd been thinking about how weird it would be to kiss a man who wasn't Peter, even although she knew that was the inevitable result of deciding to date again.

Yet now, as she walked along beside Jake, she wondered if it really would be so weird, after all.

"So, Lisa, I was wondering—"

Before he could finish what he was saying, Lisa stepped towards him, grabbed the edge of his t-shirt and pulled him close. Her heart raced as she looked up into his eyes, and when the flash of surprise on Jake's face slipped into a dark, deep look that sent her stomach into somersaults, she tilted her head up and kissed him before she could come to her senses.

The warmth of Jake's lips on hers was delicious, and when he wrapped his arms around her and pulled her closer, she couldn't help but let out a soft murmur of delight. The summer sun shone down and the birds sang in the trees and the lovely moment was as perfect as perfect could be.

When the kiss ended and Lisa opened her eyes, she found Jake blinking at her in obvious astonishment.

"I wasn't expecting that," he said, his voice a whisper.

"Me neither." She ran her fingers along the edge of his jaw, liking the feel of his skin beneath hers and his hands on her hips. "I thought I wasn't ready for this. It turns out I was wrong."

Jake held her gaze, searching her eyes. "Are you sure?"

"I'm sure."

And to prove it, she kissed him again, allowing herself to savour it this time and enjoy the way his mouth moved against hers and the weight of his hands on her waist. For so long, she'd worried about what this moment would feel like, when she finally kissed a man again after the devastation of losing Peter. She'd feared it would be too hard, too awful, too painful, and just too much of a betrayal.

But kissing Jake wasn't any of those things. Instead, it was sweet and passionate and wonderful, and it made her body hum with pleasure and her mind turn blissfully blank.

Their second kiss might have gone on for much longer had it not been for Ruby rushing over and racing around them while yapping her head off, clearly unhappy about being left out. Laughing, Jake laid a last kiss on Lisa's lips before stepping away and looking down at the little dog.

"You're not jealous, are you?" he asked the creature, and Ruby barked in response. "You'll always be my best girl, Ruby, don't you worry about that."

Lisa laughed when the dog snorted at Jake and began jumping up to be petted.

"You're a real character, Ruby," she told the dog.

"Yeah, and a real nuisance," Jake grinned, tossing Ruby a biscuit from his pocket.

While Ruby ate her treat, Jake gave Lisa a shy look.

"I almost kissed you yesterday in the car, you know," he admitted.

"I know."

"You ran away before I got the chance."

"I know." She gave an awkward smile. "I'm sorry."

"Don't be. I can't imagine how hard it must be for you, moving on again, and doing all the different things in life that moving on involves after losing someone you love."

"I thought I wanted to take things slow. And then as we were walking along together just now, I realised that wasn't what I wanted at all."

Jake smiled and took his hand in hers. "Good. Because that was a heck of a kiss."

She felt herself blushing. "Uh, thanks?" she said, and then

only blushed even more because what kind of response was that?

Jake must have sensed her mounting embarrassment, because he laughed and said, "Before you grabbed me and mauled me, I was about to ask you something."

"I didn't maul you," she laughed, enjoying his teasing.

He crooked an eyebrow and pretended to check his t-shirt for damage, which only made her laugh harder.

"Anyway, what I'd been about to ask was whether you fancied seeing a film on Wednesday," he continued. "The Willowbridge Open Air Cinema Club is showing *The Greatest Showman* in the community centre car park. Would you like to go?"

Lisa smiled. "That's a lovely idea. I'm up for that."

"Great, because I already nabbed the last couple of tickets. You don't mind sitting on a deckchair in a car park of an evening, do you?"

"It's how I usually spend my Wednesday nights."

Jake snorted out a laugh. "They have some sort of roll-away screen they attach to the wall of the community centre and project the film onto it. Everyone brings their own chairs and cushions, so I've got us covered there. I'd never heard of this open air cinema club before, but apparently they're pretty popular."

"They only started up in the spring. The club secretary has popped into the café a few times to pin event information on the notice board. It sounds like a lovely event. I'm already looking forward to it. I'll bring movie snacks."

"They'll have a hot dog cart and a popcorn machine there on the evening."

"In that case, I'll bring dessert."

"It's a deal."

They'd completed a loop around the duck pond, and Ruby was scampering along ahead of them, sniffing at the shrubs lining the water's edge. Lisa stole a glance at the man walking by her side and smiled at the sudden change in how she felt about all of this, and about what might be going on between them. Yesterday, she'd felt nothing but anxiety at the thought of Jake kissing her. Now, she couldn't wait to kiss him again. She had no idea how things could have turned around so fast, only that they had.

It felt exhilarating and freeing, as if she was balanced at the top of a rollercoaster ride and about to plunge into a thrilling adventure, one she couldn't wait to begin.

"How about another walk around the pond?" Jake asked. "I don't think Ruby has sniffed every single blade of grass yet."

Lisa laughed. "Sounds good to me."

Jake took her hand in his and smiled, and as Ruby barked and ran around their legs, Lisa felt a lightness in her heart she hadn't felt for a long time.

CHAPTER FOURTEEN

Jake eyed the set of deckchairs he'd pulled from his garden shed, wondering if the creaky old things were up to the challenge of staying upright, and with people sitting on them, for the entire duration of a film. He'd wiped away the cobwebs and spruced them up with a damp cloth, but the chairs hadn't been used in a while and were grubby from being stored in the shed. He glanced at the metal garden chairs beside the table on the patio, and wondered if he ought to haul those along to the open air cinema night instead, but quickly dismissed the idea. Not only were they heavy and not especially portable, but they had straight backs that would become uncomfortable over the course of a couple of hours spent watching a film.

So, it was the creaky deckchairs or nothing. He ought to have checked their condition earlier, because then he could've gone out and bought new ones, but it was too late for that now. He was picking Lisa up in ten minutes.

Once he'd grabbed a couple of cushions from the living room sofa, he was sure the deckchairs would be up to the job.

After saying goodbye to Ruby, who was curled up on her

bed in the living room and half-asleep after the extra-long walk she'd enjoyed when Jake got home from school, he tucked the deckchairs and cushions under his arm and walked the ten minute route to Lisa's flat in the centre of Willowbridge.

"Let me help you," Lisa said when she came down the back steps. "I should've come to your place and helped carry all this."

"It's no trouble."

Lisa took the cushions from him, anyway. Jake noticed the plastic box she was carrying and spied something chocolatey-looking inside it.

"What's in there? It looks good."

"Just some mini brownie bites I made this afternoon in the café. I thought we might enjoy them after our hot dogs and popcorn."

"I'm not sure I can wait that long," he said, eyeing the box.

Laughing, Lisa opened the lid and offered him the box. "Help yourself."

Jake took one of the brownie bites and ate it, tasting dark chocolate and soft gooey sponge and sweet hazelnuts. "Wow. Those are amazing. I'm glad you made an entire box of them for us to eat."

"These aren't all for us," she said, laughing again. "I made enough so we could share them with the other cinema guests around us."

"Share?" Jake said with a frown. "You can't be serious. Why would we share these with people we don't even know? I plan on eating the lot all by myself."

"Jake, you'd be sick if you ate all this chocolate, and..." She glanced over at him and shook her head. "And now I realise you're joking."

He grinned as they turned off the lane behind Lisa's café

and made their way up the high street towards the community centre.

"It's sweet that you made extra to share with people," he said. "You have a good heart, Lisa."

She gave a shy shrug at his compliment, and Jake saw her cheeks colour. The blush made her look even prettier than she already did, with her hair falling around her shoulders and her summer dress blowing in the evening breeze.

"We've got a gorgeous night for it," Lisa said, glancing up at the blue sky. "Although the weather forecast said something about a chance of rain later, but I don't see how that can be right. There isn't a cloud in the sky."

"The forecasters never get it right. It's definitely not going to rain."

"Yoo-hoo! Hello you two!"

Jake turned and saw Mrs Wishmore walking along the pavement behind them, carrying a large shopping bag in one hand and with her red jacket slung over her other arm.

"Mrs Wishmore, let me help you with your bag," Jake said, adjusting the deckchairs he was carrying so he could take the older lady's bag.

But Mrs Wishmore waved him off. "I'm perfectly fine, dear, but thank you. This bag isn't as heavy as it looks, and it seems you have quite enough to carry as it is. I was just picking up a few things at the supermarket before I catch my bus." She gave them both a wide smile, her eyes sparkling. "So, you're off to see a film tonight, is that right? And in the great outdoors, too?"

Lisa nodded. "It should be fun. Here, have a brownie, Mrs Wishmore. I forgot to offer you one before you finished your shift earlier."

"Thank you, Lisa, but I'm meeting an old friend for dinner tonight, and I'd better not waste my appetite. Although, I must admit, those look delicious."

"They *are* delicious," Jake said.

Mrs Wishmore chuckled. "I don't doubt it." She looked thoughtfully up at the sky for a moment and then back at Jake and Lisa. "I hope this fine weather will hold for you both. They say there might be rain on the way."

"We were just reassuring each other that the weathermen don't know what they're talking about," Lisa said. "After all the beautiful sunshine we've had this past week, it would be a shame if it started raining on the night of the open air cinema."

"Fingers crossed that your evening goes smoothly," Mrs Wishmore said. "But sometimes, a little jolt of something unexpected can be just the ticket."

Jake gazed at the older woman for a second, wondering at her odd and mysterious comment. There was a strange and knowing glint in her eye as she looked at him and winked.

"Anyway, I'd better be on my way or I'll miss my bus," Mrs Wishmore said. "Have a lovely time, you two."

"Thanks, Mrs Wishmore," Lisa said as the older lady hurried up the high street and disappeared around the corner.

"What do you think she meant by that?" Jake asked Lisa as they crossed the road towards the community centre. "A little jolt of something unexpected can be just the ticket? That's a bit cryptic, don't you think?"

Lisa laughed. "Mrs Wishmore says the oddest things, I must admit. But even although I only met the woman a little over a week ago, she seems excited that you and I are going out together, so I don't think she secretly wants us to get soaked in the rain tonight, if that's what you're thinking."

"She's excited that we're seeing each other? Why?"

Lisa gave him a confused look. "I suppose she thinks we make a nice couple. Hasn't she already said as much to you?"

"No, why would she?"

"I thought you two were good friends? At least, that's the impression I got from Mrs Wishmore."

"I've only met her a few times, and one of those was in your café."

"Oh, right." Lisa fell quiet, and Jake watched her expression as she thought about what he'd said. "I must have got my wires crossed."

Jake thought about it for a minute. "Although I wouldn't say we were exactly strangers. Whenever I've bumped into her, we've enjoyed a friendly chat."

"I must have got mixed up, that's all. Although I don't know why I'm surprised, because this isn't the first time things have become a bit confusing where Mrs Wishmore is concerned."

"What do you mean?"

"Well, when she first turned up to work in my café, I thought she was a customer instead of a waitress, and tried to shoo her away from the table she was clearing. Then there was a silly mix-up at the temping agency who sent her to me, when they said they had no record of her on their files. It turned out to be a problem with their computer system, although the explanation of what had happened was pretty confusing the more I thought about it. And then the other day, when the café was packed with tourists, it seemed that Mrs Wishmore couldn't possibly be doing all the work she actually seemed to be doing in order for us keep up."

Jake frowned. "You mean she was cutting corners on the job?"

"Oh no, not at all. In fact, the café has never run more smoothly. She's a miracle worker. It just sometimes seems..." Lisa looked up and shook her head. "Ignore me. I'm babbling. Instead of the barely functioning incompetents the temping agency usually fob me off with when I've got a staffing problem, they've sent someone who's brilliant, and all I can do is wonder if it's all too good to be true."

"I know that feeling," Jake said, looking at Lisa as they turned into the community centre grounds and wondering just how long his own good luck with her would last before he either stuffed it up or she reached the same decision every other woman he'd ever been with eventually reached—that they should just be 'good friends'.

He frowned at the stupid, negative thought, wondering where it had come from. They were here to spend time together, and continue getting to know one another better, and he shouldn't jinx it by rehashing all his romantic failures from the past. That was no way to live.

The community centre car park was bustling when they arrived, as people set up their chairs and chatted with one another, and queued to buy goodies from the hot dog stand and popcorn cart. There were couples, both young and old, families with children, groups of older women, and even a pack of giggling teenage girls loitering beside the colourful beanbags they'd hauled along to the event. At the car park entrance, members of the cinema club were greeting new arrivals, while others were dealing with the technicalities of the projection equipment. The atmosphere was relaxed and fun, and Jake was glad he'd brought Lisa along, and relieved there'd been tickets available at such late notice.

Maybe, he thought, his luck was changing when it came to romance. He hoped so, at least.

They found a space in the tarmacked car park area and set up their deckchairs. Jake fetched them hot dogs and popcorn from the vendor carts, and they settled into their chairs. He was relieved to discover that once they'd propped the sofa cushions into place, the deckchairs were reasonably comfortable, although Jake couldn't help but hear the creaking noises made by the hinges on the one he was sitting on, and hoped the thing would remain in once piece while they watched the film. As they ate their hot dogs while the folks in charge of the open air cinema club argued good-naturedly amongst themselves as they worked on setting up the projection screen, Lisa turned to Jake with a thoughtful look on her face.

"So, I've already told you about losing Peter and how hard it's been to move on again," she said, her voice soft. "But you haven't told me anything about your past relationships and I feel bad for not asking yet. Have you had any serious girlfriends or partners or anything like that?"

Jake wondered if Lisa had somehow plucked his earlier thoughts from the air. He munched on his hot dog and thought about how to answer her question.

"I've had a couple of girlfriends who've lasted for a few months," he said. "And I've had more casual dates than you could shake a stick at. But nothing long term, nothing that ever became a proper relationship."

He saw the surprise on her face at this admission and cringed inside as she tried to cover her reaction.

"You don't have to pretend it isn't a bit unusual, or maybe even downright odd," he said, "because I already know it is."

"It's not unusual or odd," Lisa said. "It's just surprising, that's all. You're a really nice guy, Jake."

Jake concentrated on his hot dog as the word Lisa had used to describe him swirled in his head. *Nice*. How often had women described him as 'nice' in his life? Countless times, and usually right before they told him that things would be better between them if they were 'just friends'.

You're so nice, Jake, but I love you as just a friend and don't see us being anything more than that.

You're the nicest guy I know, Jake! I hope we can still be friends.

I wish every man was as nice as you are, Jake. You're a great pal!

Jake, you're so sweet and nice, and I hope I don't regret this, but can we just be friends instead of something more?

"If I've learned anything," Jake said, "it's that women just don't see me as boyfriend material. Friend, yes. Boyfriend, not so much."

He laughed as he said it, wanting to making light of the whole thing, but when he glanced at Lisa, he saw she was frowning.

"I'm sorry," she said. "That doesn't make much sense to me. You're a great guy."

"Thanks," he said, and took another bite of his hot dog to cover his embarrassment at how this date he'd been looking forward to had somehow turned into a confidence-boosting exercise for his benefit.

"Uh, Jake?"

He glanced at Lisa and saw she was pointing to his shirt. When he looked down, a splodge of red ketchup was dribbling down the front.

"Bloody hell!" Jake said, grabbing a napkin and wiping at the mess he'd made. "You can't take me anywhere." He wiped ineffectually at the spill on his shirt, remembering being in the same predicament in school not two weeks ago when he'd got red paint all over his clothes, not to mention the incident in the Daffodil Café, when he'd dropped chocolate cake down the front of his jeans right before he'd met Lisa for the first time.

With a sinking feeling, he realised this was now twice she'd seen him spilling food all over himself. He was a plonker and obviously beyond all help.

"It's just a blob of sauce," Lisa said. "Stop dabbing at it and forget about it. You can hardly even see it."

Jake knew this wasn't true. His shirt was light blue and the ketchup was bright red. Anyone looking at him would see plainly that he'd squirted food down himself, like some clumsy child.

"See, this is why women think I make a good, fun pal to have around, but never see me as the significant other in their lives," Jake said, pointing to his shirt and laughing, keen to make light of his mortification. "I'm too high maintenance."

Lisa glanced one last time at the sauce blob on his shirt and shrugged. "You're making something out of nothing."

He appreciated she was making it easy for him to pretend his gaffe wasn't as embarrassing as it actually was.

"Anyway," she added, "did you want to have something more with any of these women you've been involved with in the past? I mean, were you in love with any of them and heartbroken when it ended?"

"I wasn't in love, no," he said, tucking the dirty napkin into his pocket and settling back into his deckchair. "And I wasn't heartbroken when things ended, but that doesn't mean it didn't still hurt. No one likes to be rejected, do they? And in case you're thinking this all sounds like I've had tonnes of women in my past, I haven't. I've dated a lot, but it never goes anywhere. On the few occasions things *have* gone somewhere, it's fizzled out after a few months."

"It sounds to me like you just haven't met the right woman yet," Lisa said with a smile.

Maybe she realised the implications of what she'd just said, because her eyes widened and she waved a hand in the air, as if dismissing her words.

"What I mean is, none of the women you've dated in the past, or had short-term relationships with, were meant for you, because if they had been, it wouldn't have ended," she continued. "And at least you didn't fall in love with any of them, only to have your heart broken when it ended. You're lucky, Jake."

He didn't see that way, although he wasn't about to tell Lisa that. She had, after all, been engaged to marry a man who'd ended up being killed in a horrific road accident, and so she knew all there was to know about broken hearts. Jake understood the point she was making.

"Maybe you're right," he said. "I don't know what I've been doing wrong, but I hope I can figure it out soon. I like to think that, one day, I'll have someone in my life. Someone who's there to stay for good. Someone who sees me as more than just a friend."

His gaze stayed locked on Lisa's as he spoke, and a stunning thought occurred to him.

Was she the one he'd been waiting for all this time?

The more he looked into her eyes, he couldn't help but imagine what it would be like to fall in love with her.

It would be easy, he realised. Far too easy.

At the front of the car park, the film starting rolling on the projector screen and there was a cheer and a round of applause from everyone seated around them. Lisa looked away and joined in with the clapping, smiling as she turned towards the screen, where the cinema club members were taking theatrical bows for finally getting the projection equipment working. As *The Greatest Showman* began playing on the screen, and the music blared from the hastily rigged speakers, the chatter around the car park died away and people took their seats, ready for the evening's entertainment.

Jake knew he'd been saved from yet another awkward moment. If the film hadn't started when it had, how might Lisa have responded to his much too honest admission about how he wanted to have someone in his life? He'd sounded like some desperate sad case. They'd only been out together a few times and he'd scare her off if he'd kept talking like that.

Which was the last thing he wanted to do.

"Here, have some popcorn," Jake said, passing Lisa the box he'd bought for her.

She balanced the popcorn in her lap and grinned as she passed the box of brownies to him. "You'd better help yourself to some of these before I share them around. I don't want you getting huffy if they run out."

Jake took a handful of the brownies and returned her smile, glad to be back on firmer conversational territory. "If they run out, you'll just have to bake more for me some other time."

"I think that can be arranged."

He watched as Lisa tapped the shoulders of the people seated around her, smiling as she offered them the box of brownies.

She really did have a good heart, Jake decided. Seeing the faces of all those strangers light up at the small gifts she was offering, he felt his own face light up too.

THEY'D REACHED the halfway point in *The Greatest Showman* when Lisa realised the air temperature had tumbled and the light had changed. She looked up at the sky and saw clouds rushing in from the west, blotting out the midsummer blue and the last of the evening sunshine. The clouds were tinged with dark grey and looked stormy and foreboding.

"I think the weather forecasters might have known what they were talking about after all," Lisa whispered to Jake, whose gaze was fixed on the screen as he dug the last kernels of popcorn from the bottom of his cardboard box.

He tilted his head up to the sky and his eyebrows flew up when he saw the clouds scudding in their direction.

"Maybe it won't come to anything," he said, although not with much conviction. "Are you cold?"

Lisa shook her head and pulled the light cardigan she'd brought tighter around her shoulders. "I'm fine."

No sooner had she said this than fat raindrops began falling from the darkening sky. As Barnum chased his wild circus dream up on the screen, the audience seated in the car park blinked at the rain and then leapt to their feet as it quickly turned into a torrential deluge.

"Eek!" Lisa half-screeched, half-laughed. "I think we'd better make a run for it!"

"Agreed!" Jake said.

Jumping from her chair, Lisa grabbed her deckchair to fold it up. As she closed the squeaking wooden frame, she heard a dull thudding noise beside her followed by a groan. When she turned, she was astonished to see Jake lying sprawled on the ground with his deckchair collapsed beneath him.

"Jake! What on earth happened?"

"Uh," Jake muttered, obviously a bit stunned. "My deckchair gave way as I tried to get out of it."

Lisa stared at the man lying on the ground and trying to extricate himself from the collapsed deckchair. Before she could stop herself, she burst out laughing.

"Oh, I'm sorry," she said, her helpless laughter only made worse by the faux wounded look on Jake's face. "I know it's not funny, but..."

"Don't let me stop you from having a good laugh," he grinned, rolling onto his side and pulling his arm free from the seat fabric of the deckchair, before hauling himself to his feet. "It's not like I might've broken a bone or anything serious like that."

This only made her laugh even harder. "I'm sorry, I'm so rude," she wheezed. "Are you okay?"

"I'm fine," Jake said, brushing himself down. "I'll have a

bruised backside tomorrow, and my pride took a bit of a hit, but there's nothing to be done about that now."

Lisa covered her mouth to stop another roll of laughter escaping. Even although the rain was pelting down now, and everyone around them was grabbing their belongings and making a run for their cars and homes, Lisa could hardly move because she was giggling so much.

"God, Jake, I'm really sorry," she said, forcing herself to stop laughing. "I know it's not funny."

Jake's lips twitched. "It *is* funny. My own deckchair assaulted me. It's hard not to laugh at that."

Seeing the humour on his face brought Lisa's laughter back once more, a huge belly-roll that had her clutching her sides even as the rain poured down.

"Come on," Jake said, smiling and grabbing their chairs under his arm. "Let's hurry before we get any more drenched than we already are."

Together, they ran from the swiftly emptying car park. The rain was so heavy now that it was bouncing off the pavement, and the sky was so dark with storm clouds it was as if night had suddenly fallen. They covered the distance back to Lisa's flat in a matter of minutes, and she flew up the back stairs while digging her keys from her drenched bag.

"Come inside and get dry," Lisa said after flinging open the door.

"Are you sure?" Jake said, still standing at the bottom of the steps and looking at his water-logged clothes. "That might take a while."

"You're not walking the rest of the way home in this downpour. You'll catch pneumonia, for god's sake. Come in and wait until the rain stops, or at least until it's not so heavy. I'll make us tea. I think we could do with something hot to warm us up."

Jake stood on the bottom step for about half a second,

thinking it over, before dumping the deckchairs against the wall and hurrying up the stairs and inside the flat. As they stood in the tiny hallway, shaking off the cold from the unexpected deluge, water dripped from their clothes and hair and pooled on the wooden floor.

"I'll grab some towels," Lisa said and fetched a stack from the cupboard in the bedroom where she kept her linens. They scrubbed at their hair and faces with the fresh towels, and attempted to soak up as much of the water as they could from their clothes, but even after a thorough drying off, they were still wet through.

"I think I'll have to get changed," Lisa laughed, holding up the edge of her dress and wringing it out.

"Me too." Jake gave her an uncertain look as the water continued dripping from his shirt sleeves. "Listen, I think I should head home and get into some dry clothes."

"It's much too wet to go back out there, and it's cold too, and..."

And the truth was she didn't want him to go. Their open air cinema date might have ended with them both getting drenched, but it didn't feel like a disaster.

Instead, it felt like fun, and Lisa wasn't ready for it to be over yet.

"I'll turn up the heating and we'll soon dry out," she said, already adjusting the thermostat on the wall. "At least stay for a cup of tea before you venture back out there."

To make it harder for him to say no, she hurried to the kitchen and filled the kettle to boil. When she glanced out the window, the heavy rain was now being whipped by a fierce wind.

"Look, the weather's only getting worse," she said, gesturing out the window. "It's turning into a proper summer storm. It makes sense to wait it out until it passes."

She pulled out a chair at the kitchen table and was glad

when Jake nodded and sat down, still rubbing at his hair and clothes with the towel she'd given him.

"I feel like an idiot after what happened in the car park with that stupid deckchair," Jake said, his expression sheepish as he scrubbed the towel around the back of his neck.

"I thought you handled it all very gracefully."

He coughed out a laugh. "Seeing me rolling around on the ground in the rain while wrestling with a deckchair didn't make you want to run for the hills?"

"Nope. Now, whether I would've felt the same way if it'd been *my* chair that had collapsed to the ground, I couldn't possibly speculate."

Jake laughed again. "Noted."

While the tea brewed, Lisa set out a plate of oatmeal cookies she'd baked earlier that day and turned on some music.

"More goodies," Jake said, grabbing a cookie and eating half of it in one bite. "Now I'm glad you shared those brownies with the folk at the open air cinema, or I wouldn't have room left to clear this plate of cookies."

He wiggled his eyebrows and ate the rest of the biscuit before Lisa had even brought the tea pot to the table and sat down. "See, this is nicer that wading home in the rain, isn't it?"

Jake glanced towards the window, where the rain was lashing against the glass, then around the kitchen and back at Lisa. "Much nicer. This is a great flat you've got here. I like what you've done with it. You've made it cosy and comfortable and welcoming. It suits you."

She looked around at the snug kitchen, with its wooden countertops and compact range stove and country-style dresser on which she liked to display her favourite plates and dishes and glassware.

"Home is important, especially when you live right above

your place of work," she said, pouring the tea. "When I finish a long day in the café, I like knowing I'm retreating upstairs to a place I love and that fits me like a glove. I redecorated a while ago too, just to…" Realising the direction she was about to take the conversation, she cleared her throat and set down the tea pot. "Just to freshen things up."

Jake's eyes stayed on her as they picked up their mugs. "Did Peter live here with you? Is that why you redecorated?"

"No, not exactly. We never made the jump into living together. We stayed over at each other's flats, of course, and once we got engaged and started planning our wedding, we also started talking about buying a place of our own somewhere, too." She sipped her tea, enjoying the warmth of the mug clasped in her hands. "Mentally, I'd been preparing to leave my little flat for pastures new. And then Peter died, and this place became my sanctuary while I got over it. Earlier this year I gave the place an overdue make-over. Fresh paint on the walls, some bits and pieces of new furniture. It helped keep me busy and cheered me up."

"You did a good job," Jake said, giving the place another once-over. "You have a good eye for what works when it comes to decorating. Maybe you should come over to my place sometime and give me a few pointers. I've been in my house for almost two years and haven't done a thing."

"Not even repainted?"

"The last owner painted all the rooms white before he put it on the market, and as everything was clean and smart, I didn't see much point in changing it."

"If you like white walls, you should keep them that way."

Jake looked around her kitchen again, his gaze speculative. "I like this colour better. What is it?"

"Plain old primrose yellow."

"It's warm and it works. Makes the room feel cosy. Maybe I need some primrose yellow in my kitchen, too."

"Well, that depends on what the rest of your kitchen looks like. What colour are your kitchen cupboards?"

"I don't know. Some sort of fake wood colour."

Lisa laughed. "Light or dark?"

"Dark."

"And what's on the floor? Tiles? Wood?"

"Dark grey tiles."

"Pale yellow might not work in that case. It works in here because the floor tiles are light and so are the cupboards. But against darker colours, yellow can sometimes look a little brashy, or at least that's what I think."

"So, what do you suggest?"

"I'm not sure."

"That settles it," Jake said. "You'll have to come over and look around and give me some advice."

"I'm no expert, Jake."

"But you know how to put some colour in a room and make it feel like a proper home, and that's what I need." He grabbed another cookie from the plate and took a bite. "Oh, and we'll need some sustenance while we talk colour palettes, so you ought to bake more of these and bring them with you."

"You're only interested in me for my baked goods and interior decorating tips, is that it?" Lisa laughed.

"Hardly."

Jake reached across the table and took her hand in his. The unexpected move caught her off-guard, making her breath hitch as his gaze held hers. His warm skin touching hers, and the way his damp hair fell across his forehead, and the bright look in his eyes as he watched her sent a shiver rippling down her back.

"I like you a lot, Lisa," he said. A wry smile came to his lips. "The amazing baking you do is just a bonus."

"And the decorating tips?" she said, enjoying this now.

"Maybe I just want an excuse to invite you over to my house."

She laughed, more at his warm, teasing smile than anything else. It had been too long since she'd felt this relaxed and loose in someone else's company. Feeling like this with a man—and the first man she'd spent any real time with since Peter's death—was nothing short of staggering.

She'd imagined that dating again would be almost impossible. Instead, with Jake, it felt like the easiest thing in the world.

He must have read the thought in her eyes, because he got to his feet and gently pulled her from her chair and into his arms. The warm kitchen and the soft music and the summer rain beating against the window all receded into the background as Lisa drew in a shaky breath.

Jake's lips met hers, and she fell into the sweet thrill of his kiss and the sensation of his damp body pressed against hers. When they pulled back and looked at each other, she saw humour dancing in his eyes.

"I've been looking forward to doing that ever since you started laughing at me back in the car park," he said.

"I wasn't laughing *at* you. I was laughing *with* you."

He grinned and curled a lock of her hair around his fingers as he stroked her cheek. "Your entire face lights up when you laugh and makes you look even more beautiful than you already are."

His words left her speechless and blushing and feeling oddly shy. But even although she was enjoying the sensation of being held in Jake's arms, and enjoying his compliments even more, a memory suddenly burst into her head and drained away all the pleasure of the moment.

The memory was of Peter, standing in the door of her flat just before he left to drive back to his own place after spending the day with her.

See you later, beautiful, Peter had said and thrown her a wink as he closed the door.

It was the last time she'd ever seen him.

See you later, beautiful.

Jake's compliment curdled in her ears and left a sour taste in her mouth. Before she could catch herself, or stop her runaway emotions, she felt the smile disappear from her face.

"The storm's passed," she said, stepping away from Jake and looking to the window, where the wind had dropped and the rain was now little more than a light drizzle, and evening blue skies were already peeking out from the departing clouds.

Jake threw a puzzled look out the window, then glanced back at Lisa. "Hey, are you okay?"

"I'm fine," she said, filling the sink to wash up their tea cups. "Although, the more I think about it, I should change out of these damp clothes. The central heating isn't drying them out as fast as I thought. You still look pretty wet, yourself."

Jake glanced at his jeans and shirt. "I guess you're right. Maybe I should head home and change."

"Good idea."

For a moment, he didn't move from where he stood beside the kitchen table, his eyes filled with concern as he watched her. "Did I say something wrong, Lisa? Did I do something wrong?"

"Of course not," she said and gave him a bright smile as she walked him to the door. "I just think I ought to change out of these clothes and get dried properly. Thanks again for a fun night."

"Maybe we can do it again some time?"

"I'd like that. Goodnight, Jake."

He paused for a long beat at the door before stepping outside. "Goodnight, Lisa."

At the bottom of the steps, he picked up the sodden deckchairs and cushions he'd left there, and then, with a wave goodbye, walked towards the lane and disappeared out of sight.

Lisa closed the door, her heart beating out a shaky tattoo inside her chest. Anger and confusion roared inside her head. How could her traitorous emotions have turned on her? One minute she was enjoying being held in Jake's arms and kissing him, and the next minute she was thinking of Peter and missing him so much it hurt.

Jake had been so sweet, saying she was beautiful, and in response her mind had filled with memories of Peter.

See you later, beautiful.

Was she going to behave like this every time she thought of Peter? That idea was too grim even to think about.

But Lisa knew it wasn't just any random old thought of Peter that had caused her reaction tonight. Instead, it was the realisation that having a new man in her life meant hearing that man say the same things that Peter had once said. When Jake had called her beautiful, she'd been helpless to stop her mind replaying that memory of Peter's last words to her. He'd used the word 'beautiful' as a term of endearment for Lisa, and hearing that same word on another man's lips had left her shaken.

The same way she'd been shaken just a few days earlier after their trip to the New Forest, when she'd thought Jake was about to kiss her. She might have got her head around that idea in the end, but it seemed like she was taking one step forward and two steps back.

Romance was supposed to be a lot more fun than this.

"This is just stupid," she told herself as she finished washing cups at the sink. "Just stupid, plain and simple."

Outside the window, the summer storm had disappeared altogether, leaving behind soft blue skies and streaks of late evening sunshine and a sweet stillness in the air.

Lisa only wished she felt as calm as the weather beyond her window. Instead, it seemed like the storm that had rushed through the town had now lodged itself deep inside her heart.

CHAPTER FIFTEEN

"My goodness, what's with the long face?"

Lisa looked up from the receipt she was staring at on the café counter and saw Mrs Wishmore standing before her, unbuttoning her jacket and with a concerned look on her face.

"Oh, it's nothing," Lisa said, waving the receipt in the air. "I made a mistake on the till and I'm trying to unpick it, that's all." She glanced at the clock on the wall and frowned. "You're very early this morning, Doris. It's only just gone ten o'clock."

Mrs Wishmore carried her jacket to the store cupboard and said, "I was up with the birds this morning and decided I'd make myself useful and come in early."

"We've been quiet so far and there isn't much happening yet." Lisa gestured around the café where the only customers were Mildred and Jean, tucking into their tea and cherry scones at their favourite table by the window. "Can I make you a coffee, Doris? I was about to have one myself."

"Thank you, dear."

As Lisa set aside the receipt she'd bungled and turned to the coffee machine, she felt Mrs Wishmore's gaze on her.

"How was your evening at the outdoor cinema last night with young Jake?" Mrs Wishmore asked. "When I saw those dark clouds arrive and the rain start falling, I thought of you both and hoped you didn't get caught in the downpour."

"We got a proper soaking, Doris, along with everyone else who was there," Lisa smiled. "I felt bad for the cinema club people, after all their hard work to put the event together. I just hope the torrential rain didn't damage their projection equipment."

"I bumped into one of the club members this morning on my way here, and he said they got their various bits and pieces of technical equipment out of harm's way in the nick of time."

"That's a relief." Lisa gave the older woman a puzzled look. "How do you know any of the folk in the cinema club? You really are well connected in Willowbridge, Doris, for someone who doesn't actually live here."

"I have a great many friends all over the place," she replied with a cheerful smile. "But you know, Lisa, I can't help but thinking that you look a little down this morning. Did the wind and rain put a terrible dampener on your evening with Jake?"

"No, I did that all by myself."

Mrs Wishmore watched her as she warmed milk for their coffees, and once Lisa shut off the noisy steamer nozzle, the older lady said, "Would you like to talk about what happened, dear?"

Lisa surprised herself by nodding, but it quickly turned into a head shake. "I wish I could, but I've got so many things to do this morning. There are cakes waiting to come out of the oven, and Fiona's got a dentist appointment, so I'll have to start on her lunch preparations, and we'll no doubt have more customers arriving soon, and—"

"I'm sure we can manage a few minutes to chat," Mrs Wishmore interrupted, her voice soft and soothing. "All those other jobs can wait."

She said these words with such calm confidence that Lisa found herself once more nodding. Of course those other jobs could wait. Mrs Wishmore was right. There was no hurry this morning, no need to rush. Lisa found herself thinking that it would be quite all right to sit down for a minute and try to settle her racing mind and whirling emotions. In fact, it would be *more* than all right.

The older lady smiled and picked up the mugs of coffee Lisa had prepared before guiding her towards a table on the other side of the café counter. When Lisa sat down, Mrs Wishmore gave her arm a gentle pat, and she felt comforted and relieved that her thoughtful waitress had suggested this quick coffee break.

As she sat at the table, with her coffee mug in her hands and Mrs Wishmore smiling kindly across the table, Lisa had the sudden sensation of being cocooned in a warm, comforting blanket… even although she knew that made no sense.

"So," Mrs Wishmore said, after sipping some coffee. "What's troubling you, dear?"

Lisa sighed and thought about how to explain it all. "Jake and I had such a fun night together, at least to begin with. We ran back to my flat once the rain started, and we were sitting in the kitchen with some tea and chatting about things when Jake said something that made me think of Peter, and all at once I clammed up. Although I pretended everything was fine, it wasn't fine at all, and I practically threw Jake out the door because I didn't want him to see how upset I suddenly was. I behaved like an idiot and I'm angry at myself because I can't get a hold of my feelings."

Mrs Wishmore nodded and drank some coffee. "You mustn't be so hard on yourself."

"But I like Jake. I like him a lot. I'd like to get to know him better and find out if... well, find out if there might be a chance for something between us. But that won't happen if I keep switching on and off like a dodgy lightbulb every time some memory of Peter pops into my head."

"You can't imagine that you'd just jump into a lovely new romance with a lovely new man and that it would all be plain sailing?" Mrs Wishmore said with a kind smile.

"It might be plain sailing if I could stop my stupid brain from hijacking me."

"Really?"

Lisa frowned at the older lady's question. "I think so. I like Jake. There's something about him, something that draws me to him. I don't want to drive him away before we've even got to know one another properly."

"Well, that's something, at least. You know you're interested in Jake and want to take things further. That's a big leap, Lisa, and you should be happy with yourself for making that leap. Don't forget that just a few days ago, you were agreeing to meet Fiona's friend for a drink simply in order to get the ball rolling in your life again. Already, you've found in Jake someone who you might want to have a relationship with, not just meet for a casual drink from time to time."

"But that's exactly the problem. How can I be sure I want to spend time with Jake, and yet still keep pushing him away every time he does something or says something that reminds me of Peter and what I lost when he died?"

"Our emotions are often complicated and mysterious, Lisa. When it comes to our feelings, the heart rarely works the way we want it to, and almost never responds to any instructions we might want to dispense. The heart keeps its own counsel. And it always knows best."

Lisa gave a heavy sigh. "Those sound like wise words, Doris. And I want to believe them. But I don't think my heart knows best at all. It's torturing me and making me do things that are downright horrible and confusing." She winced and closed her eyes. "Poor Jake must think I'm a nutcase."

"I'm sure he thinks nothing of the sort," Mrs Wishmore laughed. "Last night, he kissed you and said you were beautiful. Why would he do either of those things if he thought you were, as you put it, a nutcase?"

Lisa frowned at the older lady sitting across the table. "How do you know Jake kissed me and said I was beautiful?"

There was a pause before Mrs Wishmore gave an easy shrug and said, "I just know."

"But how?"

Mrs Wishmore smiled and reached across the table and squeezed Lisa's hand. "You already know the answer to that question, Lisa."

For a long moment, the café seemed suspended in perfect stillness. Lisa could hear the quiet hum of the coffee machine, and the whir of the ovens baking her cakes through in the kitchen, and the gentle murmur of conversation between Mildred and Jean at the table by the window, and the chatter of passers-by outside on the street, and the rumble of cars rushing by on the road.

But although she heard these things, everything in the world was utterly still. No one moved, not a single inch, not a single muscle. Not Mildred and Jean at the window table, who sat with their cups raised to their mouths but without taking a single sip. Not the people outside on the pavement, who stood frozen in mid-step along the street. Not the cars on the road, which were all perfectly motionless even as their tyres spun on the tarmac.

No one moved—no one, that is, except for Mrs Wishmore, who smiled as she sipped her coffee, her twinkling eyes filled with compassion and love, and wisdom that was older than the stars.

Lisa felt the sudden weight of understanding fill her mind, the magnitude of it shocking and surreal. The sun slanted through the window and fell across the table, and it seemed to Lisa like Mrs Wishmore's cloud of silvery hair appeared to be glowing, almost as if she wore a bright halo above her head.

"Doris?" Lisa said, her voice tiny as she searched for the right words to frame her incomprehensible question. "Are you a...?"

Are you a guardian angel? Lisa wanted to ask. *Are you magical? Are you some kind of fairy godmother?*

And is it possible I'm losing my mind?

"I'm just a friend," Mrs Wishmore said and gave a laugh that snapped Lisa from her reverie.

When she glanced around her, she saw the world was continuing on just as it had been before. Mildred and Jean were once more sipping their tea and eating their scones. The passers-by outside on the street were making their way along the pavement. The cars were speeding by on the road.

Lisa looked at Mrs Wishmore cheerfully sipping her coffee. She peered at the older lady's hair, which was the same silvery colour it had always been, and couldn't understand how she could have thought that it looked like a...

What had she thought Mrs Wishmore's hair looked like? Lisa couldn't remember. Nor could she even remember why she'd been wondering about such a thing.

She realised she must have wandered into a daydream for a few seconds and lost her train of thought, because she'd completely lost the gist of what they'd been talking about as she sat there at the table with Mrs Wishmore.

"Sorry, what did you say?" Lisa asked.

Mrs Wishmore chuckled. "I said, I'm just a friend, Lisa. And I want only for you to be happy. And for what it's worth, I have some advice if you'd like to hear it."

"Of course," Lisa said, remembering now that they'd been discussing Jake and the embarrassing situation she'd found herself in last night when she'd sent the poor guy packing.

"I think you should be honest with Jake about how you feel," Mrs Wishmore said. "He's a kind hearted man and I'm sure he knows it can't be easy for you to step into the world of romance and dating again after all you've been through. But pretending that everything is okay, instead of explaining how you feel, isn't giving him the chance he deserves to show you the man he is."

Lisa thought about what Mrs Wishmore had said. It all made perfect sense. "I know you're right. But I don't want to scare him off and make him think that whenever we're together, my mind is on Peter all the time. I don't want him to think I'm not ready for this."

"Maybe you aren't ready, not entirely. But maybe Jake is the one who can help you become ready."

Lisa sank back into her chair and sighed. "Everything you say makes such good sense, Doris."

Mrs Wishmore beamed at this. "Naturally."

"But it's hard knowing what to do in the heat of the moment."

"But of course it is. Your heart misses Peter. And yet it also longs for the match that will heal it. That's why being honest with young Jake is the only thing you can do. You have to trust that he'll understand."

"Will he understand, though? Last night isn't the first time I've backed off just as something was happening between us. Maybe he's already had enough of me not knowing whether I'm coming or going."

"Perhaps there's only one way to find out."

Lisa frowned. "What are you saying?"

"What I've been saying all along, Lisa. That you must trust your heart, even when you don't understand what it's telling you. And that you must be honest with Jake, even if that seems like a terrible risk."

Mrs Wishmore leaned closer across the table and patted Lisa's hand, once more filling her with that strange but welcome sensation of comfort and love.

"What is your heart telling you to do right now?" Mrs Wishmore asked.

The answer arrived instantly in her mind and it was so ridiculous that Lisa laughed out loud. "Something stupid."

"It's not stupid," Mrs Wishmore said, her tone firm. "It's not stupid at all."

"How do you know what I was thinking about? I didn't say—"

But Mrs Wishmore waved off her protest. "Don't waste your time worrying about what I know or don't know. Just tell me this—are you willing to follow your heart, right this very minute?"

Lisa had no idea how this simple chat over coffee with her elderly waitress could have turned into such a baffling and mysterious conversation. "I think so," she said, and then seeing Mrs Wishmore's arched eyebrow, added, "Yes, I am."

"Good girl," Mrs Wishmore said. "You run along and I'll hold the fort here."

"But—"

"Lisa, you know you want to do it. And you know you *have* to do it."

Lisa glanced around the café just as new customers stepped through the door and Mildred and Jean waved their hands to catch her attention and ask for their bill.

"Are you sure you can cope here by yourself for a little while?"

Rising from her chair, Mrs Wishmore laughed. "You don't still doubt me, dear, do you?"

Lisa watched her mysterious waitress for a moment, then shook her head as she, too, laughed. "No, I don't doubt you."

"Off you go, then," Mrs Wishmore said. "And good luck!"

Before she could think about what she was planning to do, never mind reflect on the bizarre conversation she'd just had with Mrs Wishmore, Lisa grabbed her bag and ran out of the café and around to where her car was parked at the back of the lane.

Her heart thundered in her chest like an out-of-control freight train. As she started the car and thought about what she was about to do, she only hoped she wasn't about to make a complete fool of herself.

"There's only one way to find out," she muttered, and sped out along the lane and towards her terrifying destination.

CHAPTER SIXTEEN

The final preparations for the Willowbridge school summer fair were underway in the playground, where the pupils were enjoying the late morning sunshine as they put the finishing touches to stall banners and painting projects and layout blueprints and any number of other tasks Jake was coordinating on his out-of-control master spreadsheet.

"Don't look so worried, sir," said Bradley, the cheeky Year Nine pupil who was standing at Jake's side with a clipboard and pen in his hands while casting a managerial eye over the other students working around them. "We're all on track to be finished in time for the fair. No need to panic or give yourself grey hairs."

Jake hid a grin. He was pleased Bradley had found his niche helping to organise the summer fair, even if the lad was too cheeky sometimes for his own good. The boy had a good heart, and that's what mattered.

"Is the work finished on all the refreshment stalls we'll be running?" Jake asked, grinning again as Bradley flicked through the pages on his clipboard with a self-important look on his face.

"Kevin and Susan were falling behind with their tuck shop stall organisation, but I stepped in and got them back up to full speed," Bradley said. "They just needed better systems in place and I gave them some pointers. They'll be fine now."

"Good lad. And the coconut shy you're running with your pal, is that all ready to go?"

"It's all done. We think we'll make a tonne of money on our stall, sir. Everyone we speak to says they'll want to have a turn, especially when we told them about the pizza vouchers my uncle donated as a prize."

"With some luck, Bradley, we'll beat last year's fundraising total by a country mile."

"Fingers crossed, sir. And even if we don't beat last year's total, you shouldn't feel bad about it. This is your first year on the summer fair committee and you've still got a lot to learn."

Bradley gave him a cheeky wink before running off to join the other pupils, who were hard at work around the playground.

"Jake, take a look at this for me, will you?"

Turning, Jake saw Marie walking towards him with some paperwork in her hands and an unhappy look on her face.

"What's the problem?" he asked.

"I think there's been a mix-up with the order we placed with the wholesaler for the tuck shop stall," Marie said. "Before I phone them, I thought you ought to look at these order numbers to double-check."

Jake glanced at the paperwork and nodded. "The numbers look iffy. Even if we pack out the summer fair with every single person who lives in Willowbridge, we'd never sell this many bags of crisps and chocolate bars in a million years."

"I'll ring them up and get to the bottom of what's happened." Marie tucked the paperwork into a folder and gave him a look. "So, how did it go last night on your cinema date with this girl you're seeing, Lisa?"

Jake winced, not wanting to think about the unhappy events of the night before. "I thought it was going fine until…"

"Until?"

He sighed, wondering if he could avoid this discussion by helping the pupils with some urgent summer fair task, but he could tell from the look on Marie's face that she wouldn't be so easily deterred from her inquiries into his love life.

"I made a total shambles of the entire night, as per usual," Jake finally said. "First, my chair collapsed while I was sitting in it, and I looked like a proper twat rolling around on the ground."

Marie's eyebrows shot up her forehead. "Jake! Tell me you're joking."

"I only wish I could. And then when it started raining we ran back to Lisa's flat, and I thought things were going fine, despite my earlier cock-up, until she suddenly clammed up and sent me on my way."

"What do you mean? She threw you out?" Marie said, her voice indignant.

"No, not exactly. We'd been getting quite close, having a nice chat in her kitchen, and then she suddenly pulled away and, well, to cut a long story short, that was that. The next thing I knew, she was showing me out the door and waving goodbye."

Jake had no idea what he'd done wrong. He'd loved having Lisa in his arms, loved kissing her, loved telling her how much he liked her and how beautiful he thought she was. One minute, it seemed like she'd been enjoying those things as much as he had, and then she'd completely shut him down. The hints she'd dropped about their clothes being wet and wanting to get properly dried off after the soaking they'd endured hadn't exactly been subtle, and Jake hadn't been interested in outstaying his welcome.

His mind returned to his clumsy catastrophe with the deckchair. Lisa had laughed at the time, and been a good sport about the ridiculous mishap that had befallen him, but it stood to reason that the incident had given her second thoughts about spending time with him. What woman would find a man attractive when he was writhing around on the ground getting soaked by the rain while wrestling with a broken deckchair?

And he shouldn't forget having dribbled ketchup down his shirt not long before that, too. He was nothing short of a complete and utter embarrassment. No wonder Lisa wasn't sure about him, or whether she wanted to spend time with him.

It was the same old story and the only thing Jake found surprising was that he kept expecting there to be a different ending.

"I'm sorry, Jake," Marie said, frowning as she watched him. "It sounded like you were keen on Lisa and I hate seeing you get fobbed off like this."

"I'll live. We'd only gone out together a few times."

"But you liked her."

He nodded. "I did. But—"

Before he could finish what he was saying, he heard a car screech to a stop beyond the school gates on the other side of the grounds, then the sound of a car door opening. Peering across the grounds, he gasped when he saw Lisa leap from the car and run towards the gates.

"Jake!" she shouted when she saw him and waved her hand in the air. "Jake, I need to talk to you!"

He was too astonished to do anything but hurry towards

the gates where she stood on the other side. Remembering at the last second that he was supposed to be supervising the two dozen pupils hard at work in the playground, he spun around to ask Marie if she could cover for him for a minute, only to find her already grinning and waving him off.

"I'll deal with this lot," Marie said, giving a final flick of her hand to send him on his way. "You go and find out what's going on."

With a grateful smile to his friend, he turned back and unbolted the gates and Lisa stepped inside the school grounds.

"Lisa, is everything okay?" he asked, worried about why she was breathless and flushed and had a bright, panicked look in her eyes.

"No, it's not okay," she said. "I was an idiot last night and I'm so sorry. I had to come and tell you I wish I hadn't ended our evening the way I did."

He wasn't sure what he'd expected her to say, but it wasn't this. "It's because I fell off that stupid deckchair, isn't it? That's why you brought the night to a halt. I made a fool of myself and you couldn't look past it any longer."

Lisa gave him a puzzled look and shook her head. "It wasn't anything to do with that. Why would you think that?"

"Because I'm a clumsy idiot and rolling around on the ground on top of a broken deckchair can't have made me look like the most attractive man on earth."

She looked at him, long and hard, her eyes searching his face. "I'm sorry I made you think that about yourself, Jake. But the truth is..."

Jake watched her draw in a deep breath, her gaze still on him as she searched for the words she wanted to say.

"Jake, here's the truth," she said.

And then she stepped towards him, pulled him close and kissed him.

He was too surprised to do anything other than kiss her back.

From across the school grounds, he heard the distant whoop of wolf-whistles from the pupils who were no doubt enjoying every minute of this unexpected romantic development, but he was too caught up in the moment to care what anyone thought.

When Lisa finally realised him, there were stars exploding in his eyes and the world had turned blurry around the edges.

"Wow," Jake said, blinking in surprise as a round of applause began from the pupils across the playground.

"I hope I haven't got you into trouble for doing that," Lisa said, eyeing the kids behind him. "It's probably against the rules for teachers to kiss people like that on school premises."

"It's definitely against the rules, but if the headteacher sacks me for it, all I can say is that it was worth it."

Lisa laughed, and as the raucous applause died down behind them, a serious look crossed her face. "I really am sorry about last night, Jake. I had to come here and tell you that. I know how it must have seemed. One minute we were getting along great and the next minute I was pushing you out the door. That's twice I've blown hot then cold with you, and it isn't fair."

Jake watched as she fidgeted for a moment and saw how much she was struggling with what she wanted to say.

"I like you a lot, Jake. I want to spend more time with you. But although I know that's what I want, my memories of Peter keep rushing to the surface and confusing me. That's what happened last night after we kissed, and that's why I panicked and pushed you away. Believe me, I know that's stupid."

"It's not stupid. I'd never rush you, Lisa, and if it seemed like that's what I was doing last night at your flat, I'm sorry."

But Lisa shook her head. "I want to be with you, Jake. And that means I need to handle all these feelings that keep popping up all over the place. Maybe it's asking too much for you to stick with me, especially after how I've behaved so far."

"I suppose I can stick with you," he said with a smile and a breezy shrug that got her laughing, just like he hoped it would. "But only if you stop running out on me. A man's confidence can only take so much before it crumbles to dust."

Lisa gave him that studied look again, the one where it seemed she could see straight into his soul. Jake liked seeing that look on her face. Loved seeing it, actually.

"Fair enough," Lisa said. "But you have to stop talking yourself down and saying you're a clumsy idiot."

"I *am* a clumsy idiot."

"Jake!"

"It's true, Lisa. If you don't see it now, you will eventually."

"Will you stop?"

Smiling, Lisa stepped closer and kissed him again, gentler this time and without the frenzied passion of the kiss she'd given him a minute ago, but with enough tenderness to send Jake's head spinning just the same.

"So, are we friends again?" Lisa said at last.

"More than friends."

"I won't run off again, Jake, I promise. I'll share how I feel, instead of bottling it up and pretending everything is okay."

"Good."

"Mrs Wishmore said I should tell you the truth about what I've been feeling. I'm glad I listened to her."

"I'm glad you did, too. I want you to trust me and be honest about what's going on inside that head of yours."

They smiled at one another as the school bell rang to announce the end of second period.

"I should get back to the café," Lisa said, turning for her car beyond the gate.

"And I should get back to this lot," Jake said, gesturing to the pupils across the playground who were already gathering up their summer fair work projects under Marie's supervision.

When Lisa reached her car, she opened the door but paused before getting in. "Come over to my flat tonight for dinner. I'd like to cook for you, to make up for last night."

"There's nothing to make up for, Lisa. But if you're cooking dinner, I'll be there."

"Ruby's welcome too."

"I'll see if she's free and let you know."

With a laugh, Lisa threw him a final wave and got into her car. When Jake turned around, Marie was walking towards him.

"Looks like you two have smoothed things over," Marie said.

"I think so. We're having dinner tonight. Lisa's cooking."

Jake grinned, but Marie's expression was thoughtful. "I hope this woman won't keep putting you through the wringer time and time again."

"It's not like that. She lost her fiancé, Marie. Seeing someone new is a big thing for her, after going through something like that."

"Of course it is. But I'm *your* friend, Jake, so it's *you* I'm worried about."

"I'll be fine."

"I hope so, Jake. I really hope so."

Marie squeezed his arm before hurrying off to supervise the kids as they hauled the last of their various summer fair tasks back inside the building. Jake was glad to have a friend like Marie, someone who was on his side. If she was doubtful about Lisa, it was only because she wanted things to go right for him in his love life.

That's all he wanted, too.

Maybe now, at last, that's what would happen.

CHAPTER SEVENTEEN

"Eek! Look at the time!" Lisa muttered to herself as she winced at the clock on the café wall and turned the door sign to 'Closed'.

It was five-thirty and the day had disappeared in a flash thanks to a packed lunch service that had morphed into an afternoon of non-stop coffee and cake orders. When a minibus had stopped across the road at four o'clock and decanted its cheerful elderly tourists straight into the café, just as Lisa had been preparing to close, she hadn't wanted to turn them away, especially when the tour guide explained that their earlier scheduled stop at another café in a village deep inside the New Forest had been cancelled because the café owner had closed at the last minute on account of a family emergency. Lisa had taken pity on the thirsty-looking sightseers and welcomed them inside, assuming they were only in search of a cup of coffee before once more hitting the road.

Instead, they'd ordered full rounds of sandwiches and cakes, and Lisa hadn't the heart to refuse them, even although the kitchen usually stopped serving at three-thirty.

The group comprised a bunch of elderly care home residents enjoying a day trip together, and Lisa hated the idea of their lovely outing being spoiled because they couldn't find somewhere with the capacity to serve the group at short notice.

And so she'd got stuck in, with help from Fiona who'd stayed late to prepare sandwich rounds, and from Mrs Wishmore who'd got to work serving cakes and muffins while Lisa cranked out tea and coffee and ferried trays of tasty treats back and forth to the chattering customers.

The group had lingered over their drinks and snacks before finally saying goodbye and returning to their minibus, and now it was five-thirty and Lisa was only just closing the café. The tables were still to be cleared, the display case and counter were still to be wiped down, not to mention any number of other daily tasks not yet done on account of the late afternoon gaggle of customers. Fiona had left fifteen minutes ago, having stayed to help far longer than she should have done, and Mrs Wishmore was busy through in the kitchen dealing with the backlog of dirty dishes.

Lisa peered around the café, wondering how she could get it tidied up and squared away and still have enough time left to run upstairs to her flat and cook dinner for Jake, like she'd promised him.

As she piled plates and cups onto a tray, she did a mental scan of her fridge contents, wondering what she could make for them to eat. When she'd asked Jake to dinner after her surprise visit to his school that morning, she'd assumed she'd have time to dash to the supermarket and buy what she'd need, but that plan had long ago bit the dust. There were eggs and cheese and vegetables in her fridge upstairs, she was sure of that, but not much else. She couldn't invite Jake over and serve him an omelette or eggs on toast, could she? Perhaps she could raid the café fridge and prepare a slap-up toasted sandwich with all the trimmings?

These weren't terrible ideas. But they weren't quite what she'd had in mind, either.

As Lisa carried the tray of dirty dishes to the back, she smelled a delicious aroma drifting from the kitchen. When she walked through the kitchen door, she found Mrs Wishmore stirring a pot at the stove and humming cheerfully to herself.

"What are you up to?" Lisa asked, glancing around the kitchen, which she was more than a little surprised to discover was clean and pristine. The counter had been piled high with dishes when she'd last stuck her head around the door to tell Fiona to finish what she was doing and go home before her hour of overtime turned into two. But now there were no signs of any dishes waiting to be washed and the counters shone like new pennies.

Mrs Wishmore turned from the stove and smiled at Lisa. "I thought you might need a nice home-cooked meal to serve to young Jake tonight, so I popped a few things into a pot to give you a head start. I hope you don't mind?"

Astonished by this, Lisa set down the tray of dishes and peeked inside the pot, where a rich bolognese sauce was bubbling away and filling the kitchen with the scents of tomatoes and garlic and herbs.

"Gosh, you didn't have to do that, Doris," Lisa said. "That's well beyond the call of duty."

"Nonsense, I was happy to help," Mrs Wishmore smiled. "You were so kind to those elderly folk from the care home who dropped by at the cafe, and I know it put a great dent in your plans to serve them and send them away happy, when you'd been about to close up for the day. You did them a good turn and so I thought you deserved a good turn yourself."

"But you've cooked an entire pot of bolognese!" Lisa said. "How did you find time to do this?"

Mrs Wishmore waved a hand. "It was the work of moments, dear. Fiona wanted to stay and help prepare it, but I know she visits her mother on Thursday evenings, so I insisted I could handle this myself. There was a pack of beef mince in the café freezer, and I found a few other bits and pieces of ingredients, too. I hope that's okay?"

"You're a life saver, Doris. I was just thinking I'd have to serve Jake eggs on toast tonight, or send out for a takeaway, and I wanted to do better than that. I can't thank you enough."

"Here, try some and tell me what you think."

Mrs Wishmore passed her a spoon and Lisa dipped it into the rich bolognese sauce.

"It's delicious," Lisa said, filled with awe. "This sauce tastes like it's been slow-cooked for hours."

"Well, if you let it simmer for another twenty minutes, it will be ready to serve. All you'll have to do is boil some spaghetti and voila! The meal will be done."

While Mrs Wishmore turned her attention to the clean dishes waiting to come out of the washer, Lisa tasted another spoonful of the bolognese and shook her head in wonder.

"I don't know how you pulled this off," Lisa said. "Ever since you came to work here, Doris, it seems like a minor miracle happens every day."

"I'm happy to help however I can," Mrs Wishmore chuckled. "Now, why don't you run upstairs and freshen up, and take the pot of bolognese with you and get it settled on your hob. I'll finish clearing up in the café and lock up behind myself when I leave."

"I can't ask you to do that."

"You're not asking, I'm offering. You did the right thing, seeking Jake out this morning and explaining things to him, and you did the right thing, inviting him over for a meal. It's time to put your happiness ahead of your café chores, Lisa."

Mrs Wishmore smiled and patted Lisa's hand. Instantly, Lisa remembered the comfort she'd felt that morning when she'd chatted with Mrs Wishmore over coffee in the quiet café, although the details of what they'd discussed were a little hazy now. How strange that she couldn't quite recall the specifics of a conversation she'd only had a few hours ago with her friendly waitress, when the specifics of her conversation with Jake outside the school just a few minutes later were crystal clear.

Not for the first time, Lisa thought there was something just a little enigmatic about the mysterious Mrs Wishmore.

"If you can deal with a little more clearing up before you leave, then the rest of it can wait until first thing tomorrow morning," Lisa said. "I'll pop back down in ten minutes and lock up. Just pull the front door behind you and the latch will catch and I'll take care of the rest."

"Fair enough." Mrs Wishmore said, then picked up the bolognese pot with a pair of oven mitts and all but forced it into Lisa's hands. "Now, get yourself upstairs this instant."

Laughing, Lisa took the pot from Mrs Wishmore and hurried out the rear door and upstairs to her flat. Once she'd set the pot on the hob on a low heat, she measured out spaghetti and set the table, and breathed a sigh of relief when she found a bottle of red wine lurking at the back of the cupboard. After taking the fastest shower she'd ever had, she spent a few minutes freshening her make-up and loosening her ponytail and attempting to style her hair into something vaguely attractive, before pulling on a pair of jeans and a soft sleeveless blouse.

When she glanced at her watch and saw it was six o'clock already, she flew back down the stairs from her flat and into the café to finish locking up. She told herself not to look at all the clearing still waiting to be done, knowing that if she began wiping down tables or washing out the cake display case or anything else, she'd still be doing it when Jake turned up for dinner, and all the effort she'd made to look halfway decent for his arrival would be for naught.

So it came as a surprise to discover that the entire café was tidy and pristine from top to bottom. All the tables were cleared and reset for the next day. The floor had been mopped, fresh dishes were stacked beneath the counter, and the glass in the display case gleamed. For a long moment, Lisa stared in amazement at the transformation that had taken place since she'd gone upstairs.

"How did Mrs Wishmore do all this in just twenty minutes?" Lisa said to the empty café. "It's impossible."

But there was no time to find an answer to her question, because Jake appeared on the other side of the café window just then, walking along the pavement with Ruby trotting at his side. When Jake saw her inside the cafe, he stopped and smiled, then raised his hand in which he held a bunch of flowers, which he waved in her direction.

"I was just about to walk around to the lane," he said through the window.

"Come through this way instead," Lisa said and unlatched the café door to let Jake and Ruby inside. "I only popped down to finish locking up."

"Anything you need a hand with down here?"

"No, Mrs Wishmore took care of everything. Quite how she managed it I have no idea, but she whipped this place into order in record time."

Lisa thought of how quickly Mrs Wishmore had turned around the café kitchen and the backlog of dirty dishes, and now she'd done the same thing at the front of house. There'd be no need for Lisa to arrive downstairs earlier than usual tomorrow morning in order to knock the café into shape, because Mrs Wishmore had done it for her.

"Are you okay?" Jake said, peering at her. "You seem confused about something."

"No, I..." Lisa laughed and shook her head. "Doris just never ceases to surprise me, that's all. We were miles behind on our clear-up this afternoon, but somehow she's taken care of everything and got us back on track. As usual, I'm looking a gift horse in the mouth."

She finally noticed the beautiful bunch of flowers Jake was holding, a summery mix of white daisies and soft pink roses. When he saw her looking at them, he held them out to her.

"To thank you for having me over to dinner," he said. "And for inviting Ruby over, too."

"These are beautiful," she said, admiring the sweet blooms. "But don't thank me too soon. You haven't eaten anything yet, and I didn't even..."

She caught herself before she confessed that she hadn't even been the one who'd cooked their meal. After all the wavering she'd done with this man over these last few days, and the mixed signals she'd sent, it didn't seem like a good idea to tell him she hadn't even made time to cook a meal for him, after asking him over here for precisely that purpose.

"I didn't even have time to start the spaghetti boiling yet," Lisa said instead. "Come upstairs and I'll get the pasta cooking and we can open some wine while we wait."

As they walked through the café and beyond the kitchen, Lisa checked the equipment was turned off and switched off the lights before locking the rear door. When they went upstairs to Lisa's flat, Jake let out an appreciative grumble the moment they walked through the door.

"Something smells amazing," he said, unclipping Ruby's lead so she could dash off and explore her new surroundings.

"It's spaghetti bolognese. I hope that's okay?"

"It's perfect. In fact, it's my favourite meal. You couldn't have chosen better."

Another win for Mrs Wishmore, Lisa thought with a wry smile as she boiled the kettle for the pasta. After opening the bottle of red wine, she poured them each a glass.

"Thanks for coming over tonight," Lisa said when she clinked her glass against Jake's. "And thanks for giving me another chance after yesterday."

"Thanks for inviting me. And it's not about giving you another chance, Lisa. I like your company and I like you. Maybe we both just need to relax a bit and stop waiting for things to go wrong."

"I'll drink to that."

They sipped more wine and Lisa started the pasta cooking on the hob. While she stirred the bolognese sauce and searched her fridge for a wedge of parmesan cheese, Jake wandered to the display cabinet on the other side of the kitchen table and eyed the shelves.

"Do you collect these plates and dishes and so on?" he asked. "You have a lot of them."

Lisa cast an eye over the display shelves, which were groaning beneath her hodgepodge collection of tableware items. There were old fashioned china teacups and saucers, stacks of delicately painted plates, and more teapots, sugar bowls and milk jugs than one person could ever hope to need.

"I'm a bit of a hopeless case when it comes to buying things in second-hand shops and jumble sales. I'm always on the lookout for vintage tableware for the café, but I can't help keeping some of the special items for myself. Whenever I see a plate with a pretty decoration on it, or a serving jug with a sweet shape, I'm a goner."

Jake laughed and continued examining the hoard of plates and teacups, before picking up a pale blue sugar bowl decorated with tiny little daffodils around the rim. "You've got a thing for daffodils."

"I love them. They're my favourite spring flower, which is why I named my café after them. After every long winter, the daffodils arrive with their cheerful yellow flowers and remind us that spring always comes, eventually."

She let out a soft sigh, knowing she wasn't just talking about the seasons changing, and that Jake understood this. With a tender expression on his face, he set down the sugar bowl he'd been admiring and looked further along the shelf.

"This is a great photograph of you and Peter."

Lisa turned again from the stove and saw Jake pointing at a framed photograph on one of the display shelves. The photograph showed Lisa and Peter together on the beach, the blue waves of the sea breaking on the shore behind them as the sun shone down.

"We had a holiday together in Cornwall a few weeks before Peter died," Lisa said. "It was a wonderful trip, and we got lucky with sunshine and blue skies the entire time we were there." She walked across to join Jake at the cabinet. "I should take down some of these photographs of the two of us, but..."

"But you like being reminded of the times you spent together," Jake said with a soft smile.

Lisa nodded, then searched Jake's expression for a moment. "Does it make you uncomfortable seeing photographs of Peter around the place? It's no trouble to move them out of the way."

She reached for the framed photo, but Jake's hand stopped her. "Don't do that. Seeing this photo of the two of you just got me wondering, that's all. Tell me about him. What was he like?"

"I'm sure you don't want to hear me talking about Peter," Lisa said with a nervous laugh.

"I do," Jake said. "You haven't told me much about him. In fact, you haven't told me anything about him. He was a huge part of your life and you loved him. I'd like to at least know who he was."

Lisa looked at Jake, then back at the framed photograph of Peter and herself on that sun-kissed Cornish beach. Peter's smile shone and his eyes were bright as he held Lisa close, and for a moment she could almost smell the salty sea air and feel the sun on her skin and Peter's arm around her waist.

"He was the kindest person you could ever meet," Lisa said, her gaze still on the framed photograph. "One of those wonderful people that there just aren't enough of in this world. He was kind to strangers and doted on his family and never had a bad word to say about anyone. He believed there was good in everyone and didn't have a cynical bone in his body."

Jake smiled and glanced back at the photograph. "He sounds like quite a guy."

"Oh, he had his faults, like we all do. Sometimes he was too trusting of people when he ought to have been more careful, and that got him into trouble sometimes. Actually, it was one of the few things we argued about. In his job, he worked for a charity that raised funds for cancer research, and he believed that everyone else who worked there was as committed to the cause as he was. He believed in the charity and believed the work they did could change lives, which, of course it did. But he sometimes forgot that some of the other employees simply saw it as a job, not a calling, and he didn't always realise when they were exploiting his good nature."

Jake raised an eyebrow. "You realised it, though."

"He'd often work late to cover for other members of staff who didn't think twice about off-loading their unfinished tasks onto him, knowing he'd deal with it all because what mattered to Peter was making sure the charity raised money.

He wanted to change the world and make it a better place and if that meant working late, so be it. But some of his lazier colleagues didn't see things the same way. I didn't like knowing Peter was being used like that, but whenever we had cross words about it, he told me I was being cynical."

"Every couple argues from time to time."

"True. And we weren't exactly at each other's throats over it or anything like that. Some couples out there find a lot more to argue about than we ever did, and I know we were lucky. Peter wasn't interested in making a tonne of money or chasing after material things. He saw the possibility of a better world for people and worked hard to turn that better world into a reality. He believed with all his heart that one day the scientists and researchers would find a cure for cancer, and all he wanted was to help them do it, however he could. That was Peter."

Talking like this was stirring emotions Lisa was determined to keep in check. When she looked away from the photograph on the display shelf, she saw a thoughtful look on Jake's face, and something else too, something harder to read. She found herself torn between the aching memories of Peter she'd been remembering and a deep desire to know just what was going through Jake's head as he watched her with that unreadable expression in his eyes.

The spaghetti pot on the stove boiled over just then, hissing and spitting as the water hit the gas flames. Grateful for the interruption, Lisa hurried across the kitchen to deal with the pot and turn down the heat.

"A few more minutes and the pasta will be ready," she said, stirring the spaghetti and then the bolognese, relieved that both tasks needed her attention.

As she stirred the pots, the kitchen fell into silence. When she glanced over her shoulder, she found Jake still studying the framed photograph on the shelf.

"I can hear in your voice how much Peter meant to you," Jake said at last. "I can hear how much it still hurts that you lost him. I appreciate you sharing something about him with me, even if it wasn't easy."

"It gets a little easier every day. And I don't want you to feel I'm shutting you out or keeping you at a distance. That isn't fair. I know I need to talk about Peter and share how I feel, even if the feelings I have are hard to explain sometimes. Thanks for listening."

That same unreadable expression once more clouded Jake's expression. Lisa almost opened her mouth to ask what was on his mind. Was it something she'd said while talking about Peter?

Before she could analyse things any more, Ruby trotted into the kitchen and planted herself on the floor at Lisa's feet and gave her a hopeful look.

"Dinner's almost ready, Ruby," Lisa laughed. "Although I'm not sure if you're allowed bolognese."

"I already fed her," Jake said. "She's just trying her luck."

Ruby barked in protest at this summary of her motivations. When Lisa looked over at Jake, she saw his expression had shifted and that the unreadable look of just a moment before had been replaced with a smile as he ruffled the dog's ears.

Despite Jake's insistence that he wanted to know more about Peter, Lisa wondered if she should've kept her reminiscences to herself. Perhaps it was just too weird for Jake to hear Lisa talk about the man she would've been married to by now had tragedy not struck.

But that wasn't all she wondered about as she drained the pasta and ladled bolognese sauce onto their plates. Talking to Jake about Peter was weird for her, too.

She'd loved Peter so much. But when she was with Jake,

she also felt something flickering to life inside her, something that had been cold and dormant for so long.

What would it mean if that tiny flame kindled into something more? She hadn't expected to feel this way with the first man she started seeing after losing Peter, and certainly not to feel this way so quickly.

Did that mean she was betraying Peter's memory and all they'd meant to each other?

Or did it mean that moving on was just as complicated as she'd always feared it would be?

"Jake," Lisa said, setting aside the pots and stepping across to the table where he was setting down his wine glass and pulling out a chair.

She wanted to say something, something that might explain these strange, contradictory feelings racing through her, to help Jake understand. But she scarcely understood it herself and the words she searched for remained unspoken.

Instead, she pulled Jake close and kissed him. The move caught him off-guard and she heard his surprised gasp as her lips met his. Wrapping her arms around him, she sank into his embrace and into the delicious kiss—a kiss that chased away her swirling worries and unanswerable questions, and replaced them with a warm glow and a feeling that everything was right with the world once more.

When she opened her eyes and drew in some air, she smiled and said, "I like you, Jake, in case you hadn't noticed."

"I noticed," he said, a wry grin tugging at his mouth.

"If you want to know more about Peter, I'll tell you about him. But maybe tonight we owe it to each other to enjoy some conversation that doesn't leave either of us thinking about the past."

A shadow across his expression, but only for a moment. "That makes perfect sense to me."

"Good. Let's eat. I'm starving after the day I've had." Lisa set their plates on the table and brought the wine over to top up their glasses.

"You should hear about the day I had," Jake said. "This crazy woman turned up my place of work and kissed me in front of a playground filled with impressionable teenagers."

Lisa laughed. "She sounds like a mad person."

"Totally bonkers." Jake dug into his meal with his fork. As he chewed his first mouthful of food, his eyebrows shot up his forehead. "But this woman is also an amazing cook, so I think I'll stick with her and see how it goes. This bolognese is fantastic."

Lisa looked at her plate and then back at Jake. "I have a confession. I didn't cook the bolognese sauce."

He paused with another forkful of spaghetti halfway to his mouth. "You didn't?"

"Mrs Wishmore made it. I planned to cook something for us, but we had a coach-load of old age pensioners turn up at the café just before we were closing and I didn't want to turn them away. They had a café booking somewhere else, but it fell through, and the poor old folks looked like they needed a nice cup of tea and a slice of cake. By the time we'd served them all, I'd run out of time to cook something from scratch, which was when I discovered Mrs Wishmore had done it for me..."

She trailed off, feeling a little foolish. "I know it's just some dinner, but I couldn't sit here accepting compliments on the food when I wasn't even the one who cooked it. I thought I should come clean."

Jake's gaze scanned her face for a long moment before he laughed softly. "Peter wasn't the only one with a good heart, Lisa." He squeezed her hand across the table and picked up his fork again. "I'll be sure to thank Mrs Wishmore for the meal next time I see her, if that makes you feel any better."

"It does."

Jake laughed again then raised his wine glass. "To Mrs Wishmore and her last minute spaghetti bolognese."

"I'll drink to that." Lisa tapped her glass to Jake's and sent out a silent prayer of thanks to the mysterious woman with the kind eyes and cloud of silvery hair who'd rescued her dinner plans. "To Mrs Wishmore."

She picked up her fork and ate some food and realised how comfortable and at ease she felt, sitting at the kitchen table with Jake, sharing an evening meal together and enjoying his company. Something about the man made every tension in her body disappear.

"So, what shall we talk about, Jake?" she said.

"Anything and everything," he said, smiling over his wine glass.

As they ate the meal Mrs Wishmore had cooked for them, that's just what they did—they talked and talked, about anything and everything, and all the good stuff in-between.

JAKE ATE his food while Lisa told him more about her busy afternoon in the café, and about the crowd of old folks who'd turned up looking for tea and cake right before she'd been about to close up for the day, and about how she wouldn't have got through the day at all had it not been for her reliable cook, Fiona, and her helpful temporary waitress, Doris Wishmore.

He liked listening to Lisa talk, liked listening to her chatter about her day and the trials and triumphs she'd had, and liked listening to the way she talked about her café staff and how much she treasured them and all their hard work.

He'd liked hearing her talking earlier about Peter, too, when he'd asked about the photograph of the two of them on the kitchen dresser. The man had been a big part of Lisa's life and Jake didn't want her to pretend he didn't exist, or think she had to spare his feelings. It was obvious from what Lisa said that Peter had been a good man. After all, Lisa had fallen in love with him and agreed to marry him, which meant the man couldn't have been anything other than good. Jake knew enough about Lisa by now to understand she'd never give her heart to someone who wasn't worthy.

But although he'd liked hearing her talk about her late fiancé and what they'd meant to one another, Jake had still felt an icy sliver of unease as he'd absorbed what Lisa told him about the man she'd been engaged to marry. He couldn't help but wonder whether any other man could ever compare to Peter's memory.

And he couldn't help but wonder how many men Lisa would have to date before she put enough distance between her late fiancé and the future she said she wanted to embrace.

It hadn't escaped his noticed that while Lisa had talked about Peter and the life they'd shared, her hand had moved to the necklace she wore and the diamond engagement ring attached to it, her fingers closing around the ring almost automatically. Judging by her expression, Lisa hadn't even realised she'd done it. Jake wondered how often she reached for that ring each day, seeking its comfort and a reminder of the future it had once promised.

He couldn't deny that seeing Lisa cradling that engagement ring between her fingers had made him wonder just how ready she was to move on. When their conversation was interrupted by the pasta pot boiling over on the hob, he'd been relieved. Watching her drop the ring pendant back beneath her top in one fluid move before hurrying off to deal with the pasta, Jake had sensed the size of what he was up against.

Lisa's fiancé had been a great guy and it wouldn't be easy

moving on. She still wore the engagement ring he'd given her, albeit it on a necklace and not on her finger, and surely that said it all? The way she fidgeted with that ring whenever she talked about Peter only underlined what Jake already knew.

Lisa wasn't ready to launch into a new relationship. She might be ready for some casual dating, but surely anything more than that was out of the question?

So where did that leave him?

Jake pushed away the stupid thought. He'd only gone out with Lisa a few times and it was far too early to worry about something like that. And if the woman made him feel things he hadn't felt before with any other girl, well, that was his problem, not Lisa's. Instead of thinking about these big questions, he should just enjoy their evening together and find out if Lisa was interested in finishing that bottle of wine they'd opened. He ought to take things as he found them and see where it led.

"I'm stuffed," Jake said, finishing his last forkful of spaghetti bolognese and pushing away his plate. "My greedy brain wants second helpings, but if I eat any more, I might explode."

"That's a shame, because I've got some dessert in the fridge," Lisa said.

Jake perked up at this. "Dessert? I thought you didn't have time to make anything for dinner tonight?"

"I'm a baker, Jake," Lisa said with a laugh as she cleared their plates away. "There's always something sweet to enjoy in this house. I made meringues in the café today and there were a couple left over. There are strawberries going spare from a Victoria sponge I made yesterday, and whipped cream, too. I can make Eton Mess, if you're interested?"

"I think I could force down some Eton Mess. It would be rude not to."

Laughing, Lisa turned to the counter where she began breaking up the meringues and slicing the strawberries. Jake walked to the sink and filled it with hot water, and got to work on the dinner plates.

"You're my guest, you don't have to wash dishes," Lisa said as she assembled their puddings.

"I'm happy to make myself useful."

As Jake washed and rinsed the plates, his gaze kept returning to Lisa working at the counter beside him. The evening light was slanting through the kitchen window and catching her face and hair, giving her skin a warm glow and making Jake's heart fill with longing. She was so beautiful, standing there absorbed in her work while the sunlight washed over her. It was all he could do not to abandon the dishes at the sink and haul her into his arms and kiss her until he ran out of breath.

Lisa must have sensed him watching her, because she turned from her chopping board and pudding preparation and gave him a smile.

"Everything okay?" she asked.

"Oh, sure, everything's fine," he said and rubbed at a bit of bolognese sauce on the dinner plate he was washing. "So, how did you end up becoming a baker and running your own café? I'm curious about the story behind the best cakes in all of Willowbridge."

Lisa laughed. "Thanks for the compliment. It's not much of a story, to be honest. My mother always baked when I was growing up and I enjoyed helping her. She taught me how to make sponges and scones and the simple stuff that isn't too complicated. Once I had all that under my belt, I wanted to know more, but that was as much as my mother knew about baking. She was a good home baker, she still is, but the advanced stuff didn't interest her. So, I started working my way through her baking books and trying things she never had, like bread and complicated pastry and that sort of thing. I think I was fourteen when I mastered the art of choux pastry."

"You were some kind of child prodigy," Jake grinned.

"Hardly. There were lots of disasters before I learned the techniques. I'm sure my parents still haven't forgiven me for all the undercooked bread and pastry I fed them while I was finding my feet. My father never wanted to hurt my feelings by not eating the things I baked, and I'm sure at one point he was working his way through a packet of indigestion tablets every day."

Jake laughed, enjoying hearing her talk about her past and her family. "They must be very proud of you."

"They are. To hear my mother talk, you'd think I was the CEO of my very own multinational patisserie chain, instead of a little café in the countryside." Lisa rolled her eyes and smiled, then continued mixing the Eton Mess puddings.

"So why did you decide to open a café?" Jake asked. "Why did you take that route?"

"I always loved the idea of owning my own little place. After I finished catering college, I worked for a while in restaurant and hotel kitchens as a pastry chef, but it wasn't for me. I wanted the chance to meet the customers who were eating my food and feel like I was part of a community, and that's difficult when you're stuck in a kitchen most of the time. With my own café, I get to enjoy baking cakes and goodies, but I can also run the front of house. A café is a different culinary experience compared to a restaurant meal or fine dining venue. When people visit a café they want good, wholesome food and they want delicious home baking, and that's what my café gives them, and I'm proud of that."

"You should be."

"Plus, when I was working in restaurant kitchens, I didn't enjoy the long shifts that lasted so late into the night. I wanted more from life than just earning a living and working myself to the bone in someone else's kitchen. My café is only open during the day, and although there's always plenty of work to keep me busy outside of opening hours, there's at least the chance of a social life and, maybe one day, a..."

When she trailed off, Jake glanced up from the dishes he was drying and saw a wistful look on her face. "What were you about to say?" he asked.

She threw him an awkward smile. "I was about to say that maybe one day, there's the chance of a family life, too, but then I realised..."

Jake watched her frown and blow out a breath before continuing.

"I realised I don't want to make you uncomfortable talking about something like that," she said.

He set aside the tea towel he'd been using to dry the dishes. "That's what you planned with Peter?"

"Yes, but..." She finished working on the puddings and turned around. "I don't want to talk about any of that. It's not fair to you. And, if I'm being honest, it's not fair to us."

Jake held her gaze, thinking about what she'd said. "There's an 'us'?"

"There could be, if I don't keep talking about my dead fiancé," she said with a soft, sad smile. She glanced back at the strawberries on the chopping board, as if gathering her thoughts, and when she looked at Jake again, her soft smile had turned into something more playful. "And anyway, we've only been on a few dates, and I'm sure the last thing you want to hear about is me talking about all the kids I want to have some day."

Jake gave an exaggerated shocked reaction, his eyebrows climbing up his forehead. "You want to have kids? That's insane. I've never heard of anyone our age wanting kids before. If I'd known this, I wouldn't have agreed to come here for dinner. You're clearly deranged."

Lisa laughed, her eyes bright, and Jake decided he could listen to the sound of her laughter for the rest of his life.

He pushed away the idea, knowing it wasn't the first time he'd thought something like this where Lisa was concerned. They'd only just met and the dates they'd had so far hadn't exactly gone without a hitch. And yet here he was, thinking about forever and what it might look like if he spent it with Lisa.

"Well, our desserts are ready," Lisa said, carrying two bowls to the table. "So I hope you won't run out of here just yet."

Jake had no intention of running. As he pulled out his chair, Lisa took his other hand and looked deep into his eyes.

"I'm sorry if I spooked you when I said what I said about wanting kids someday," she said.

"You didn't spook me. Everyone wants kids, right?"

"I suppose so."

He narrowed his gaze. "You don't want them right now, do you? Because we should shut Ruby in another room before we rip each other's clothes off. I don't want my poor dog being traumatised."

For a long moment, Lisa only stared at him, her eyes wide. Jake feared he'd taken the joke—or the pretence of the joke—too far. But then, at last, her shocked expression dissolved into a volley of laughter, and she threw her arms around his neck and planted a kiss on his cheek.

"You're funny, Jake. So, so funny," she said between rolls of laughter.

"I try my best to keep the ladies entertained."

This only seemed to make her laugh harder, although Jake had no idea why. What he'd said wasn't particularly funny or witty. Their laughter brought Ruby back into the kitchen from the living room, where she'd been curled up on the floor fast asleep, and the little dog scampered around their legs, panting and barking in response to the noise and fun. Lisa ruffled the little dog's ears and then reached up to Jake and pulled his face closer to hers and kissed him so tenderly it made him forget where he was.

"You're the best thing that's happened to me in a long time, Jake," Lisa said. "Thank you."

His head still spinning from Lisa's kiss, he replied, "It's all part of the service, ma'am."

She laughed again, her eyes twinkling. "Come on, let's eat this pudding before the whipped cream makes the meringue too soggy. No one likes soggy meringue."

They sat down and ate their desserts, feeding Ruby dog biscuit treats as she begged at their feet and pretended to be starving. Later they made coffee, and a little later after that they finished the last of the red wine still open on the table.

They talked and talked as the evening turned pink and golden beyond the kitchen windows, and as the hours ticked by, Jake realised something as he listened to Lisa chattering away and watched the candles she'd lit dancing in her eyes.

He was on the verge of falling for her.

And he wasn't sure there was anything he could do to stop himself falling hard.

CHAPTER EIGHTEEN

The next morning, Lisa was piling chocolate tiffin squares onto a plate inside the café's display case in preparation for opening when there was a knock at the door. When she looked up, Jake was smiling through the glass and waving.

"Morning!" Lisa said when she turned the locks and stepped outside. "What brings you here so early?"

"I was driving to school and thought I'd take a detour and stop by to say thanks again for dinner last night," he said. "I had a great time."

"Me too, Jake."

It was true. They'd talked for hours at her kitchen table, polishing off the bottle of red wine and lingering over several cups of coffee as the summer twilight had deepened outside. The candles she'd lit had filled the kitchen with a warm glow and kept the conversation going even longer, neither of them seeming to want the evening to end while the candlelight shimmered and the balmy scents of summer drifted through the open window.

After feeling awkward and torn about sharing her memories of Peter with Jake, the conversation had come easily once they were eating their food and enjoying their wine, much to Lisa's relief. She suspected that throwing herself at Jake and kissing his face off had helped lighten the mood. It had certainly put a smile on her face that had lasted the rest of the night.

As they'd made themselves comfortable at the kitchen table, she'd enjoyed hearing Jake talk about his life as a teacher, and the upcoming school summer fair, and funny stories from his time at the chalk face. Over dessert, they'd swapped stories from childhood, compared holidays they'd taken in the past and discussed places they'd like to visit in the future, and shared details about their families and friends.

It had all been wonderful. The searing kiss they'd shared as Jake was leaving at the end of the evening had been the delicious cherry on top.

"Are you free tonight?" Jake now asked.

"Yes. What did you have in mind?"

"I thought we could take a drive and find a nice sunny beer garden somewhere and have a drink together. What do you think?"

Lisa nodded. "I'm up for that. I was planning on working on some baking for the stall at your school's summer fair, but thanks to my freeze-ahead recipes I'm okay with my preparations and a drink sounds more fun."

"What have you baked so far?" Jake said, intrigued.

"It's a surprise."

"If you bake one of your amazing chocolate cakes, I'll put a hefty donation into the collection bucket if I'm allowed to claim the entire cake as mine."

"Consider it done."

They smiled at each other as the early morning sunshine bathed them in warmth and a soft breeze rustled the leaves in the trees further down the high street on the village green. It seemed like a perfect moment, Lisa thought—another perfect moment on top of the many other perfect moments they'd shared last night over dinner in her cosy kitchen.

Lisa felt a great rush of excitement in her stomach as Jake's eyes darkened and his gaze ranged over her face. When he pulled her against him and tilted her chin up and kissed her, her head spun with pleasure.

Another perfect moment, captured inside her heart and making her feel things she'd thought she might never feel again.

"What on *earth* is going on?"

The sharp voice behind them abruptly ended their kiss. When Lisa opened her eyes and saw who was standing there on the pavement, the sweet pleasure she'd been enjoying evaporated in an instant.

"Joan!" Lisa cried, taking in the unexpected sight of Peter's mother and the stunned expression on the woman's face as she glanced between Lisa and Jake. "Uh, listen, I can explain—"

"Can you?" Joan said, almost spitting out the words. "How could you betray Peter like this? It was the one-year anniversary of his death just a few days ago!"

"Joan, please—"

"He would turn in his grave if he knew you were making a fool of yourself out here in the street with some other man, kissing and carrying on like this and making a fool of yourself for the entire world to see!"

"Hang on!" Jake said, the confused surprise on his face turning into anger. "I don't know who you are, but you can't talk to Lisa like that!"

"Jake, please, don't get upset," Lisa said, and then turned once more to Joan. "Joan, this is all just a misunderstanding. It's just a mistake."

Jake's gaze now narrowed on Lisa. "A mistake?"

"What I mean is, I need to speak to Joan privately," Lisa said, her cheeks now burning with embarrassment as her stomach churned with anxiety. "Can we talk later, Jake?"

Jake frowned at her for a long moment, before throwing an unhappy look at Joan and then checking his watch. "I suppose I'd better get to school or I'll be late."

He almost leaned closer to kiss her goodbye, but she saw the troubled look on his face as he thought better of it. With an inscrutable nod, he turned and walked down the high street to where his car was parked in a free spot. Lisa turned to Joan, who was still scowling, her face bunched into angry lines of unhappiness.

"Joan, come inside and we can talk," Lisa said.

"I don't think I care to do that, Lisa," Joan replied with a sniff, tugging at the light scarf around her neck. "I'm appalled by what I've witnessed here this morning. Utterly appalled."

"Joan, listen—"

"I came here to see how you were coping," Joan interrupted. "After all the kindnesses you've shown me this past year, I thought it was only right that I check up on you and see how you were. I know how hard these past weeks have been on me, so I assumed they'd been hard on you, too. Now I realise I was mistaken."

"If you'd just let me explain—"

"There I was imagining you were grieving Peter and his death. But instead, you've been having a grand old time and acting as if Peter never existed!"

"Joan, that's not true!"

"My goodness, ladies!" said a voice behind them. "Is everything all right?"

This time when Lisa turned, it was Mrs Wishmore she saw, hurrying towards them along the pavement, her eyes filled with concern.

"No," Lisa sighed. "It's not all right."

"Of course it isn't!" Joan cried. "I shouldn't have come here this morning, Lisa. But don't worry, I won't make that mistake again."

Joan straightened her shoulders, her knuckles white from clasping her shoulder bag against her body, and then she turned on her heel and marched off up the street.

"Joan! Wait!" Lisa called out. It broke her heart to see Joan's pencil-thin frame lurching along the pavement, and she could almost feel the woman's anguish pouring from her in fierce waves. Joan had almost become her mother-in-law, and was as close to a proper member of her family as it was possible to be, and she ached to see the woman plunged into such misery and to know that she herself had caused it.

Lisa was about to take off along the pavement to catch up with Joan when she felt Mrs Wishmore's hand grab her arm and stop her.

"Let me go after her," Mrs Wishmore said.

"You? But you don't even know her," Lisa frowned.

"Which is why it might be best if I can say a few words to calm her down. They might have more effect coming from a stranger than from someone she loves so dearly, don't you think?"

Lisa wasn't so sure, either about Mrs Wishmore's logic or about her assumption that Joan felt anything for her now other than anger and disgust. But Mrs Wishmore's hand on her arm was firm, her expression unwavering, and Lisa found herself nodding.

Mrs Wishmore smiled and set off up the street in pursuit of Joan, who was already heading towards the turn at the junction, her burst of speed no doubt a result of the upset she'd just experienced. When Mrs Wishmore caught up with her, Lisa watched her gently take hold of Joan's arm and bring her to a halt. Joan shrugged her off, shaking her head and attempting to continue on her journey, but Mrs Wishmore wasn't dissuaded, once more reaching out and laying her hand on Joan's arm.

Lisa watched in wonder as Joan stopped walking again and this time turned to Mrs Wishmore and listened while the older woman spoke to her. Lisa hadn't thought it would be possible to reason with poor Joan when she was so upset, but Mrs Wishmore seemed to be succeeding. Joan said nothing while Mrs Wishmore spoke, and Lisa only wished she knew what Doris was saying. Mrs Wishmore's hand remained on Joan's arm as she talked, and even at this distance Lisa saw the kind smile on Doris's face and the warmth in her eyes.

She thought, too, that even at this distance she could feel the soothing vibes radiating from Mrs Wishmore like sunbeams. As she watched Mrs Wishmore gently squeeze Joan's arm, Lisa remembered the deep comfort of the older woman's touch when they'd sat together in the café just yesterday morning, and hoped that same deep comfort was now helping Joan.

Lisa let out a breath of relief as Mrs Wishmore at last turned Joan around on the pavement and walked with her back towards the café.

"Joan would like to come inside for a nice cup of tea and a chat, wouldn't you, Joan?" Mrs Wishmore said once they returned to the café.

Joan cut her eyes towards Lisa and glanced away again. "I suppose so."

If Mrs Wishmore heard the reluctance in Joan's voice, she didn't let on. Instead, she only smiled as she led Joan inside the café and steered her towards a table in the corner.

"Thank you for coming back, Joan," Lisa said, following behind the two older women. "I would've hated for you to rush off without talking to me. I don't want you to be upset or angry."

Joan unwound the summery scarf around her neck and sat down at the table. "Your friend here, Doris, persuaded me that it's better to talk about these things and get them out in the open, to avoid misunderstandings. Personally, I don't see how I could have misunderstood what I witnessed out on that street—"

"But I'm sure a nice hot cup of tea will help settle everyone down," Mrs Wishmore interrupted. "Why don't you two make yourselves comfortable and I'll deal with the tea things."

Mrs Wishmore threw an encouraging wink at Lisa and gestured for her to sit down at the table with Joan. Lisa turned the lock on the café door, as it wasn't yet time to open and she knew it would be better if she and Joan could talk without being interrupted by early bird customers.

"Joan, I'm so sorry you got upset," Lisa said as she sat down across from Joan. "That was the last thing I wanted."

"I'm astonished by what I saw this morning, Lisa. And after all we've endured together, I'm disappointed in you."

Joan's words stung, but she tried not to let it show on her face. "I wouldn't want to hurt you for the world."

"Well, that's exactly what you did, Lisa. You hurt me, very badly."

"I had no idea you planned on coming by the café this morning, Joan. If I'd known…"

"If you'd known, you would've done what?" Joan snapped. "Kept your fancy man hidden away until I was gone?"

"No! It's not like that. And please don't say things that make it all sound like something tawdry."

"Maybe tawdry is exactly what it is."

"Now you're deliberately being hurtful, Joan. I didn't

mean to hurt you. But you're saying things you must know will hurt my feelings and that isn't fair."

Joan scowled and opened her mouth to respond, and Lisa feared another angry onslaught was coming her way. But Joan must have noticed the anguished look on Lisa's face because the older woman plopped her mouth closed and sighed.

"I'm sorry you feel that I'm trying to hurt you," Joan said, her mouth an angry thin line. "That's not my intention. But I cannot pretend I'm not betrayed and shattered by the scene I just witnessed outside on that street."

Lisa let out an unhappy sigh of her own. This conversation was going nowhere and judging by the indignant look on Joan's face, it never would.

Mrs Wishmore returned to their table carrying a tray bearing a teapot and cups. After setting down the tray and stirring the pot, Mrs Wishmore joined them at the table.

"Here we go," she said, pouring the tea and offering the milk jug to both women. "Nice and strong, just the way we need it."

Lisa sipped her tea, grateful for the strong brew. Joan clasped her cup in her hands, as if drawing the warmth from the cup and into herself. The unhappy look on the poor woman's face filled Lisa with sadness and brought a lump to her throat.

"Joan, please can we talk about this like adults?" Lisa said, determined to sort this out. "I want to explain, if you'll let me."

"I'm not stopping you from saying whatever you want to say," Joan sniffed.

"I think what Lisa means is that it's difficult to be open and honest about things sometimes," Mrs Wishmore said softly. "Especially when the person we most need to be open and honest with isn't truly listening."

Joan protested, but Mrs Wishmore only smiled and laid her hand on Joan's. Immediately, Joan's expression softened.

"Perhaps that's true," Joan nodded, glancing at Lisa. "I'm upset and angry, and because of that, I don't want to hear what you want to tell me, Lisa. But that won't get us anywhere." She let out a long sigh and stared into her tea cup. "Peter wouldn't have wanted me to be angry like this, not at you, even if I believe I have good reasons. He was always kind and generous with the people in his life, even when they'd done him wrong. He never held a grudge or shut people out. I have to remember that, especially right now, when I can hardly bear to look at you, Lisa."

Tears welled in Joan's eyes as she uttered these last words, and the sudden twists and turns in what she'd said left Lisa with a wave of emotion rushing through her.

"Please try," Lisa said, her voice a whisper.

Her bereft tone must have got through Joan's defences, because the older woman glanced up at last, her eyes rimmed with tears as their gazes met. It was a breakthrough of sorts, and Lisa decided it was now or never.

"The man you saw me with outside is Jake Reid," she said. "He's a teacher at the local secondary school. We only met recently and we've only gone out together a few times. It's too early to know if we're in a relationship, or if we're just two people who like each other and want to spend more time together, getting to know one another a little better."

Joan seemed to consider this. "What I saw didn't look like two people who were unsure of their feelings for each other."

"That's fair," Lisa said, blushing at the truth of the matter. "I like Jake a lot, far more than I expected to. When we first met, all I wanted was to get back out into the world and start living my life again. I've been so lonely, Joan, and I've missed Peter so much this last year. Sometimes I thought I wouldn't survive losing him."

Lisa's voice broke and Joan's expression crumpled as she pulled a handkerchief from her bag and dabbed at her eyes.

"I don't want to be lonely anymore," Lisa continued, struggling to keep her voice even. "And that means moving on. It means beginning my life again. It means meeting new people. Until recently, I couldn't imagine what it might mean to spend time with a man who wasn't Peter, or become close to a man who wasn't Peter. But since I met Jake, it's something I can imagine more and more clearly every day."

Joan let out a sob and pressed her handkerchief against her nose, shaking her head as if to deny what Lisa was saying.

"That's the truth, Joan," Lisa said quietly. "I sobbed for Peter and grieved for him until I was wrung out. Nothing will ever change what I felt for him and I'll love him for as long as I live. But I have to move on. I *want* to move on. It's not easy. But it's time."

The quiet of the café was broken only by the sound of Joan's smothered sobs. Lisa fought to keep her own tears at bay. She felt wretched enough without adding a crying jag into the mix.

"Joan," Mrs Wishmore said, patting the other woman's hand across the table. "You're obviously very troubled and upset by what Lisa has told you."

Joan nodded, still pressing the handkerchief to her face, her eyes closed tight.

"Maybe it will help you both if you can explain why you're so troubled," Mrs Wishmore continued.

"Isn't it obvious?" Joan hiccupped through a loud sob.

"Perhaps it is," Mrs Wishmore said. "That doesn't mean it won't help to say it out loud."

"For goodness' sakes, it's gut-wrenching to see Lisa replace Peter with another man! There, I've said it!"

Joan's gaze raked across Lisa before she lowered her head and turned her attention back to her sodden handkerchief.

"But that's not the real reason you're upset, is it?" Mrs Wishmore said in a low voice.

Lisa frowned, wondering what Mrs Wishmore meant. She glanced at Joan, who was still turning her handkerchief over in her hands. A long moment passed before Joan drew in a deep breath and slowly shook her head.

"No, it's not the real reason I'm upset," Joan said at last.

Puzzled, Lisa waited for Joan to explain. The frail woman was clearly struggling to find the words she wanted to say.

"It's all right, Joan," Mrs Wishmore said. "You are among friends here."

Joan gave Mrs Wishmore a grateful look and then turned towards Lisa.

"The real reason I'm upset is because when I saw you with that young man outside, Jake, it showed me you're moving on," Joan said. "And that only reminded me that I'm not moving on, and that I can't."

Fresh tears rolled down Joan's pale cheeks. Lisa reached across the table and clutched the older woman's hand into her own.

"Oh, Joan," she said. "Of course you can move on."

Joan shook her head. "No, I can't. The day I buried my son, my life might as well have ended. No parent should have to bury their child. All the lights went out the day Peter died and they won't come back on again, not for me. I'm an old woman, Lisa, older than my years because of what happened to Peter. It feels like there is no future for me, no future I'd want, at any rate."

"But, Joan, Peter wouldn't have wanted you to stop living. He wouldn't have wanted you to give up, because..."

Joan's tears only fell all the harder at Lisa's words, making her stop talking mid-sentence. She wanted to comfort the heart-broken woman, not make her feel even worse.

"I know that," Joan said. "I know he would have wanted me to be happy and that only makes it worse. Peter was a good man. A wonderful, good man. It isn't fair that he's gone! It's cruel! How can I move on in life when all I can think about is how it *isn't fair* that Peter is dead! My lovely, sweet son!"

Joan's voice rose with every word she spoke, anger dancing in her eyes, but as she said these last words, she sobbed once more.

"Oh, Joan," Lisa said, holding the woman's hand tight. "You can't go on like this."

"I know," Joan said, shaking her head. "I know I have to find a way out of this misery. But it's so hard. Sometimes I don't see the point in finding a way out. It feels like I have very little left to live for."

"I wish I'd realised just how terribly unhappy you were," Lisa said. "I knew you were struggling, but I didn't realise how dark things had become for you. I should've spent more time with you and helped you more."

Joan shook her head. "I'm not your responsibility. You have your own life, you have a business to run, you have your own daily challenges. I have no one to blame but myself for the way I feel."

"Now, don't be so hard on yourself," Mrs Wishmore said. "Grief is a terrible thing, and you suffered the worst grief of all when you lost your son. Don't make it worse by piling more misery on yourself because of how you feel. Instead, perhaps you ought to give yourself a pat on the back for opening up and sharing with others just how much you're struggling."

"I've made a terrible scene this morning. There's no cause for self-congratulation in that."

"Everyone lets their emotions run wild from time to time," Mrs Wishmore smiled. "It's just part of being human. What matters now is that you find a way out of this prison in which you've put yourself, Joan."

Joan looked up from her handkerchief. "Prison?"

"That's what it is, isn't it? A prison. You've locked yourself away so that you don't have to be in a world in which Peter no longer lives. But he does live, Joan. He lives inside your heart."

Mrs Wishmore's words brought tears to Lisa's eyes. She watched as Joan slowly nodded and as Mrs Wishmore once more laid her hand on Joan's arm.

"Perhaps it's time to find the key that unlocks that prison cell of yours," Mrs Wishmore said.

"I know you're right," Joan nodded again. "But how do I do it?"

Mrs Wishmore picked up the teapot and refilled Joan's teacup. "Take a sip of tea."

For a moment, Joan looked puzzled, but she did as Mrs Wishmore told her.

"What was it like to take that sip of tea?" Mrs Wishmore asked.

"Uh, I'm not sure." Joan glanced at her cup. "It was comforting, I suppose. The tea tastes nice and strong and warming."

"You enjoyed the sip of tea?" Mrs Wishmore asked.

Joan considered the question. "Yes."

"Well, that's how you can escape from your unhappy prison cell, Joan," Mrs Wishmore said. "You find pleasure in small things and allow yourself to enjoy them. That's how you begin to live again. That is, if you truly want to live again."

Joan stared at Mrs Wishmore for several long beats. Lisa found herself staring, too. Mrs Wishmore's words were so simple and obvious, and yet filled with such wisdom, and it seemed to her that both she and Joan were caught and spellbound by the promise they offered.

Joan looked back at her tea cup. She raised it to her lips and drank. A small smile creased her mouth, and Lisa realised it was the first time she'd seen the woman smile in more than a year.

"This tea is good," Joan said. "Perhaps we could brew another pot?"

With a warm laugh, Mrs Wishmore rose from her chair. "Coming right up. And perhaps you'd enjoy a lovely toasted teacake too, Joan?"

"Yes, I'd like that," Joan said. "I just realised I'm rather hungry."

Lisa almost gasped, thinking of all the times she'd offered food to Joan during her visits over the past year and all the times she'd refused. To hear her say she was hungry was nothing short of astonishing.

"I could make you a bacon roll instead," Lisa said. "Or scrambled eggs?"

"No, a toasted teacake will be fine," Joan said and gave a weak smile. "Small steps."

While Mrs Wishmore busied herself behind the counter, Lisa watched Joan drink more tea.

"I'm sorry you were so upset when you saw me with Jake," Lisa said. "I don't want you to think I was keeping secrets from you. But as we've only been out together a few times, it didn't seem like something I should share with you, at least not yet."

"Now that I've calmed down and remembered my manners, I feel ashamed for how I behaved earlier. It was wrong and I'm sorry for the things I said. I hope you can forgive me."

"Of course I can forgive you. You mean so much to me, Joan. I don't want us to fall out."

"Neither do I. And it's only right that you start living your life again. Although it's strange indeed for me to think of you becoming involved with another man, knowing as I do how much you and Peter loved each other, the fact remains that you're a young woman and you deserve to be happy. It will take time for me to adjust to whatever romantic relationships may develop in your future, Lisa, but I promise I'll never react again the way I did this morning."

Lisa smiled. "I should have told you I'd started dating again. I should have trusted you with important news about what was going on in my life."

"Perhaps all this happened this way for a reason. I'm embarrassed by how I reacted and will be for quite some time. But I feel better for having talked like this."

"I'm so happy to hear that."

Joan glanced towards the counter, where Mrs Wishmore was setting out a fresh tea tray. "She's a wise old bird, this new waitress of yours."

"No argument there."

"I don't know how she did it, but after talking to her, and sitting with her here and sharing a cup of tea, I feel better than I have in as long as I can remember."

"I know just what you mean," Lisa replied.

"I'd like to apologise to your friend, Jake," Joan said. "I was horribly rude to him this morning, and I'd like to make amends."

"Don't worry about that right now. When I see him later, I'll explain everything."

Joan cleared her throat and a tortured expression crossed her face. "Perhaps if things continue going well between the two of you, I'll be able to meet him properly one day and get to know him better."

Lisa saw what it cost Joan to say this. Reaching across the table, she squeezed the older woman's hand. "Let's stick to small steps for now, just like you said."

A mixture of relief and gratitude flashed in Joan's eyes. "Yes, you're quite right. Small steps."

There was a knock at the café door, and when Lisa turned around, she saw Mildred and Jean smiling through the glass and waiting to get in.

"It's time to open the café," Lisa said, rising from her chair just as Mrs Wishmore returned to the table with Joan's fresh pot of tea and a plate of toasted teacakes.

"I'll keep Joan company while you see to Mildred and Jean," Mrs Wishmore said, sitting down and pouring tea for them both. "It's always nice to make a new friend, don't you think, Joan?"

"Yes, you're quite right," Joan said with a surprised smile.

"A person can never have too many friends," Mrs Wishmore said. "Now, tuck into those toasted teacakes, Joan, and enjoy them while they're still hot."

As Lisa unlocked the café door and welcomed Mildred and Jean inside, and waited behind the counter while the two ladies pondered the contents of the cake display case and debated their choices, she couldn't help but steal a glance towards the table in the corner where Joan and Mrs Wishmore were drinking tea and chatting to one another and enjoying their toasted teacakes. Lisa saw a light in Joan's eyes that had been gone for much too long, and as she watched Mrs Wishmore top up their teacups, she knew beyond all doubt that she had her mysterious temporary waitress to thank for the unexpected alteration.

Mrs Wishmore's kindness and empathy knew no bounds. The woman seemed to know just what to say in order to soothe someone's troubled heart and help them find their way back to the path from which they'd strayed. Lisa felt a surge of gratitude to the silver-haired lady who'd come into her life when she'd needed a helping hand, and who was now also lending a helping hand to Joan, too.

Lisa wished there were more people like Mrs Wishmore in the world and wondered just how she'd cope when Vicki returned to work once her ankle injury was healed and Doris's time as a waitress at the Daffodil Café came to an end.

She pushed the thought away. There was no point worrying about that just yet. Mrs Wishmore was here right now, and thank goodness for it, too.

Lisa hoped Joan might now turn a corner in her life. She knew only too well just how hard that was to do and resolved to be there for Joan and help her however she could. If she'd known how bleak things were for Joan, she would have moved heaven and earth to be more help to her already. Now that the truth was out in the open, and Joan was being honest about the deep difficulties she faced getting over Peter's death, Lisa would be there at Joan's side as she took these tough next steps in life.

Lisa had long ago accepted that Peter wouldn't have wanted her to waste her life after he died. He wouldn't have wanted his mother to waste her life, either. Lisa owed it to his memory to help his mother find her way once more, and one day find the happiness she deserved.

Serving up the cakes that Mildred and Jean pointed to in the display case, Lisa's thoughts turned to Jake, and her stomach clenched at their abrupt parting outside the café and his obvious dismay at the scene to which he'd been a party. She hoped she could explain Joan's outburst in a way he'd understand. She hoped, too, that the mortifying altercation with Peter's mother wouldn't cause things to sour between them. After all, no man wanted to be shouted at and embarrassed in the middle of the street by the mother of his new girlfriend's deceased fiancé.

Remembering the unhappy look on his face as he'd turned and walked away, she couldn't help but worry that he was wondering just what he'd got himself into, and whether it was worth all the effort.

Lisa sighed and got to work at the coffee machine. After the fun she'd had with Jake last night, their fledging romance suddenly felt as uncertain as ever.

CHAPTER NINETEEN

The classroom was quiet as Jake's pupils focused on the short quiz he'd assigned them, and he was pleased to grab a moment of peace during the busy school morning to organise his thoughts. Those thoughts needed organising, following the astonishing scene he'd found himself caught up in outside Lisa's café just a few hours earlier, a scene from which he was still reeling.

At his desk at the front of the room, Jake watched his pupils hunch over their reading materials and scribble on their worksheets. The task he'd given them involved reading a historical document and then answering a series of quiz questions about it. The aim was to develop their critical thinking skills and ability to judge whether the information in the historical source was trustworthy and why some of it might not be so reliable. After emitting their usual round of groans and complaints when he'd announced the quiz at the start of the class, the kids had become absorbed in the task once they'd applied themselves to the reading. Jake knew they liked thinking for themselves and liked being given space to make their own judgements about the history topics they studied in class, and about whether something was 'fact' or 'opinion'. These were important skills they'd need out there in the big wide world, as Jake knew only too well.

In life, it was too easy to make assumptions about how things were, and those assumptions didn't always stand up to scrutiny, as he'd discovered this morning. He'd assumed things were going well between him and Lisa, especially after last night and the long conversation they'd enjoyed over dinner in her kitchen. The more he learned about Lisa, the more he liked her, and the more time they spent together, the more he hoped that their casual dating might turn into something that looked like an actual relationship.

But the astonishing altercation that morning outside her café now made Jake question everything he'd thought was going on between them.

The older woman who'd turned up and made a scene could only be Peter's mother, he now realised, although he hadn't quite made that connection this morning in the heat of the moment. Lisa had already mentioned Joan to him, and Jake understood she cared for the woman a great deal. She'd almost become her daughter-in-law, and it stood to reason that the two women would have stuck together after their awful bereavement. Lisa had a good heart and Jake knew she'd want to help her late fiancé's mother in any way she could, and that Lisa's relationship with Joan would continue even although the man who'd connected them was gone.

What troubled Jake about the scene outside Lisa's café wasn't just Joan's outburst, although he could have done without being humiliated in the street by a stranger for doing nothing more scandalous than kissing his new girlfriend goodbye.

What troubled him more was Lisa's reaction to it.

She'd told Joan that what she'd seen was just a 'misunderstanding' and a 'mistake'.

What was there to misunderstand? Jake and Lisa had been kissing, which was what people did from time to time when they were romantically involved. He was smart enough to realise that Joan would find it difficult to see the young woman who'd almost become her son's wife kissing another man. But Joan's horrified reaction suggested that she hadn't known Lisa was seeing someone new and that it had all come as a terrible shock.

If Joan and Lisa were as close as Lisa had told him, why hadn't she mentioned Jake by now?

There were many plausible and understandable reasons why Lisa would keep things to herself for now, and Jake rattled those reasons off inside his head with ease. They'd only been dating for a short time, and Lisa might want to see if anything would come of it before sharing the news with Joan. That made perfect sense. It would be hard enough for Joan to hear about a new man in Lisa's life after the death of her son, and Lisa would want to tread carefully with the poor woman's emotions and find the right time to explain that she was dating again. That also made perfect sense.

But after Joan saw them kissing outside the café, Jake couldn't help but feel the cat was well and truly out of the bag. While that didn't mean that Lisa should have launched into a full and frank explanation of who Jake was and what was going on between them, did she really have to brush him off as a 'misunderstanding'?

Worse, did she have to brush him off as a 'mistake'?

Was that all he was? A silly misunderstanding and a stupid mistake?

If he was feeling generous, he might chalk up Lisa's choice of words to the embarrassment and panic of the moment causing her to reach for some quick excuse that would explain an awkward situation, and what better way to do it than to pretend things didn't look the way they seemed.

But he wasn't feeling generous. What she'd said, and the ease with which she'd said it, left him wondering if he was the one who'd 'misunderstood' what was going on between them, and if he was the one who'd made the 'mistake'.

The school bell rang to mark the end of the period, pulling Jake from his unhappy thoughts. The pupils got to their feet and grabbed their school bags from beneath their desks.

"Everyone bring your worksheets down to the front and pile them up on the desk on your way out," Jake said, shouting above the din of the chattering students. "We'll discuss your answers next time."

Once the kids had shuffled from the classroom, Jake stacked the pile of worksheets and stuffed them in a folder for marking. As he made his way to the staff room, he bumped into his friend, Marie, exiting her classroom further along the corridor.

"What's with the long face?" she said, her own smile disappearing as soon as she saw him.

"Sorry, I don't mean to look like a miserable git," Jake laughed, before waving his folder of marking in the air. "Just feeling snowed under with work at the moment, that's all."

They fell into step as they walked along the corridor. "You're always snowed under. We all are. So that can't be it." Her gaze narrowed and then she said, "It's this Lisa woman, isn't it? What's happened now?"

"How'd you work that out?" Jake said, astonished.

"I'm your friend. It's my job to know who's upsetting you so I can hate them."

Jake laughed again as they pushed through the doors and down the stairs. "Lisa and I had a misunderstanding this morning," he said with a wry smile.

"What happened?"

"I swung by Lisa's café on my way to school to thank her

for dinner last night. We'd had a great evening together, the nicest we've had since we started dating, and I wanted her to know how much I enjoyed it."

Jake paused, realising the next part of the story sounded a bit daft. When Marie gestured for him to keep talking, he sighed and said, "I was kissing Lisa goodbye outside the café when the mother of her late fiancé turned up and flipped out. She started shouting about how it was disgraceful to see Lisa carrying on with another man, as she put it, and that Peter—her son—would be turning in his grave. She obviously knew nothing about Lisa and I spending time together, and was upset by what she saw, which I can understand, and—"

"Wait a minute," Lisa interrupted. "I thought Lisa's fiancé had died over a year ago?"

"Well, yes, he did—"

"But his mother thinks Lisa should never be involved with another man ever again? That's ridiculous! And what business is it of hers, anyway?"

Jake made a calming gesture with his hands. "Look, it's not the over-reaction from the poor would-have-been mother-in-law that I'm worried about. It was embarrassing, yes, and I wish it hadn't happened, but the woman lost her son and that can't be easy to deal with, even a year down the line. The real problem is how Lisa reacted."

"What did she do?"

They'd reached the staff room entrance by now, but Jake didn't feel like continuing their discussion inside, where his colleagues would be sure to overhear them talking. The whole thing was embarrassing enough already, having no doubt been witnessed by the passers-by on Willowbridge high street without further adding to the rumour mill by venting his feelings about it all in the busy teachers' staff room.

"Let's take a walk outside," Jake said, and steered them both towards a nearby exit. Once they were outside in the school grounds, they found a shady spot beneath the trees near the playing fields where some kids were kicking a football around.

"So, are you going to tell me what happened or not?" Marie said.

"We should've grabbed our sandwiches from the staff room fridge," Jake said, peering back at the main building with regret.

"We've got plenty of time for lunch. Stop stalling and tell me what happened."

Jake sighed. "When this woman—Joan, her name is—when she saw Lisa and I kissing and started yelling her head off about it, Lisa told her it was a misunderstanding and that it was just... a mistake."

Marie peered at Jake and frowned. "A mistake? As in she was mistaken in thinking you were kissing?"

"No, I don't think there was any mistaking that. It was, er, quite a kiss."

Marie's frown only deepened. "What, then?"

"That's what I've been thinking about all morning. Maybe Lisa was just trying to spare the woman's feelings, which I can understand. She would have been Joan's daughter-in-law if Peter hadn't died, and the poor woman's been through the wringer enough already. I understand why she'd want to make it seem like it was nothing."

"I can't understand it," Marie said angrily. "It's not like Lisa's fiancé only passed away last week and she's already off snogging some new bloke. But I also appreciate that you want to give her the benefit of the doubt where the feelings of a bereaved mother are concerned. That's honourable and generous of you."

Jake shrugged. "The problem is that I can't help but think

about how Lisa shrugged off the two of us kissing as a 'mistake'. The way she said it, I'm beginning to wonder if it's true."

"You think she wishes the two of you weren't dating? But you were kissing each other! And you just said you had a great time together last night."

"We did! At least, I thought we did. Now I'm wondering if..."

Sighing, Jake looked off across the playing fields, watching the boys tackling one another on the football pitch while he searched for the words he needed to explain all this.

"Lisa's been hot and cold since we first met," he said. "When she explained what happened to her fiancé, I understood how hard it must be for her to date again after losing the man she wanted to marry. And although we've only been out a handful of times, I didn't want to rush her into any kind of dating or relationship deal that she wasn't ready for. I figured we'd take things one day at a time, and one date at a time, until we figured out if we wanted more from each other."

"That's because you're a lovely, sweet man, Jake," Marie said with a smile.

"The problem, though, is it isn't working. I don't think Lisa is ready for any kind of relationship, no matter how casual or relaxed, despite what she's told me. She says she wants to move on from Peter, and I believe she believes that's true, but I don't believe she can actually do it. If she could do it, she would never have described us as a mistake this morning, when she found herself on the spot like that. Although I want to believe she was trying to spare Joan's feelings, I'm not sure I'm even convincing myself on that score. There were plenty of other things she could've said to explain it. She could've said, 'Joan, this is Jake, and we've been seeing each other, and although it's early days, we quite like spending a bit of time together, but it's nothing more serious than that, and if it gets more serious than that, you'll be the first to know'."

Jake waved his hands in the air, as if scooping up the words he'd just put into Lisa's mouth and setting them out for examination. "Saying something along those lines would've been fine, wouldn't it? Joan might still have been upset about what she'd seen, and the poor woman would've needed a minute to digest what was happening. But Lisa didn't say that, or anything like it. Instead, she said it was a misunderstanding. She said it was a mistake. Maybe she was right."

"Look, I'm not trying to defend Lisa here, because I think she's got this all wrong and I hate that she's hurt you like this," Marie said. "But I know you like her, and so maybe—"

"That's the problem, Marie," Jake interrupted. "I do like her. I like her an awful lot. A couple of weeks ago, I was putting you off when you tried to set me up with that friend of yours, because I wasn't interested in getting involved with anyone, because it only ever ends in me being dumped. I'm fed up hearing women tell me they want to be my friend, and only that, which is why I wasn't interested in getting involved again." Jake sighed and raked a hand through his hair. "And then I met Lisa and everything changed."

Marie watched him carefully. "Meaning?"

"Meaning I'm falling for her, Marie," Jake said with an unhappy sigh. "I'm a stupid bloody fool and I'm falling for her."

"You've only been out a few times."

"I know. It doesn't matter. I know what I'm feeling. Give it another few weeks—bloody hell, give it another few days—and I'm a goner. That's how I feel about her."

Jake shook his head at the admission, as if denying what

he'd just said. "But after this morning, I realise the mistake I'm making. I can't fall in love with a woman who, when pressed, describes what we have together as a mistake. It doesn't matter what her reasons are for doing it. I can't put myself in that position. I *won't* put myself in that position. Because I know what's happening here. Lisa's only just started dating again after a gruesome, horrible bereavement. There's no way she's going to fall for the first bloke she starts seeing after something like that. And so while I'm busy falling head-over-heels for her, she's doing nothing more than stretching her legs in the dating world and blowing away a few cobwebs. She might have fun with me while she's doing it, but that's all it is. Fun. Eventually, she'll realise that I'm a great pal but a non-starter as a boyfriend, and she'll disappear. And listen, after the loss she suffered, it's only fair that she gets to enjoy herself at last and have some fun. Bloody hell, it's the least she should expect. Which is why I'm not about to hang around like some idiot, falling in love with her, when I know that, in the end, she's only going to break my heart."

Jake blew out a breath, feeling stunned at the words that had just poured out of him.

"Wow," Marie said, slanting a wry grin in his direction. "Are you finished or is there more still to come? Because if there's more, I want to pop back to the staff room for my sandwich after all, or I'll never get my lunch at this rate."

Jake laughed, relieved that Marie's easy humour had punctured the intensity of what he'd just shared.

"I'm finished," he said. "In more ways than one."

She rolled her eyes at this. "Don't say daft things like that. Okay, do you want my honest opinion?"

"I'm not sure. How brutal will it sound?"

"Pretty brutal."

"Then, no, I don't want your honest opinion."

"Tough, because it's impossible for me to be anything other than straight down the line, which is why you love me."

Jake grinned, rocking on his heels as he turned his gaze towards the boys' football match. One of the kids had scored a goal and his teammates were running around like maniacs as they celebrated, while the losing team trudged back up the pitch and yelled angry instructions to one another about what they ought to do to turn the game around. When the language the kids were using became too colourful for Jake to ignore, he called out a warning and received a few raised hands in apology as the game resumed.

"Okay," Jake said to Marie when the footballers were once more engrossed in their game. "What's your honest opinion?"

Marie, who'd also been watching the young boys kicking the ball around, raised her eyebrows and cleared her throat.

"My honest opinion, Jake, is that you've had a lot of bad luck in the past when it comes to women, but you've let it get the better of you, and that's a shame," Marie said. "It's made you too cautious. And now you think you're falling in love with Lisa and you're scared to death because you don't want to get hurt again if she doesn't feel the same way you do. My honest opinion is that you're looking for a way out before you get in any deeper, and this business that happened this morning, when Lisa described things between you as a 'mistake', well, I think you're latching on to that as an excuse to get out while you still can."

Jake turned and stared at Marie in total surprise. "Hang on. A moment ago, you were livid about what Lisa had said and how she'd handled things this morning. But now you're on her side?"

"It's not about sides, Jake. And if it was about sides, you know I'd be on yours, always. But I've listened to what you've said and now I'm telling you what I think about it. That situation this morning probably *was* just a misunderstanding, Jake. This woman, Joan, knew nothing about the two of you seeing one another. All she saw was Lisa kissing some random guy, and it upset her. If it's a misunderstanding, it's because Joan didn't know what was going on. You said that yourself. You said you understood Lisa's reasons for not telling this woman what was going on."

"But?"

"But you also said that wasn't the issue. And it's not. It's not about some poor bereaved mother getting upset about her dead son being replaced in another woman's affections. It's not about a bereaved fiancé feeling unsure about the new man in her life and not being ready to explain it all, chapter and verse, to the people she loves and who love her. What it's really about is you smothering your feelings rather than facing up to them. You're being a coward."

Jake stared for a moment, taking in what his friend had said. "Marie, that's harsh, even for you."

"But it's the truth, Jake. You're scared Lisa won't feel the same way about you as you feel about her. You're scared to fall in love with her in case she doesn't love you back. But that's the risk we all take. Falling in love isn't a choice we make, or a decision we can control. You can't decide not to love someone just to avoid being hurt. It doesn't work that way."

Jake said nothing. Marie's words were just a little too close to the bone.

"But if you like Lisa," Marie continued, "and if you think you might be falling in love with her, and yet you still walk away from her because of some stupid notion you have about protecting yourself, then you're not giving her the chance to find out if she might one day feel the same way you do."

Jake watched the boys kick their football around for a

moment, his thoughts swirling. "You want me to make an idiot of myself, even although I know I'll end up hurt."

"No, of course not. But just because none of your other relationships have lasted doesn't mean this one won't."

"So, what are you suggesting I do? Do you want me to blurt out to Lisa that I think I'm falling for her?"

"I don't think that's the right move. You've only just started seeing one another."

Jake frowned. "What then? I don't understand what you're saying."

"It's not what *I'm* saying that's important here. It's what *you're* saying."

"Look, if you're just going to talk in riddles, then let's forget this entire conversation even happened," he frowned, and turned to leave.

Marie grabbed his arm, and when he looked back at her, there was a knowing—and very irritating—smile on her face.

"Jake, the fact that you're getting upset like this just proves my point," Marie said. "You never get upset, and yet here you are, just about ready to tear your hair out with frustration."

"No wonder! You're supposed to be helping me work out what to do, not confusing me with all these cryptic comments."

"Jake," Marie said, raising her hands up in a calming gesture. "Have you ever been in love with a woman before?"

Jake scowled. "No, I don't think so, although—"

"You haven't," Marie interrupted. "Once it happens, believe me, there's no room for doubt. You've had girlfriends, and you've dated, and you've been fond of women and cared for them a lot, that's true. But you've never fallen in love."

"Great, well, thanks Marie for pointing out yet another defect in my character."

"Don't be an idiot. It's not a character defect. It's just the way it is. You just haven't found the right woman in all these years."

Jake realised where Marie might be going with this.

"You just told me you're falling for Lisa," Marie continued. "After all the ups and downs you've had with women, and all the times you've been dumped—"

"Again, thanks for that summary."

"—it never hurt as much as it might have done, because you didn't love any of those other women. Now, you're falling in love with Lisa, and so you want to be the one to dump her before things go any further."

"Exactly. Marie, if all you're going to do is parrot back what I just said to you when I tried to explain this whole mess, then you're no help to me at all."

"Jake, don't you see? You can't end things just to stop yourself from getting hurt. What if she's the one you've been waiting for all this time? Can you really walk away from something that might turn out to be the best thing that ever happened to you?"

Jake sighed. "That might not be my choice to make."

"But it is your choice not to throw a spanner in the works before you find out for sure. You want to call things off before they get any more serious and you want to use what Lisa said this morning as an excuse to do it."

"It's not an excuse! What's wrong with not wanting to get hurt, Marie?"

Marie shrugged. "Nothing's wrong with it. But if you call things off with this woman for no other reason than you're scared by what you feel for her, then you'll regret it for the rest of your life, Jake."

"I don't know that for sure."

Marie watched him for a long moment. "Look, just don't do anything too rash."

"Says the woman who thinks I should go right ahead and

fall in love with someone who's only ever going to break my heart."

"You don't know that for sure," Marie said, throwing his words back at him.

Jake grinned. "You're not helping."

"Sorry."

"What should I do?"

"Tell her how you feel."

"You just told me not to do anything rash! You told me not to tell her I'm falling in love with her!"

"But you should tell her you're annoyed about what happened this morning, and that the reason you're annoyed is that you like her so much. Saying you like someone isn't the same as telling them you love them. And telling her how you feel about all this is just being honest, not rash."

Jake saw her sly grin and laughed. "Okay, I've had enough of your linguistic trickery for now. All you've done is confuse me."

"You confused yourself. That's what happens to people when they're in the middle of falling in love with someone, Jake. They can't hold a single coherent thought inside their heads and they don't have the faintest what's going on from one minute to the next."

Jake sighed and raked a hand through his hair in frustration. "Is that what happened to you when you met Scott?"

Marie smiled. "I was a complete disaster."

"You've always been a complete disaster, Marie. Don't blame it on your poor husband."

She gave him a playful punch on the arm and smiled. "Jake, listen, I understand why you want to back away from whatever you feel for Lisa. And my advice is, don't do it. Don't run away. Stay and see what happens."

"Stay?"

"Stay," Marie nodded.

"That's like something I tell Ruby to do. Ruby, stay! Ruby, sit!"

Marie gave him another playful swat. "Well, you're being such an idiot about this. Maybe you need to think about in terms of simple instructions you can easily follow."

"What would I do without you as my friend Marie, and without these terrific boosts to my confidence?"

"Honestly, I have no idea what you'd do, Jake."

They grinned at one another and watched the boys finish their football match out on the playing fields before heading back to the staff room to collect their lunches. Although Jake was glad they'd ended their chat on an upbeat note, he hadn't found the conversation particularly helpful. He'd assumed that Marie would have endorsed his gut reaction to end things with Lisa before they went any further. After all, Marie hadn't exactly been enamoured with Lisa when Jake told her about how skittish she'd been about spending time with him. Knowing all she did about his rotten luck with women, Jake thought Marie would've agreed that it made sense to call things off with Lisa before his feelings for her got any deeper.

Instead, Marie had told him to do the exact opposite—to stay with Lisa, not call things off, and to tell her how he felt, at least some of it.

The problem was, Lisa already knew Jake liked her. That much was obvious. They'd both said they enjoyed being together, in their own awkward and fumbling way, and so far that had been enough for Jake.

But something unexpected had happened since then. Last night over dinner, he'd realised that he didn't just like Lisa, but was on the verge of falling in love with her. And then this morning, the light-headed rush of that knowledge had been shattered by the realisation that Lisa didn't feel the same way and probably never would.

Jake couldn't help but think he was nothing more than a pleasant romantic diversion for Lisa after the grief and loss she'd suffered. It was inconceivable that any woman would fall in love with the first man she began dating after the death of her beloved fiancé. He was a fool to hope otherwise.

As Jake geared up for the start of his next teaching period, he thought about Marie's advice and her warning that he shouldn't make assumptions about what Lisa might or might not feel for him in the future. Was Marie right? Was he being rash in wanting to back out of this thing before it got any more complicated? Should he wait and see what might happen?

Part of him wanted nothing more than to find out if Lisa might just fall in love with him one day. But another part of him feared the hurt he'd feel when that day didn't come.

With a sigh, Jake realised Marie was right about one thing —he had to talk to Lisa.

Quite what he'd say to her, though, he had no idea.

CHAPTER TWENTY

Lisa hurried into the park, hoping Jake hadn't given up and already gone home. It was after seven-fifteen and they'd agreed to meet by the duck pond at seven o'clock, and she was annoyed to be running late thanks to another hectic day at the café.

When she'd received a text message from Jake cancelling the evening drive they'd arranged earlier and asking to meet in the park for a walk instead, she'd agreed straight away. She'd been embarrassed by her botched handling of the situation outside the café that morning, and it was obvious that Jake had been confused and hurt by her reaction when she'd downplayed the kiss that Joan had witnessed. Lisa knew she had to straighten things out between them both.

And now she was running late for their meet-up in the park. While whipping up a batch of tray bakes that would keep until the Willowbridge School summer fair in a few days, one of the café's ovens had gone on the blink, forcing her to shuttle half the trays up to her flat for baking while also spending time on the phone with an appliance repair company to arrange an emergency call-out to fix the broken oven. By the time the repair call-out was arranged and a contingency plan was in place for the next day in the café to compensate for the broken oven, it was almost seven o'clock. Lisa barely had time to change her clothes, drag a brush through her hair, and douse herself in deodorant before hurrying up Willowbridge high street towards the park and hoping she didn't look as exhausted as she felt.

It was only as she dashed through the park gates that it occurred to her that Jake might not have waited around. She was more than fifteen minutes late and hadn't even had time to send him a message explaining the delay. After the embarrassing episode outside her café that morning, and now her inability to turn up on time to meet the poor man, Lisa wouldn't blame him if he decided she wasn't worth the trouble.

As soon as the thought occurred to her, Lisa clenched at the idea of it. She'd hate for things to stall between them because of what had happened earlier. Her thoughts kept turning to last night, and to the sweet and romantic evening she'd spent with Jake, lingering over dinner in her kitchen. For the first time in a long time, she'd felt completely at ease.

And for the first time since Peter's death, her heart was no longer filled with sadness and loss whenever she thought about her late fiancé. She didn't feel the confusing sense of betrayal she'd felt only a few days ago when it came to enjoying Jake's company. Instead, all she felt was a desire to be with Jake even more. Talking to Jake last night about Peter had helped in a way she hadn't imagined possible. Lisa was as astonished by this as she was thrilled and excited by it, and now that she'd taken this huge step forward in her life, she didn't want to stumble in her fledging relationship because of this morning's misunderstanding with Joan, and definitely not because she was running late.

She wanted Jake to know he meant something to her. She

had to put things right after this morning's debacle, and she couldn't do that if he'd already left the park because she couldn't even turn up on time.

When Lisa rounded the path and saw Jake walking around the pond with Ruby at his side, she knew instantly, and beyond any doubt, that she wanted things to work out between them. Seeing Jake's tall frame and thoughtful gaze as he watched Ruby frolicking beside the pond made Lisa realise how much she'd grown to like him over the course of only a few dates together.

And just how much more she wanted from him.

"Jake!" she called out as she neared the pond. "I'm so sorry I'm late."

Jake turned at her voice and smiled. Lisa's stomach somersaulted at the sight of that smile and its warmth.

But as quickly as his smile appeared, it was gone, and Lisa felt her excitement evaporate.

"I didn't mean to keep you waiting," she said as Ruby rushed over and pressed her nose against Lisa's knees. "One of the café's ovens broke down, and I was on the phone for ages trying to arrange a repair. I hope you're not too annoyed with me."

She searched his expression, but it wasn't easy to read. He wasn't frowning, but he wasn't smiling either. Something that looked like either frustration or uncertainty clouded his face.

"Don't worry about it," Jake said. "I know how busy things are at your café. It's your business and you don't have to apologise for running it."

"I was so glad you wanted to meet after what happened this morning with Joan," Lisa said, ruffling Ruby's ears and then straightening up to look at Jake. "The last thing I wanted was to leave you standing here by yourself and wondering where on earth I was."

Jake ran a hand over his chin and gave a dry laugh. "Yeah, that was quite a scene this morning. Is your mother-in-law... sorry, I mean, is Peter's mother, Joan... is she okay?"

Lisa saw Jake's doubt about how he should refer to Peter's mother. It wasn't a straightforward situation to grasp, she supposed, and realising that he wanted to refer to Joan with respect and care touched her.

"Joan's fine, or at least she is now," Lisa said. "We had a long talk after you left, and it helped to get things out in the open. I knew Joan was struggling, especially with the anniversary of Peter's death, but I didn't realise just how bad things were for her. But chatting always makes these troubles feel a little lighter, and Mrs Wishmore was so much help, too, and..."

She realised she was babbling. She hadn't come here to talk about Joan. She'd come here to sort things out with Jake.

"Jake, I'm sorry about how Joan reacted when she saw us kissing outside the café this morning," Lisa said, stepping closer. "Joan is sorry, too, and wants to apologise to you in person. It's all my fault, because I didn't tell her I was involved with you, and so it all came as a big surprise, and—"

"I understand," Jake said, holding up his hands and smiling. "It must have been hard for her to see you with another man, considering you were once engaged to her son. There's no need to apologise for Joan or for her reaction. It's fine."

Lisa nodded, but it was obvious from his expression that everything wasn't fine at all.

"I also want to apologise for how I reacted," Lisa said. "I was so shocked and surprised when Joan turned up out of the blue and saw us kissing, and that's why I made it seem like there was nothing happening between us. But that was stupid of me. I know I hurt your feelings when I said it was all just a misunderstanding and a mistake. I'm sorry."

Jake looked towards the pond, where the ducks were flapping their wings and quacking at one another. "Do you think this is a mistake, Lisa? You and I, being together—is it a mistake?"

Lisa shook her head so quickly she almost made herself dizzy. "Of course not! It was a stupid thing to say, but I couldn't stand the idea of hurting Joan. She's gone through so much pain since Peter died. I hated knowing I was making things worse by kissing you right in front of her, and so I said something stupid, something that didn't even make any sense."

She had no idea if she was convincing him or not. His gaze was unreadable.

"You're not a mistake, Jake," she said. "And us going out together and spending time together. That's not a mistake, either."

Jake watched her for a long moment. He was about to say something when Ruby let out a volley of barks further along the path.

"Let's catch up with Ruby before she disappears from sight," Jake said, and started walking. Lisa fell into step beside him, wishing she could explain this properly, because she obviously wasn't doing a good enough job of it so far.

"Look, we all say silly things from time to time," Jake said, his tone mild. "But what you said this morning, and how you described us, isn't really the problem here."

Lisa frowned. "What *is* the problem, then?"

Jake looked away, his attention absorbed by Ruby, who was greeting another dog further along the path, her tail wagging as the canines sniffed one another before beginning a game of chase across the grass.

"What do you see happening between us, Lisa?" Jake said, and slid his gaze in her direction, his eyes searching her face.

She hadn't expected this question. The sudden turn in the conversation threw her off-balance.

"I don't know." She wished she'd come up with something better to say, something more meaningful. "What I mean is that I don't look too far into the future anymore, not after what happened to Peter. I just can't do it. I don't know what might happen between us because I'm only thinking about right now."

Jake nodded, but said nothing.

"But I know I like spending time with you, Jake. I want to spend more time with you. Being with you..." She searched for the words she wanted to say, knowing she didn't want to mess this up. "Being with you makes me realise I can live my life and be happy again. It makes me believe I can move on and that, one day, everything will feel right again in the world."

"One day?" Jake said, his gaze holding hers.

"Yes, one day. I didn't think I could feel as comfortable with a man as I feel with you, Jake. I thought I'd never feel that way again. You've shown me what's possible. I don't want to lose what we have because of what happened today."

Jake looked at her for a long beat. She had no idea what he was thinking, or what he thought about what she'd just said. Was this what he wanted to hear or not? And was this what she wanted to say or not?

"I don't know what you want me to say, Jake," Lisa sighed. "I want us to keep seeing each other. I want to get to know you better. And, yes, I want to find out if we might have something together, something that isn't just dating, but..."

"But?" Jake said softly.

"But I can't predict the future," she said and laughed softly. "No one can. But we can enjoy each other's company, can't we? We can have fun together. Everyone deserves a little fun in life."

Once more, Jake nodded and looked out across the sunlit park. "You're right, Lisa. Everyone deserves a little fun, and after what you've gone through, no one deserves it more than you. You've been through hell and you survived, and now that you've made it through to the other side of all that loss and grief, you ought to have all the fun you can handle."

He turned and smiled then, and it was a smile filled with so much sadness that it made Lisa's breath catch.

"But I don't think I'm the person you ought to be having all that fun with," Jake said at last.

Lisa could only stare as she tried to absorb what Jake had said. "What do you mean?"

"I think we've had a few fun dates together, Lisa, and I think you're a terrific person," he said, his eyes not quite meeting hers. "But we're looking for different things in life and we're going in different directions, and I think it's best that we don't see each other anymore."

Frowning, Lisa opened her mouth and closed it again. She had no idea how to respond to what Jake had said, because it had taken her so completely by surprise.

"I don't understand," she said. "I said I'm sorry about what happened this morning and I meant it. I thought you were okay with it. I thought *we* were okay."

"It's not about that. But what happened this morning made me realise that we're in completely different places, Lisa. You're just starting to date again after a terrible loss and I'm..." He paused, as if he'd been about to say something he didn't want to say. "This is all just a lot more complicated than I thought it would be when we started seeing each other."

"It doesn't have to be complicated. I said I'm sorry about this morning. Can't we just move on?"

Jake looked away. "I don't think we can. You've got a lot of emotional baggage that you don't seem to want to put down... and I'm not the right person to help you carry it."

Lisa was too stunned to respond. The words he'd used

sliced straight through to her heart. For a long moment, she could only stand and stare as she tried to process what he'd said and the words he'd chosen to use.

Emotional baggage. Was that how he thought of her? As someone clinging to the grief and hurt of the past, unwilling to let go?

"The last thing I want is to be thought of as emotional baggage," she said, hurt now bubbling in her voice. "Maybe you're right. Maybe we ought to quit before we go any further."

Jake nodded, but kept his gaze fixed on some point across the park. She'd thought he was kind and sensitive and understanding, but the fact that he wouldn't even look at her made her wonder if she'd misjudged the sort of man he was.

"You really want to end this?" she demanded, unable to stop herself from asking, because some contrary part of her wanted to force him to say it.

"Yes, I really want to end this," he said. "It's for the best."

There would've been tears in her eyes had it not been for the anger burning inside her, although whether she was more angry at Jake or at herself, she couldn't say. She'd come here to apologise for the embarrassing incident outside her café that morning, and to move on from it. Instead, Jake was ending things between them for reasons she didn't understand.

"I see," Lisa said, her voice a whisper. She almost added that she was sorry, but caught herself before the words got out. She'd apologised enough in the last ten minutes and it hadn't got her anywhere. There was no point saying sorry yet again, especially when she no longer knew what she was supposed to be sorry for.

Jake whistled for Ruby, and when the little dog abandoned her chase with her canine friend on the grass and trotted over, he clipped on her lead and turned to Lisa with a sad smile.

"Take care, Lisa," he said. "And, for what it's worth, I hope you find what you're looking for."

He leaned closer, and for one awful moment Lisa thought he was about to kiss her goodbye and make the whole wretched moment even worse than it already was. Instead, he reached out and squeezed her arm, and the touch of his hand against her skin made her head spin with longing.

"Bye," Jake whispered and turned towards the park gates, Ruby trotting at his heels. As they rounded the corner, Ruby glanced back at Lisa and barked, as if adding her own goodbye, and then they both disappeared from sight beyond the trees.

Lisa stood by the duck pond as the evening sun slanted down through the trees, wondering how on earth any of this had happened. Even as she'd hurried here this evening, worried about arriving late and having to apologise for the stupid comments she'd made in front of Joan, she hadn't thought it possible that Jake would end things between them because of it. And yet, that's just what had happened.

The birds in the trees sang their evening songs. Dog walkers passed by on their journeys around the park. Families played together and kids raced by on bikes and the world kept turning around her, even as she stood rooted to the spot, trying to make sense of the unexpected end of something she'd thought was rather wonderful.

She'd misunderstood everything about Jake and what was going on between them, that much was now clear. He'd told her he was fine with what had happened outside the café that morning, but it was obvious that he wasn't fine with it at all.

Worse, he'd said she was carrying emotional baggage that she wasn't prepared to set aside. That had hurt. She hadn't thought Jake could be cruel, but he'd shown his true colours in the end.

So much for getting back out into the world of dating and rediscovering the fun of romance. If this was as much fun as she could look forward to, then she'd rather not bother, thanks very much. No casual romance was worth this trouble and heartache.

Jake wasn't the man she'd thought he was. She had no idea who he was at all.

She'd had a lucky escape, Lisa decided as she turned for home.

And if there were tears burning in her eyes, it was only because she was relieved that things had ended with Jake before she'd invested any more of herself into an obviously doomed romance.

Lisa wiped away a tear before it fell and left the park behind.

CHAPTER TWENTY-ONE

After days of dazzling sunshine and blue skies, the weather turned cold and grey and gloomy just in time for the weekend, and the overcast Saturday morning reflected Lisa's mood. The Daffodil Café was due to open in twenty minutes, and Lisa was putting the finishing touches to a lemon drizzle cake she'd baked for the customers, but as she poured icing over the sponge and grated lemon zest across the top for decoration, her mind was about as far from her work as it was possible to get.

No matter how hard she tried, she couldn't stop thinking about Jake and their awful parting last night in the park. How could things be going so well between them one minute, and then be over and finished the next?

Worse, Jake's last words to her wouldn't stop swirling in her head. She'd been honest about the pain she'd endured after Peter's death, and yet he'd flippantly described her as carrying 'emotional baggage'. What he'd said had hurt. She hadn't thought him capable of being so insensitive.

Beyond the kitchen, Lisa heard a knock at the café front door. Wiping her hands on a tea towel to dust off any stray icing sugar, she walked through to the café and saw Mrs Wishmore outside, smiling through the glass pane of the door.

"You're very early, Doris," Lisa said, unlocking the door to let her inside. "We agreed you wouldn't start until nine-thirty today and I don't expect you to come in ahead of time like this."

"I was just sitting at home twiddling my thumbs and thought I'd make myself useful," Mrs Wishmore said as she walked into the café. "I'm sure there's plenty I can do to help you prepare for a busy Saturday of café service."

Lisa locked the door again and followed Mrs Wishmore through to the back of the café. While the older lady hung up her jacket and bag in the cupboard, Lisa turned her attention to the tray of chocolate brownies that were ready to come out of the oven.

"Well, considering you only have one working oven in this place, it looks like you've handled things wonderfully," Mrs Wishmore said, eyeing all the baking that was cooling on the counters. "How did you do all this with just one oven?"

"I baked half the stock upstairs last night in the oven in my flat," Lisa said, turning out a gingerbread loaf that had finished cooling in its tin and was ready to be taken through to the display case.

"I thought you were meeting young Jake last night?"

"We were only together for a few minutes in the end, and once I got home, I thought I might as well get a head start on today's baking. The oven repair man won't be here until eleven at the earliest, so it made sense to do what I could last night to stay ahead of the game."

Lisa picked up the plate of gingerbread and walked through to the café counter with it, and Mrs Wishmore followed with a batch of cherry scones that were also cool enough for display. While Lisa slid the gingerbread into place behind the glass, Mrs Wishmore tied on an apron and stacked the cherry scones onto a plate. Lisa could feel the older woman's gaze upon her as they worked.

"Did you and young Jake smooth things over last night?" Mrs Wishmore asked.

Lisa let out a long sigh. "No, we didn't. We broke up."

Mrs Wishmore slid the plate of scones onto the glass shelf and turned to Lisa, her eyes wide. "You broke up? Good grief, what happened?"

"I'm not sure what happened, Doris. Jake said he was okay about the embarrassing scene with Joan yesterday morning and was happy to forget it had happened. But in the next breath, he said it would be best if we stopped seeing each other, that we were looking for different things and he didn't see us having any future together."

Mrs Wishmore frowned. "That seems rather strange. And what did you say?"

"What could I say? I wasn't about to beg Jake not to break up with me. His mind was made up and although I like him—correction, *liked* him—we've only gone out together a few times and it's not as if I know him that well or anything..."

"But?"

Lisa sighed. "That's the thing. I feel like I *do* know him well, even after just a few dates. I thought we'd made a connection, or at least the beginnings of one. But clearly I got it all wrong and Jake isn't who I thought he was. He said something incredibly hurtful last night that he should be ashamed of, if he has any decency."

Mrs Wishmore loaded a second plate with fresh scones, and it seemed to Lisa like the woman's gaze was boring straight into her. "What did he say?"

"He said I was still carrying a lot of emotional baggage because of Peter and that I wasn't willing to put it down."

Lisa scowled as she remembered Jake's words, feeling the same hurt and anger bubble up as she'd felt last night.

"And do you think Jake might have a point?"

Stunned, Lisa turned to Mrs Wishmore. "Doris, you've listened to me talk about how much I want to move on again, how much I want to start living again. It hurts to leave Peter behind in the past, but I know I have to do it. That's what I'm trying to do."

"And yet there's some part of your heart that won't let Peter go," Mrs Wishmore said, her gaze travelling to the necklace Lisa was wearing, the one on which she kept her engagement ring, and which she hadn't even realised she was fidgeting with as she spoke.

Lisa squeezed the diamond ring between her fingers, then dropped the necklace back beneath the collar of her shirt. "Moving on shouldn't mean I have to forget Peter altogether or pretend like he never existed. I can't do that."

"Of course you can't. And I'm sure Jake didn't mean that at all, dear."

When Mrs Wishmore said nothing further, and busied herself arranging the plates of treats in the display case, Lisa frowned. Her hand travelled once more to the necklace and the engagement ring attached to it, her fingers tracing the outline of the slim gold band and the pretty diamond suspended beneath the fabric of her shirt.

"I'd forgotten I was still wearing this diamond ring on my necklace," Lisa murmured. "I don't know how I could have forgotten, but I did."

"You got used to it being there," Mrs Wishmore said. "Perhaps in the beginning it brought you comfort to touch the ring and think of Peter, and now you don't even realise you're doing it."

Lisa realised this might just be true. When she'd removed the engagement ring from her finger almost a year ago, she'd cried until there were no more tears left. She couldn't bring herself to put the ring back into the box it had come in, and couldn't bring herself to part with it. The ring had signified the life she thought she'd been about to share with the man she loved. Threading it through a plain necklace and wearing it around her neck had indeed brought her comfort. She couldn't bear to keep wearing the ring on her finger, but she couldn't bear to be separated from it, either. Hanging it as a pendant was a compromise she'd made with herself and her broken heart until she was ready to take the next step.

But she'd never taken that next step, because the ring was still hanging on that necklace all this time later. How often did she touch it each day, drawing comfort from its slight weight and from the memories it held? How often did her fingers seek it out? How often did she touch that ring without even realising she was doing it, as she'd just done in front of Mrs Wishmore?

A thought leapt into Lisa's mind, of the evening she'd spent with Jake at her flat, enjoying the spaghetti bolognese that Mrs Wishmore had cooked for them. Before they'd sat down to eat, Jake had asked about the framed photograph of her and Peter, and he'd seemed interested in hearing more about her late fiancé. And yet, as she'd talked about Peter, sharing memories of the man she'd loved, she'd noticed an odd expression on Jake's face, an expression she couldn't decipher. She'd wondered if Jake had wanted to hear about Peter after all, or if he was just being polite.

Now, though, as she thought back to that evening and pictured it in her mind, she realised that as she'd been talking about Peter, she'd been fidgeting with the engagement ring hanging on her necklace.

No wonder Jake had looked troubled. Seeing her twirling her engagement ring while she spoke must have left Jake wondering about her emotional state of mind and her readiness to move on.

Was there something to what Jake had said last night, after all? Was she carrying emotional baggage that she didn't want to leave behind?

Lisa realised she didn't know the answer to those questions, after all.

"You think I should stop wearing the engagement ring on my necklace," Lisa now said, slanting a glance towards Mrs Wishmore.

When the older lady only shook her head, Lisa frowned in confusion.

"What I think you should do is neither here nor there," Mrs Wishmore said with a smile. "I'm not here to tell you what to do, Lisa. You must find your own way."

Mrs Wishmore reached out and touched Lisa's hand. Immediately, Lisa felt that same soothing peace flow through her that she'd felt before when Mrs Wishmore had held her hand, and her clouded thoughts cleared.

"Maybe I should take this ring off the necklace," Lisa said, pulling the pendant from beneath her shirt and looking down at the diamond setting as it twinkled beneath the café's lights. "Maybe there are things I'm carrying from my past and I'm not even aware of them."

Mrs Wishmore only gave an enigmatic smile and said nothing.

"But surely Jake didn't break up with me because I have a habit of twirling a ring on a necklace, a ring that means rather a lot to me?" Lisa said, feeling frustrated. "Yes, it was an engagement ring, and yes, it represents something in my life that's gone forever, and yes, I can see how it might be strange for Jake to see me still wearing it when he and I are supposed to be together. But he could just have asked me about it, and talked about it with me. The ring isn't why Jake walked away."

"No, it's not," Mrs Wishmore said. "Although, as you've said yourself, your reasons for still wearing that ring have made Jake wonder about things. But don't forget that it takes two people to make a relationship, and it takes two people to break a relationship, too."

Lisa scratched her head, confused. "What are you saying?"

"Only that Jake may well have his own emotional baggage —baggage that he, too, can't quite leave behind."

"Like what?"

Mrs Wishmore laughed. "Well, how would I know that, dear? You're the one who was involved in a budding romantic relationship with the young man. I'm sure you must have a better idea than I would."

"I don't have the faintest idea," Lisa said.

"Really?"

There was a knowing smile on Mrs Wishmore's face as she said this, a knowing smile that Lisa found rather annoying.

"We only went out a few times, Doris. It's not like I discovered his entire life history in the past two weeks."

Lisa finished arranging the plates in the display case. She'd only been pushing the same plates around the same space for the last few minutes anyway, while her conversation with Mrs Wishmore progressed. The café would open shortly, and she ought to bring through the rest of the baking stock and add it to the display case before her first customers arrived. Today of all days, she didn't want to be on the back foot in the café, not with the oven still out of commission in the kitchen, and with it being a Saturday, which was her busiest day of the week. She was already out of sorts as it was after last night's unhappy split with Jake without adding any café fiascos into the mix.

"Anyway, we'd better get cracking, Doris," Lisa said. "It might be dull and grey outside, but that won't stop the tourists and visitors from getting out and about, and we ought to be ready for them."

"You're quite right," Mrs Wishmore said, then offered Lisa a smile and patted her hand. "I'm certainly sorry things didn't work out with young Jake."

"It wasn't meant to be."

Mrs Wishmore gave a small nod and turned towards the coffee machine. "Oh, before I forget Lisa, I was hoping you wouldn't mind if I leave half an hour early today. I have an errand to run for a friend who could use my help."

"That's fine. You came in early today, Doris, so you should get that time back, it's only fair."

"Thank you, dear," Mrs Wishmore said. "Now, let's get everything organised so we can welcome some customers through the door."

While Mrs Wishmore warmed up the coffee machine and refilled the sugar sachet bowls on the café tables, Lisa brought more cakes and goodies through from the kitchen for the display case, and then busied herself setting out the pots and pans for the hot roll orders that would soon stack up once the customers arrived. Fiona would come in soon for her shift, and Lisa enjoyed helping her cook get a head start with the work.

As she beat eggs in a jug and laid out strips of bacon on a pan and counted out sausages for the grill, Lisa's mind turned to her conversation with Mrs Wishmore.

She'd hoped the older lady might have had more words of wisdom to impart, but Doris's comments had only left her feeling more frustrated than she'd felt before. If only her waitress had come up with some dazzling insight into just what had gone wrong last night with Jake, Lisa would have been all ears. Instead, when she'd explained Jake's hurtful words about the 'emotional baggage' he claimed she was refusing to let go of, Mrs Wishmore had agreed with him!

Given how often she'd talked with Doris since the woman had begun waitressing at the café, and how much she'd confided in the older lady about her deep desire to move on and start living again after Peter's death, she'd thought Mrs Wishmore would have understood that she was trying hard to put her grief and bereavement behind her and to get back out into the world again.

Instead, Mrs Wishmore had glanced at the engagement ring pendant around Lisa's neck and made her question just how far she'd come, after all.

Lisa's hand automatically moved to the necklace, and the ring attached to it. She stopped herself before her fingers found the delicate gold band. Maybe it really was time to take off this engagement ring and put it away and out of sight.

But Lisa wondered if the simple matter of a precious keepsake was the only issue here. Mrs Wishmore had said that perhaps Jake, too, had emotional baggage of his own to deal with.

Well, if he did, Lisa didn't know what she could do about it, not after what had happened last night.

Still, Lisa felt a surge of regret roll through her at the realisation that her short romance was over. She'd had a good feeling about Jake, and a good feeling about what was happening between them. It was a shame things had fallen apart, just when she'd begun to imagine a future that had seemed impossible only a few weeks ago.

But there was nothing she could do about it now. Jake had made himself clear last night. They were finished. Lisa wasn't about to put herself through the wringer about it, or worry for a single moment longer about what had happened, or about what might have really caused Jake's sudden change of heart.

It was time to open the café and greet her first customers of the day. As Lisa unlocked the door, she hoped for a busy Saturday that would keep her occupied. Working hard and running her lovely little Daffodil Café had got her through tougher times than this. With customers to serve, and food and drinks to prepare, and the oven repair man coming soon, there was plenty to get on with.

And plenty to keep Jake out of her mind for the rest of the day.

CHAPTER TWENTY-TWO

Jake glanced around the Willowbridge School playground and smiled at the sight of what his students had achieved in just a few short hours. The place was completely transformed and he couldn't have been prouder of the kids who'd worked so hard to make it all happen.

It was almost four o'clock on Saturday afternoon, and everyone involved in the school summer fair had worked non-stop since lunchtime tidying the school grounds, erecting stalls and signage, and decorating the area with bunting and posters. Teachers and parent volunteers were working hand-in-hand with the students, bolting stalls into place, pinning up banners, and organising things inside the school hall so that stock and supplies were ready to be brought out the next morning and set up before the fair opened at noon.

Jake had spent the last hour fine-tuning the schedule of activities for tomorrow afternoon, from the talent show to the grand raffle, making sure there were staff assigned to each event and enough time for everyone to work through their programmes. With help from cheeky Bradley and his sidekick, Jake had avoided a clash between the water balloon contest and a short play being put on by the drama club, and the two pupils had shown a real knack for organisational finesse and problem-solving. Jake was proud of the boys, and of all the kids who'd put in so much effort to make this fundraising fair happen.

With most of the work now completed, people were preparing to leave for the day and were making their way towards the school gates. A few of the students waved to Jake as they departed, some parents stopped by to ask what time everyone should be there the next day to deal with the final preparations before the fair opened, and his teacher colleagues gave him weary thumbs-up as they finished dealing with their tasks and looked around the school grounds to check everything was where it was supposed to be.

It had been a good day's work, and the crammed afternoon had kept Jake's mind busy. Now, with the preparation work winding down, he found unhappy thoughts once more pushing to the surface, thoughts that made him cringe inside, and before he could stop them, the words he'd said to Lisa last night in the park came roaring through his head.

You've got a lot of emotional baggage and you don't seem to want to put it down.

Had he really said that to her? Of course he had. Even now, when he remembered the look on Lisa's face as he'd said those words, he wanted to curl up into a ball and die. Knowing he'd said those things, and had hurt Lisa by saying them, made him sick to his stomach and made his cheeks burn with shame.

"Mr Reid, what should we do with this extra bunting?"

Jake turned to see Bradley and his sidekick pal walking towards him, each carrying an armload of colourful bunting.

"Take it through to the assembly hall, lads," Jake said. "If we've got time tomorrow morning, we'll see if there are any bare patches we've missed that could use a bit of decoration and brightening up."

"I don't think there's a single bare patch anywhere, sir," Bradley said, glancing around the school grounds. "This place looks like a rainbow exploded."

"Maybe we could put the spare bunting around the school gates, sir?" Bradley's sidekick pal suggested. "We might need more decorations around the banner hanging above the entrance."

"Good idea, son," Jake said. "We'll wait until tomorrow before we put it up. I think you've both put in a long enough shift already."

"See you tomorrow, sir," Bradley said and then gave Jake a wink. "Don't forget, ten o'clock on the dot. No sleeping in."

Jake laughed as the boys hurried off to the double doors that led inside the school building. He suspected that at some point tomorrow, Bradley's enthusiasm and cheek would earn him a stern telling-off from a teacher, a telling-off that would no doubt roll off the boy like water off a duck's back.

Tucking his clipboard and tablet under his arm, Jake picked up a box containing scissors and sticky tape and other paraphernalia that was waiting to go back inside the school building. He'd only taken a few steps towards the double doors through which Bradley and his little friend had disappeared when he heard a familiar voice behind him calling his name.

"Jake, hello! I hope I haven't caught you at a bad time."

When Jake turned, he was surprised to see Mrs Wishmore making her way across the school grounds towards him, hauling a carrier bag in one hand.

"Mrs Wishmore, what brings you here?" he asked with a smile.

The older woman returned his grin as she drew closer. "A friend of mine discovered a few knick-knacks at home that she has no more use of, and which she thought might make a nice addition to one of your summer fair jumble sale stalls," Mrs Wishmore said, opening the carrier bag she was holding so Jake could look inside. "I promised her I'd see if you could make use of these items. So, what do you think?"

Jake peered inside the carrier bag and saw a collection of ornaments and trinkets, all covered in bubble wrap. He lifted out one item near the top of the pile for a closer look. Pulling back the bubble wrap, he discovered a delicate little rose vase made from pink glass and etched with rose-shaped markings along the rim.

"This is a pretty item, Mrs Wishmore," Jake said. "Are you sure your friend wants to part with it?"

"Quite sure," Mrs Wishmore nodded. "She's having a bit of a clear out because she's selling her house and moving up north to be closer to her daughter, and is happy to see these things find new homes. She'll be happier still if she knows that some money has been raised for your school funds in the process."

Jake took the bag Mrs Wishmore was holding out. "Thanks very much, Mrs Wishmore, and please thank your friend, too. Some of our students are running a bric-à-brac stall and they'll be glad to add these items to their collection."

"I'm so pleased to hear that, and my friend will be pleased, too." Mrs Wishmore glanced around the school grounds and grinned. "It looks like it will be a fabulous event tomorrow. Look at all these stalls! And the children have done such a wonderful job with the decorations and making everything look so colourful and fun."

"They've worked very hard. We're very proud of all of them."

"And so you should be." Mrs Wishmore peered further

across the grounds, squinting against the sunshine that had put in a late appearance at the end of an otherwise overcast afternoon. "Is that a stage I see over there beside the football pitches?"

Jake nodded. "The parents of one of our pupils runs an outdoor events company and donated the stage free of charge. The kids have organised a talent show, and there will be a couple of bands playing, and we've also got the drama club putting on a play they wrote themselves for tomorrow. If we can pull it all off, it should be quite a show."

"Well, I can't tell you how impressed I am," Mrs Wishmore beamed. "And will you be performing on stage tomorrow, Jake?"

Jake laughed and shook his head. "I dodged that bullet. Unfortunately, when I refused to take part in the talent show, the kids dished out a little punishment by putting my name down for the water balloon contest."

"The water balloon contest? And what does that involve?"

"It involves me sitting on a stool wearing an enormous top hat on my head while people pay money to throw water balloons at me," Jake sighed. "Whoever knocks the top hat off my head the most times wins a prize."

Mrs Wishmore stared at him for a moment and then let out a loud rumble of laughter. "I can't say that sounds like it will be much fun for you, Jake. Perhaps you should have agreed to take part in the talent contest? That sounds far less embarrassing."

"And far less painful, too, I'd imagine. I think some of the kids who don't enjoy my history classes might throw those water balloons hard enough to leave some nasty bruises."

"Well, if it all gets too much, just remember, it's for a worthy cause."

"I'll try." Jake laughed, then gestured to the box of craft supplies he was still holding in one hand and the bag of knick-knacks that Mrs Wishmore had given him in the other. "I'd better get this lot inside. Thanks again for these donations."

"You're quite welcome, dear," Mrs Wishmore said. "But before you go, I wanted to say how sorry I am to hear that things didn't work out between you and Lisa."

Jake's smile faded at the change in conversation topic. "Sometimes, these things just aren't meant to be."

"Hmm, I suppose that's true. Although I must admit, I was rather surprised when Lisa told me what happened. I thought it was all going rather nicely between the two of you? I had the impression that you were quite fond of Lisa. I know for certain that she was fond of you."

Jake set down the box of school craft supplies and the bag of donated knick-knacks, so he didn't have to juggle the load in his arms while he replied. "We had fun and I like Lisa a lot. But I'm not the right man for her."

"What makes you so sure?"

Jake peered at the older woman, wondering about her questions. "Did she send you here to ask me about this?"

"Certainly not. In fact, she was reluctant to talk about it at all this morning in the café. I think the only reason she told me anything was because she was so upset and confused about what had happened."

Hearing this made Jake's chest squeeze. He knew he'd hurt Lisa last night, but hearing Mrs Wishmore describe her reaction this morning only made him feel more wretched about what he'd said.

"I'm sorry I upset her," Jake said. "But it's for the best."

"Hmm." Mrs Wishmore eyed him carefully. "If you and Lisa breaking up is for the best, then why do you both look so miserable about it?"

Jake opened his mouth to reply, but plopped it closed

again, unable to think of anything to say. Mrs Wishmore continued studying him, her gaze searching his face.

"Lisa told me you said something rather hurtful to her last night," she said. "I must say, I found that hard to believe. You seem like such a nice, kind young man."

"I didn't mean to be hurtful."

"I'm not sure that's true, Jake."

Jake frowned and raked a hand through his hair. "Mrs Wishmore, you and I hardly know one another and I don't appreciate you insinuating—"

"You told Lisa she had emotional baggage that she was refusing to set down," Mrs Wishmore interrupted, her voice steady and quiet. "Surely you knew that would hurt her terribly? After everything she told you about the death of her fiancé and the struggle she's had moving on, you had to know that accusing her of not trying hard enough to begin again in life would hurt her deeply."

"No, that's not what I wanted."

"Then what did you want?"

"I wanted to push her away!" Jake blurted out in frustration. "I wanted to push her away so that she wouldn't want to know me anymore."

Mrs Wishmore nodded, as if she already knew this, although Jake had no idea how that could be possible. "Why would you want to do such a thing?"

"Because Lisa's on a different path to the one I'm on." Jake wondered why he was explaining himself to this woman he hardly knew, but was helpless to stop himself from talking. "She wants to date men and get back out there again and have lots of fun. After what happened to her fiancé, the world owes her that. But I realised pretty quickly that..."

Mrs Wishmore's mild gaze stayed fixed on him as he scratched his head, still wondering how he'd got into this conversation. The older woman reached out and laid her hand on his arm, giving him a gentle pat as she smiled. Jake's frustration evaporated, as if a gentle wave had washed it from his mind, and in its place he felt the hard edges of the truth he'd been avoiding.

"I realised I was falling in love with her," Jake almost whispered. "And I can't fall in love with her, Mrs Wishmore, because I know she won't ever fall in love with me."

"How can you be so sure?" the older lady asked.

"Because women never stay with me long enough for that to happen. Eventually, they decide they don't want me to be anything more than a friend. That's always the way it goes."

Jake sighed and looked around the school grounds, where there were only a few people still hanging around, putting the finishing touches to the stalls they were working on.

"Look, Mrs Wishmore, I finished things with Lisa, and that's that. I don't want to talk about it anymore, and it's getting late. I need to clear everyone out of here and lock up."

"I understand," Mrs Wishmore said with a smile. "Although I must say I'm sorry the advice your friend, Marie, gave you didn't help."

Jake frowned in surprise. "How do you know what Marie said about this?"

Mrs Wishmore waved a hand, as if this detail didn't much matter. "For what it's worth, I think Marie was right when she counselled you not to run away from something that might turn out to be wonderful, just because you're afraid."

"Hey, how do you know what Marie told me? I don't understand how—"

"Never mind that," Mrs Wishmore said, once more waving a hand as if to illustrate how unimportant this minor detail was.

Jake was frowning so hard that his eyebrows were almost merging along his forehead. How could this woman—this stranger!—know what he'd talked to Marie about? It didn't make any sense.

But the older woman's bright blue eyes and her kind expression had the effect of making Jake realise that perhaps it didn't matter how Mrs Wishmore knew about his private conversation with Marie, and it occurred to him that this odd puzzle was the last thing he ought to focus on right now.

"It's hard when we lose something precious to us," Mrs Wishmore said. "But it's harder still if we never believe that we might be precious to others, too."

Jake watched the older lady, thinking about this. "That's not a million miles away from what Marie said."

Mrs Wishmore chuckled. "She sounds like a wise young lady, this friend of yours." She checked her watch and smiled. "Well, I must go, Jake. I'll see you tomorrow for the summer fair."

Jake blinked and drew in a deep breath, feeling as if he'd been caught up in a strange spell while talking to the mysterious older lady. "I didn't realise you planned on coming along tomorrow, Mrs Wishmore."

"I wouldn't miss it for the world," she replied with an enigmatic smile and turned towards the school gates.

Jake watched the woman shuffle off across the school grounds and through the exit gate. She really was an oddity, he decided, as she disappeared from sight. And yet something about their strange conversation had brought comfort, although he couldn't explain how or why. The woman hadn't said anything remotely helpful.

He picked up the box of school supplies and the bag of donations Mrs Wishmore had dropped off and carried them inside the school building. After setting the craft supplies on a table in the assembly hall so they could be found easily tomorrow, he opened the donation bag to take a better look at what was inside. It would help the kids running the bric-à-brac stall if he gave them a steer on what prices to stick on the new donations before they added them to their stall along with the rest of the wares they hoped to sell tomorrow.

The donations were all good quality items. Along with the glass rosebud vase he'd already looked at, there were two porcelain trinket boxes, some ornamental figurines, a collection of cute crystal dogs, and some other bits and pieces that he was sure would find willing buyers on the bric-à-brac stall. After scribbling out a quick note to the kids in charge of the stall offering advice on prices, Jake was about to replace the donations in the bag alongside his note when he saw something he'd missed at the bottom beneath a scrunched-up ball of bubble wrap.

Jake reached inside and pulled out the overlooked item. It was a delicate milk jug in palest yellow porcelain and decorated with painted daffodils.

Immediately, Jake's mind filled with thoughts of Lisa.

He thought of the cosy, welcoming atmosphere of the Daffodil Café. He thought of the cluttered display dresser upstairs in Lisa's flat, laden with cups and saucers, teapots and jugs, bowls and plates, and all the other mismatched tableware she'd confessed to being unable to resist when she came across them in jumble sales and second-hand shops.

And he thought, too, of her beautiful smile and her bright laugh and her good heart, and how hard it was to walk away from her.

Jake turned the delicate milk jug over in his hands. An urge raced through him to buy the little jug and give it to Lisa. She would love the sweet item and he imagined her face lighting up when she saw it, imagined her eyes sparkling as she admired the slim, elegant handle and the soft painted daffodils around the rim. The milk jug belonged to Lisa, he decided, and he suddenly wanted nothing more than to give it to her and see that smile spread across her face.

His heartbeat raced as the idea took hold, along with all the possibilities that might come along with it.

Like the chance to tell Lisa he was sorry for being a fool and to beg for another chance.

As soon as this notion flashed through Jake's mind, the milk jug slipped through his fingers and fell to the wooden floor, where it shattered into pieces.

For a long moment, he could only stare at the fragments of the lovely milk jug scattered at his feet. The sharp ache of loss hit him hard deep inside his heart, not just for the broken pottery, but for Lisa, too. As he looked at the shards of porcelain, their painted daffodils now splintered across so many sharp edges, one grim thought gripped him.

He'd made a terrible mistake when he'd ended things with Lisa. A terrible and stupid mistake.

But it was too late now to do anything about it. What he'd said to Lisa yesterday in the park was unforgiveable. He'd hurt her in order to push her away and there was no going back now.

Jake fetched a dustpan and brush to clean up the broken milk jug. As he leaned down, he took one last look at the shattered porcelain and the fragments of painted daffodils, and wondered what might have been between himself and Lisa, if things had been different and if he'd been braver.

With a sigh, he swept up the broken jug and dumped the pieces in the rubbish bin. There was no point in dreaming about those things now.

It was time to lock up the school and send the remaining volunteers home before turning his thoughts to the final preparations for tomorrow's summer fair, where they belonged.

CHAPTER TWENTY-THREE

Lisa hummed along to the song playing on the radio as she boxed the cakes and treats she'd baked for the Willowbridge School summer fair. She was proud of all the goodies she'd produced to help with the fundraising efforts, and glad she'd used her tried and tested freeze-ahead sponge recipes to bake as much as she could.

Arrayed on the counter of the Daffodil Café's kitchen was a Victoria sponge, a carrot cake, a coffee and walnut cake, and a clementine cake, and Lisa was sure the towering sponges with their pretty decorations would be a big hit on the home-baking stall. She'd also whipped up batches of blueberry muffins, lemon and poppy seed muffins, two trays of double chocolate brownies and two trays of rocky road. Then there was the banana bread she'd made late last night, along with a gingerbread loaf and a cherry madeira loaf.

It was possible she'd gone overboard with the amount of baking she'd done. Still, it had given her something to do on a quiet Saturday night, and the extra work she'd put in to produce the tray bakes and loaf cakes had stopped her brain from picking over all the unpleasant thoughts she kept having about Jake.

After the hurt she'd felt on Friday evening in the park, and her confusion about how things could have ended so suddenly and so quickly between them, her Saturday night spent baking had helped her realise something important.

Jake Reid was nothing but a big jerk.

"That's right, he's a big jerk and I'm glad he's gone," Lisa muttered to herself as she lifted the Victoria sponge into a cardboard cake box and closed the lid. "I don't need that kind of nonsense in my life."

Nodding to confirm the wisdom of what she'd just said, she packed the rest of the sponges into boxes and shuttled them out to her car. Lisa had phoned the head teacher at Willowbridge School to confirm a drop off time for the baked goods, and they'd agreed that anytime between eleven-thirty and noon would be just fine. Lisa had decided to wait until closer to noon before arriving at the school, because that was when the summer fair officially opened, which would hopefully mean that Jake was too busy welcoming visitors and overseeing the students to notice her.

That last thing she wanted was to see him or, worse, bump into him. She was more than happy to do her bit to help the school's fundraising efforts. But she wasn't interested in seeing Jake Reid, or talking to Jake Reid, or having anything whatsoever to do with Jake Reid. She planned to drop off the cakes and goodies and then leave.

Lisa returned to the kitchen for the next load of cake boxes to pack into her car, and paused at the counter, frowning at the iced chocolate cake that sat on a plate behind the remaining boxes, its future as yet undecided.

She'd baked the chocolate sponges ahead of time for the freezer, because Jake had said he loved her chocolate cake and she'd wanted to include one in her donations because she knew it would make him smile. Now, though, the sight of the indulgent chocolate cake with its rich buttercream icing and chocolate curls only annoyed her. The chocolate cake recipe was her pride and joy, honed and perfected through much trial and error, and knowing how much Jake loved it made her wish that the cake wasn't the one she considered her signature—and best—bake.

The chocolate cake made her remember the first time she'd met Jake, when he'd come into her café and ordered a slice of it which he'd then spilled down the front of himself when the café door had blown open and wafted his school paperwork to the floor.

The memory brought a reluctant smile to Lisa's mouth at the image of Jake leaping to his feet and sending his cake flying, before staring in bewilderment at the chocolatey mess all over his jeans. His stunned and comical expression had stayed with her, and the generous way he'd responded to the embarrassing situation had touched her.

How could the Jake Reid who'd laughed off the embarrassment of making a fool of himself in front of a café full of customers by spilling chocolate cake everywhere be the same man who'd hurt her with the things he'd said when he broke up with her?

And how could she be so upset about breaking up with someone when they'd only known each other for a few weeks?

Lisa had no idea. Nor did she have any idea what to do about the iced chocolate cake waiting on the counter. She knew it would sell quickly and guarantee a nice chunk of money for the school. But she wasn't sure if she should donate the cake at all. Why should she donate Jake's favourite cake after how horrible he'd been?

It was a foolish and childish way to think, but she couldn't help it. Part of her wanted to claim at least one tiny victory in this upsetting situation, and withholding her prized chocolate cake was one way to do it. There was plenty of cake to donate to the school as it was, and if she kept the chocolate cake, it would be one less thing to bake for the café opening on Monday morning.

Jake wouldn't notice the cake on the stall anyway, and if he did, why would he even care? He'd made his feelings about her clear on Friday night.

So why was she fixating on this? Lisa only wished she knew the answer to that mystery.

"Hello? Lisa, are you there?"

Lisa was pulled from her ridiculous thoughts by the voice outside the rear kitchen door. When she turned from the counter, she saw her friend and Daffodil Café waitress, Vicki, walking in.

"Vicki!" Lisa said, smiling in surprise as she took in the sight of her friend walking into the kitchen without the cumbersome space boot on her injured foot. Lisa had dropped by to visit her unlucky waitress a couple of days after her tumble down the stairs and commiserate over homemade cake, and she knew how upset Vicki was to be sore and laid up. She also hadn't expected to see her out and about for another few weeks. "Look at you! You don't have your space boot on!"

Vicki grinned and lifted her foot to show it off. "I had a check-up on Friday afternoon and the doctor said it was healing nicely. I've been lumbering around in that silly space boot ever since the accident, and the rest and support have both done the trick. I'm as good as new."

"Vicki, that's wonderful. You must be so relieved."

"I was horrified when they said I might need to wear the

space boot for a month or more. You know me, I don't like sitting around doing nothing. And I hated not being able to work. But it's been the right thing to do, and the injury healed quickly because of it. It's also possible that the injury wasn't as bad as they first thought. I get the impression these things can be a bit hard to pin down when it comes to making firm diagnoses about all those little bones and muscles in our feet."

"I can't tell you how happy I am for you, Vicki," Lisa smiled. "I felt so bad for you after your accident, and I've missed you at the café."

"And I've missed being here. The good news is that I can come back to work tomorrow if you want me to. That's why I popped over, so I could tell you in person."

Lisa glanced at her friend's foot. "I don't know, Vicki. Are you sure you're up for a long café shift already?

"Lisa, if I don't get out of the house and do something useful with my time, I might kill my mother, or my mother might kill me," Vicki said, a wry smile on her lips. "You'd be doing us both a favour by letting me come back and saving the police the trouble of a murder investigation."

Lisa laughed. "Well, if you're sure you're ready. And as it happens, I had a phone call from Helen yesterday," she added, referring to the other Daffodil Café waitress who'd also been on extended leave. "Her father's feeling much better and all the post-surgery checks suggest he's well on the way to recovery, so Helen will be home and back at work by the middle of the week. All my lovely waitresses will be back where they belong."

"That's great news."

"Once we're all back together, we ought to have a mini-celebration one day after we close the café. I'll bake a cake, and Fiona will whip up some of her famous toasted sandwiches, and we'll open a bottle of prosecco to congratulate ourselves on making it through a tough few weeks."

"I'd love that," Vicki said. "I've missed the café, and I've missed seeing the customers and catching up with all the gossip. Mildred and Jean will have to bring me up to date."

"I'm sure they'll enjoy that," Lisa laughed.

A thoughtful look crossed Vicki's face. "Hang on, I forgot about the temporary waitress you've had working here. Have you already promised her some shifts next week? If you have, don't worry about bringing me back just yet. That wouldn't be fair."

"I'll chat to Mrs Wishmore and the temping agency," Lisa said. "I'm sure they don't have a shortage of jobs for a good waitress like her, but if she wants to stay on for a few more days, maybe that's not a bad idea while you adjust to the work again after sitting with your feet up in front of the television and doing nothing."

Lisa grinned at Vicki's mock insulted expression and pulled her friend into a hug.

"It'll be lovely to have you back, Vicki," Lisa said. "Although I must say that Mrs Wishmore is a waitressing wonder, and I'll miss her once she's gone."

She'd been more than just an amazing waitress, Lisa realised. Doris had become a real friend in just a few short weeks, and she couldn't help but think the café wouldn't feel the same without the older woman with the sparkling blue eyes and cloud of silvery hair, bustling around and bringing warmth and cheer to the café and its customers.

"Maybe you should ask her to stay on," Vicki said. "The café's always so popular and busy. I'm sure you could use an extra pair of hands around the place, especially during busy lunch times on Fridays and Saturdays."

It was a good idea. Things sometimes got a little hairy

during the busier lunch services, and an extra body working in the café to serve customers and clear tables would be a big help. Although margins were tight in hospitality, Lisa wondered if the extra money spent on staff wages, even if only for a few hours a week, might be worth it if it meant faster service and increased turnover of tables in the café. The Daffodil Café was doing well, after all. Perhaps it was time to invest in more staff?

And if so, perhaps Mrs Wishmore might be interested in staying on?

Lisa liked the idea. It couldn't hurt to ask.

"I'll have a chat with her and see what she thinks," Lisa said. "She might not be interested in staying on for only a few hours a week, but who knows?"

Vicki nodded, and then her gaze travelled to the boxed cakes on the counters. "What's all this for?"

While Lisa explained about the goodies she was donating to the school summer fair, Vicki helped her carry the remaining boxes out to the car. When they returned to the kitchen, Vicki pointed to the chocolate cake still sitting on a plate at the back of the counter.

"Shall I box this last cake up, too?" Vicki asked.

Lisa stared at the cake for a long moment. She realised Vicki knew nothing about the brief romance she'd had with Jake Reid. Perhaps that was just as well.

"No," Lisa said, deciding on the fate of the chocolate cake, even if that decision made her feel a little childish. "I'm keeping that for the café stock tomorrow."

Vicki nodded and then gave Lisa a careful look. "I know these past weeks can't have been easy for you, Lisa, with the anniversary of Peter's death, and then me being injured and off work. I'm sorry I haven't been here for you."

Touched by her friend's words, Lisa smiled. "There's nothing to be sorry for."

"Are you doing okay now that the anniversary has been and gone?"

Lisa thought about Vicki's question. She thought about the kindness of Mrs Wishmore over these past weeks, and all the chats they'd shared and the good advice the older lady had offered. And she thought about Jake, too. Hurt and angry though she was by how things had ended, Jake had helped her realise that there was life for her beyond Peter's death, after all.

All things considered, it had been a surprising and strange few weeks.

"I'm doing just fine," Lisa told Vicki with a smile. "And it feels like there are better times ahead."

"Good, because you deserve them."

The two friends smiled at one another and then Lisa glanced at her watch. "Gosh, I'd better get moving. I promised to drop these cakes off at the school fair before noon."

They said their goodbyes, and Lisa locked the back door of the café and got in behind the wheel of her car. After the unexpected news about Vicki's speedy recovery and planned return to work, her thoughts clouded over once more at the prospect of driving to Willowbridge School with her load of cakes.

She hoped she wouldn't run into Jake while she was there.

Thinking of Jake made her think, again, of the iced chocolate cake still sitting on the counter in the café's kitchen. The silliness of refusing to include the cake with the rest of the donated goodies, simply because Jake loved it and it reminded her of the first moment she'd met him, was too childish for her to endure.

Lisa got out of the car and hurried back inside the café's kitchen. For a few seconds, she stared at the lovely chocolate cake sitting on the counter, wondering why this one tiny matter was causing her so much indecision. As the thought tumbled through her head, she realised her fingers had moved to the necklace she wore and were fidgeting with the diamond ring that hung at her collar.

The gesture had been so unconscious, she hadn't even realised she'd done it. Once more, she wondered how often that happen on any given day. How often did she pause in some task and touch that engagement ring, drawing comfort from its delicate curve and sweet diamonds and the memories it evoked?

A sudden and unexpected realisation hit Lisa square in the chest—if she'd once found comfort from having that ring so close to her heart, she didn't anymore.

Instead, as she gazed down at the ring and its twinkling gemstones, she had the distinct sensation of the past shifting away from her like a wave retreating from the beach with the outgoing tide. An image filled her head of Peter, far out in the distance, a gentle smile on his face as he disappeared into the endless horizon.

Lisa felt a bolt of melancholy rush through her soul. But in its place came a crisp understanding about what she had to do now.

Reaching up, she unhooked the necklace and slid the diamond engagement ring into her palm. A bright memory filled her mind of Peter down on one knee, offering that ring to her and promising a lifetime of happiness.

Lisa cherished that memory. She always would. But it was time to let it go. Not because of what Jake had said about the emotional baggage she was carrying, and not because Mrs Wishmore had made her wonder if Jake might have a point.

But because her heart had relinquished the terrible ache that had burned deep inside it, and in that moment of release, it seemed to Lisa as if everything had changed.

She left the café kitchen and unlocked her flat, and

carried the engagement ring through to her bedroom. She'd kept the velvet ring box in amongst her small collection of jewellery, and she took it out and opened the lid.

For the tiniest moment, she paused. And then, with a soft sigh, she placed the diamond ring on the cushion and closed the lid.

It was done. Lisa had imagined this moment would be too upsetting to bear, that finally removing Peter's ring and putting it away for good would leave her in pieces. Instead, it felt like a great weight had lifted from her shoulders and all she felt was relief that an impossible task hadn't turned out to be impossible after all.

She opened the jewellery box that sat on top of her chest of drawers and rummaged around her small collection of items. When she found a silver necklace with an enamel daffodil pendant, she pulled it out and put it on, admiring the pretty daffodil and the way its yellow colour caught the light. The necklace had been a gift from her parents when she opened the café, and it had been too long since she'd worn it. It had been too long since she'd worn any of the necklaces in her small collection. Maybe now that would change.

Lisa headed back downstairs to the café kitchen and glanced at the chocolate cake waiting on the counter. After pulling a cardboard box from the stack in the cupboard and slotting it together, she slid the chocolate cake into place inside. She'd baked the cake for the school summer fair and that's where it ought to go.

As she turned once more for the door, bright memories of that first meeting with Jake rolled through her mind. She remembered his shocked expression when the chocolate cake splattered over his jeans, and the warm smile he'd given her as he apologised for the mess, his eyes bright with an irresistible mix of reluctant amusement and awkward embarrassment.

Lisa realised how much she would miss that smile of Jake's and wished that things had turned out differently between them.

She pushed the thought away. There was no use crying over spilled milk—or spilled chocolate cake, she told herself with a wry smile.

Wishing wouldn't change anything. After all she'd been through this last year, Lisa knew that only too well.

CHAPTER TWENTY-FOUR

When Lisa arrived at Willowbridge School on the other side of town, the place was so busy it took her almost ten minutes to find a parking space. The school car park was jammed with vehicles and parked cars lined the road outside from one end to the other. Fearing she'd have to haul her car load of cake donations from one of the surrounding streets further away, Lisa thanked her lucky stars when a space opened up on her third pass outside the school gates, and she pulled into it without even turning on her indicator light, earning an irritated horn toot from the driver in the car behind her.

The summer fair that was spread out around the school grounds looked amazing, and the staff and students had outdone themselves, decorating the place with colourful bunting and bright balloons. As Lisa pulled the first couple of cake boxes from the back of her car, she noticed the queue that had already formed at the main entrance as people waited to get inside, and was pleased she'd gone overboard with the amount of baking she was donating. With all these folk roaming the stalls and enjoying themselves, the school would have a bumper fundraising year, and Lisa was glad her batches of cakes and goodies would play their part in filling the coffers.

As she juggled cake boxes in her arms while locking her car, Lisa saw the welcome sight of Mrs Wishmore making her way towards her.

"Looks like I got here just in time to help you carry that load," Mrs Wishmore said. "Here, give me some of those boxes."

"Thanks, you're a lifesaver." Lisa passed two of the lighter boxes to the older lady. "I'll have to come back for the rest of the goodies. I don't want to risk dropping anything while carrying all these boxes to the home-baking stall."

"I can help, too."

Lisa turned in surprise at the voice behind her, and saw Peter's mother, Joan, walking through the main entrance gates and towards Lisa's car.

"Joan! I didn't know you were coming here today!"

Joan grinned as she drew near. "When I heard about the school summer fair from Doris when we chatted the other day in your café, I couldn't resist her invitation to join her for a nice wander around the stalls," she said and gestured to the gin-clear skies overhead. "And after all, it's such a glorious day. It would be a shame not to get out and enjoy it."

"I'm glad you could make it," Mrs Wishmore said, smiling at Joan. "The two of us will have a wonderful time, I'm sure of it."

Lisa was astonished, not just at Joan coming along to the summer fair, but at the woman's transformed appearance. She wore a cheerful summer dress with a bright pink scarf draped around her shoulders, her hair was cut and coloured, and a light dusting of make-up brightened her face. Lisa couldn't remember the last time she'd seen Joan look this smart or take such an interest in her appearance. Although still much too thin, there was a bright spark in Joan's eyes that had been missing for far too long.

"Joan, you look fantastic!" Lisa said, wishing she wasn't still balancing cake boxes in her arms because she wanted to haul Joan into a hug.

"I thought it was time I made a bit of an effort," Joan said, cutting her glance towards Mrs Wishmore. "What Doris said the other day about deserving some happiness in my life got me thinking. And I feel rather good for having put my face on today. I'd forgotten how nice it was to have my hair done and wear a nice dress and splash on a bit of lipstick. Now, I won't ask again, Lisa. Give me at least one of those cake boxes. I'm determined to make myself useful."

Lisa passed a box to Joan and unlocked her car to collect more to carry herself. With Joan and Doris lending a hand, she'd have the stock delivered to the cake stall in no time. Laden with their boxes, the three women headed towards the main avenue of stalls that ran down the middle of the school grounds, and Lisa was relieved when she spied the head teacher approaching them. As she listened to the head teacher's directions for the home-baking stall, Lisa glanced around for any sign of Jake. When she saw him talking to a bunch of students near a stage that was set up on the other side of the fair and flicking through some paperwork on a clipboard, she was pleased to see that he was busy. Perhaps she could deliver her cakes and make a quick dash for the exit and avoid him altogether, just as she'd hoped.

Lisa found the home-baking stall with no trouble, and was greeted by the three teenage girls who were running it and who thanked her for the cake delivery. As Lisa, Joan and Mrs Wishmore deposited the boxes at the stall, the girls opened each one and exclaimed in delight at the treats inside. Before the girls had even begun putting the cakes on display and slicing them up, there were already buyers lining up at the stall, pointing inside the cake boxes and pulling out their wallets. When Lisa spied her two favourite Daffodil Café customers, Mildred and Jean, standing in the cake queue and eyeing up the delivery of cherry scones, she smiled in happy satisfaction.

"You've done these girls a good turn," Mrs Wishmore said with a grin as they left the teenagers to serve their customers. "Their cash box will be jingling with money once the guests catch a glimpse of your wonderful baking."

"It looks like they have lots of goodies to sell," Lisa said, glancing at the other delicious treats on the stall as they walked off. "People have put their shoulder to the wheel to help raise money for the school."

"I'm sure they'll appreciate every penny."

Just then, the crowd moving past the lines of stalls parted and Lisa heard a woman walking towards them let out a surprised gasp.

"Joan King!" the woman cried. "I can't believe it's you!"

"Lena!" Joan said, laughing in surprise as the woman grabbed her into a hug. "How lovely to see you."

"It's been too long since I last saw you out and about," Lena said, releasing Joan from the embrace. "I'd just about given up on ever seeing you walking around in the world again."

"I know," Joan said with a frown. "But I've hidden myself away for long enough." Joan turned to Lisa and Mrs Wishmore and said, "Ladies, this is my friend Lena. We used to see each other every week at the local amateur dramatics society up in Winchester until I stopped going."

"You ought to come along again to our meetings, Joan," Lena said. "We're in the middle of planning our Christmas production and we could use you back on the team."

"Well, I think I'd like that."

"In fact, a few of the other amateur dramatics folks are

over at the coffee stall as we speak," Lena said. "I was just making my way over to them. Why don't you join me and we can all have a good catch up?"

"I'd love to, but maybe we could meet later. I promised my friend here, Doris, that I'd enjoy a walk around the stalls with her, you see."

"Oh, we have all day to enjoy the stalls together," Mrs Wishmore said with a laugh. "Why don't you say hello to your friends, and in the meantime, I'll help Lisa carry the rest of her cakes to the home-baking stall."

Joan looked torn for a moment, unhappy at abandoning Doris so soon after arriving at the fair. But Mrs Wishmore only smiled.

"Please don't keep those nice ladies waiting on my account," Mrs Wishmore said. "When the chance comes to renew old acquaintances, we should always take it."

Joan finally smiled and nodded. "You're right, Doris. Thank you. I'll see you later?"

"I'll look forward to it."

Lisa watched Joan walk off into the crowds with her friend Lena, the two of them already laughing and deep in conversation.

"I'm completely astonished," Lisa told Mrs Wishmore as they made their way back towards her car to collect the remaining cake boxes. "A few days ago in the café, I was amazed when Joan started opening up about things. Now, she looks like a woman transformed. What you said to her has worked wonders, Doris."

"Oh, I didn't say anything that Joan didn't already know for herself. All she needed was a little nudge in the right direction."

"Well, I'm glad you knew how to give her that nudge. Nothing I said ever made any difference. And it seems like the two of you have hit it off if you're spending time here together at the summer fair."

"I'm glad Joan bumped into old friends of her own," Mrs Wishmore said. "She needs that right now."

They reached Lisa's car, and she opened the door to take out the last of the boxes.

"You've made such a big difference in so many ways since you started working at my café, Doris," Lisa said, passing the smaller of the remaining boxes to the older lady.

"That's lovely to hear," Mrs Wishmore smiled.

"I spoke to my permanent waitress, Vicki, this morning. She's recovered from her injury and is ready to come back to work, and so I was wondering—"

"That's wonderful news!" Mrs Wishmore interrupted, her smile now even wider. "You will be so pleased to have her back in the café, I'm sure."

"Of course, but I don't want to lose you, Doris," Lisa said as they retraced their steps towards the baking stall. "I hoped that perhaps you'd like to keep working with us. With the café becoming more and more popular, I think it's time to expand my staff. Would you be interested in staying on and working the lunch shifts on Fridays and Saturdays? I'd love it if you could join our little Daffodil Café team permanently."

Lisa smiled at Mrs Wishmore, hoping she'd say yes. She hadn't realised until now just how much she'd grown to like the older lady with the sparkling blue eyes and warm smile.

"Is your friend Vicki ready to come back to work right away?" Mrs Wishmore asked as they reached the cake stall and handed over the boxed donations.

"Well, yes, but you and I already agreed the shifts you'd work next week, and Vicki is happy to wait a little longer before returning to her regular hours. It wouldn't be fair to you, otherwise."

"I think that if your lovely young waitress is ready to

come back right away, then that's what should happen," Mrs Wishmore said.

"But—"

"I had a phone call from the job agency yesterday afternoon, you see," Mrs Wishmore interrupted. "There's a position they thought I might be interested in. It seems they'd forgotten I was still working with you at the Daffodil Café when they thought of me for this other job. Some mix-up with their files and records, as I understand it."

Mrs Wishmore laughed and Lisa joined her. "They always seem to get their files and records mixed up where you're concerned."

The older lady laughed. "You're quite right. When I reminded them about my temporary position in your café, the agent was rather sorry about it, and I got the distinct impression that they're looking for someone with a specific skill set for this other job that has come up. However, if your own waitress is ready and able to get back to work, then perhaps I should call the agency and let them know I'm free to take on this other job after all. It would be a shame to let their client down."

"Well, yes, I understand. But would you still be interested in staying on at the café and working a few hours on Fridays and Saturdays?" Lisa felt a little desperate at the idea of Mrs Wishmore leaving so soon. "Maybe you could fit in this other job around working at the Daffodil Café?"

Mrs Wishmore smiled. "I don't think so, dear. When I take on a new job, I always like to give it my full attention." Her gaze shifted to the new necklace Lisa was wearing and her smile softened. "And anyway, I think my work here is done."

Lisa's hand moved to the daffodil pendant she'd fastened around her neck after taking off the necklace with her engagement ring on it. She ran her fingers over the lovely silvery jewellery, liking the feel of it and liking even more the big step forward the little daffodil pendant necklace represented in her own mind.

As Mrs Wishmore's gaze stayed on the pendant, Lisa thought about how much the older lady had helped her navigate these last difficult weeks and the anniversary of Peter's death.

"I'll be sorry to see you go," Lisa said. "I feel like we've become good friends since you started working at the café."

"And friends we shall remain," Mrs Wishmore smiled.

"I'll miss our chats and all your good advice. They've meant a lot to me these last few weeks and helped me more than you could ever know."

"I'm so pleased to hear it. I think you're going to do just fine, Lisa." Her expression softened, and she reached out and squeezed Lisa's arm. "Just listen to your heart. You have a good one and it won't ever lead you astray."

Lisa felt a warm feeling of comfort and strength flow through her as Mrs Wishmore squeezed her arm. "Thank you, Doris."

The older lady's gaze shifted across the summer fair, as if something had caught her attention. "Will you excuse me, dear? I just saw someone I'd like to have a quick word with."

Lisa nodded as Mrs Wishmore hurried off into the crowd and disappeared from sight. She realised that now would be a great time to make good her escape from the fair in order to avoid running into Jake. She'd delivered her cakes and had no reason to stay any longer. But she didn't want to hurry off without speaking to Joan, and she also felt as if there was some unfinished business with Mrs Wishmore still waiting to be dealt with, although quite what that could be she had no idea.

Lisa was sorry that the temporary waitress wouldn't be staying on at the café any longer, and wished she could have changed her mind about taking on those lunch shifts they'd discussed, but she understood that the woman's excellent services would be in high demand elsewhere.

Mrs Wishmore was leaving the Daffodil Café and Vicki was returning, along with Helen later in the week. Everything was returning to normal, which was what Lisa had wanted all along.

Except that wasn't quite true. Everything wasn't returning to normal because something significant had happened during these last few weeks. She'd met Jake and discovered that it was possible to move on from Peter's death and start feeling things she'd thought she'd never feel again.

Angry and confused though she still was because of Jake and what he'd said when they'd parted ways, Lisa was grown-up enough to admit that she'd miss him, even if that admission made her clench her teeth in frustration.

She once more turned towards the school gates, now more keen than ever to leave the summer fair before running into Jake. But she'd only managed two steps towards the exit when she saw Joan waving towards her from the coffee stall and gesturing for her to come over.

Lisa glanced around to make sure there was no sign of Jake before hurrying over to catch up with Joan, hoping her luck would hold for at least another couple of minutes.

JAKE HAD NEVER BEEN BUSIER in his life and quite how he was keeping up with everything that had to be done was a complete mystery.

In the last half hour, the Willowbridge School summer fair had officially opened, and it looked as if the entire town had turned up to support it. The stalls were doing a roaring trade, the entertainments were keeping everyone amused, and the talent show would begin up on the stage in the next twenty minutes. All the students who were involved in organising and running the event were throwing themselves into their tasks and making sure everything was working as planned. As Jake glanced at the busy scene around him, he smiled at what the staff and the school kids had achieved.

Ruby, who was trotting along at Jake's side with the air of his second-in-command, was also proving popular with the crowds. The school kids had been delighted to see his scruffy dog scampering beside him, and one of them had come up with the bright idea of attaching a little coin bag to Ruby's collar and pinning a request for donations to the jaunty neckerchief Jake had put on her that morning. So far, the ruse had worked and Jake had already had to empty the coin bag twice to avoid the poor dog being weighed down.

Ruby was obviously loving the attention being lavished on her by the adoring school kids, and was happily charming the socks off anyone who might be in possession of either a dog treat or a few pennies in need of donation to a worthy cause.

"Ready for your scheduled soaking, sir?"

Jake turned to see Bradley and his sidekick pal approaching, the two of them grinning from ear to ear. After patting Ruby, Bradley glanced at the clipboard he was carrying and ran his finger down the page of scheduled activities.

"According to our timetable," Bradley said with an evil grin, "the water balloon contest starts in ten minutes and you're the star target."

"Thanks for the reminder," Jake laughed. "But maybe someone else should take my place in the hot seat, so I can keep an eye on what's going on around here."

Bradley and his pal shook their heads. "Mrs Hanlon told us you might say that," Bradley said, pointing to a stall across the school grounds where Marie was helping the students serve customers. "She says she'll keep watch on proceedings while you're getting hit with water balloons."

Jake laughed again. It stood to reason that his friend would make sure he had no way out of the embarrassment and humiliation that awaited him once the water balloon contest got underway. As the teacher in charge of running the summer fair committee this year and keeping the kids focused and in line, he expected a long queue of students would turn up to lob water balloons at him, and it wouldn't be fair to deny them the opportunity of giving him a thorough soaking. He wouldn't be surprised if Marie was at the head of the queue.

"You lads have done a good job here today," Jake told the two boys. "How's it going on your coconut shy?"

"Brilliant," Bradley said. "We've already done almost twenty quid of business. We're on our way over there now to take over from the boys so they can take part in the talent contest."

"Off you go then, don't keep them waiting," Jake told them both and watched as they hurried off through the crowds.

He was about to consult his clipboard to see what task he ought to check up on next when he realised he was standing across from the bric-à-brac stall. The girls and boys running it were busy arranging the donated stock on the table top and serving the customers who'd stopped to inspect the items for sale. On one side of the table, Jake saw the pink glass rosebud vase that had been inside the bag of donations that Mrs Wishmore had dropped off yesterday on behalf of her friend, and clustered beside the vase sat the cute collection of crystal dogs and the little trinket boxes that had also been part of the donation.

But there was something else on the bric-à-brac stall, too —something that didn't make any sense.

Jake stepped over to the stall and peered at the item he'd spied tucked in beside the crystal dogs and trinket boxes.

It was the pale yellow milk jug with the painted daffodils around the side—the same milk jug Jake had dropped in the school assembly hall yesterday and smashed to pieces.

And yet there it was, sitting on the bric-à-brac stall and looking as good as new. Jake frowned in confusion and bewilderment as he stared at the little milk jug, trying to make sense of what he was seeing.

But he couldn't make any sense of it. The jug had been broken and beyond repair. He'd swept up the smashed pieces and tossed them into the rubbish bin.

Was it possible that there'd been another milk jug in that bag of donations? Jake knew that couldn't be the explanation, because he'd checked the bag himself.

Perhaps someone else had donated an identical milk jug to the bric-à-brac stall? No, that seemed even less likely. The milk jug he'd broken had been old and unique. Those daffodils had looked hand-painted and there had been a small chip at the base of the handle...

Jake picked up the yellow milk jug and inspected the handle, and found the small chip he'd remembered in the same place as it had been on the milk jug he'd broken yesterday afternoon. This was the same milk jug, there was no question about that. But how could that be?

He scratched his head, wondering what on earth was going on.

"Well, isn't that a pretty thing? Are you thinking of buying it?"

Jake turned and found Mrs Wishmore standing at his side, smiling as she looked at the milk jug he was holding. While Ruby greeted Mrs Wishmore with a wriggling wag of her tail, Jake frowned again at the jug, turning it over in his hands.

"Are you all right, dear?" Mrs Wishmore asked. "You seem a little befuddled."

"Uh, I'm not sure." Jake shook his head, trying to clear his thoughts. "This will sound strange, but this milk jug was in the bag of donations you dropped off yesterday, Mrs Wishmore."

The older lady's eyes widened. "Was it? I'm afraid I didn't have time to take a good snoop around in the bag my friend handed me before I dropped it off. But I don't understand what's so strange about that?"

"Well, the thing is, I had an accident and dropped this milk jug and it shattered into pieces," Jake said, then held the jug up for closer inspection. "And yet, here it is, back in one piece and as good as new. I'm wondering if I'm losing my mind."

Mrs Wishmore chuckled. "I'm sure that your mind is quite fine, Jake. And I'm sure there's a simple explanation for this mix-up."

Jake was sure there had to be a simple explanation, too. He just couldn't think what it might be.

"This is a sweet little item," Mrs Wishmore said, looking at the milk jug. "And so delicately decorated, too."

"The daffodils made me think of…" Jake tailed off and sighed. "They made me think of Lisa and her café."

Mrs Wishmore nodded. "I can see why. A milk jug painted with daffodils would be right at home in a place called the Daffodil Café."

"She collects things like this," Jake said, his voice wistful. "She has a display cabinet in her kitchen crammed with mismatched tableware and cups and so on."

"Perhaps this little trinket would be right at home there with her," Mrs Wishmore said and smiled. "And perhaps you would be, too."

Jake let out a surprised laugh and shook his head. "I

missed my chance, Doris. And I wasn't brave enough to take the risk I'd have to take to show her what she means to me."

"It's never too late to do the things we need to do, Jake." Mrs Wishmore's smile brightened. "And if you're looking for a sign, perhaps that little milk jug you're holding is it."

"What do you mean?" Jake frowned.

"Broken things can always be fixed," Mrs Wishmore said, her gaze soft. "Even when we believe they're beyond repair."

Jake turned the milk jug over in his hands, wondering about the strange trinket that had been broken and yet was now whole again, and wondering about other things, too.

"I said a terrible thing to Lisa," he said, shame already burning his cheeks. "Something that was stupid and wrong and I can't take it back. She won't want anything to do with me now."

"And yet I happen to believe that isn't true." Mrs Wishmore pointed across the fair to where the home-baking stall was doing a roaring trade. "Do you see that beautiful chocolate cake over there?"

Jake peered at the home-baking stall and nodded.

"Lisa baked that, along with many other delicious things being sold on the home-baking stall," Mrs Wishmore said.

Jake turned to the older woman in amazement. "She donated cakes to the summer fair even although we broke up?"

Mrs Wishmore laughed. "Well, of course she did, Jake. She has a good heart, and she promised your head teacher that she'd provide baking for the students to sell, and so that's what she did. You don't think for a minute that she'd let some silly falling out between the two of you stop her from fulfilling an important promise that she made, do you?"

Jake didn't even have to think about it. Lisa wasn't capable of being petty or small-minded. "No, of course she wouldn't."

"Although I happen to know she was rather torn about bringing along that chocolate cake that she baked," Mrs Wishmore continued, nodding back towards the home-baking stall. "You are rather fond of Lisa's chocolate cake, isn't that right?"

Jake nodded and let out a pained laugh. "When I visited her café for the first time, Lisa's chocolate cake was what I ordered, on your recommendation."

"Indeed," Mrs Wishmore said, a smile at her lips. "You had a rather amusing accident with the cake."

"Don't remind me." Jake groaned, recalling his mortification that day when he'd knocked the plate of chocolate cake all over himself. What had Lisa ever saw in him?

"Lisa thought fondly of that moment when you both met, while she considered whether to bring that chocolate cake along today," Mrs Wishmore said. "I think she wishes things had turned out differently between you, just as you do."

"How can you know that?" Jake said, frowning at the mysterious older lady who seemed to have such an astonishing insight into things.

"I just know," Mrs Wishmore said. "But perhaps you ought to find out for yourself."

Jake let out a long breath. "I don't know…"

A gap opened amongst the crowds meandering up and down the avenue of stalls and Jake let out a stunned gasp when he saw Lisa in the distance, walking away from the coffee cart on the other side of the school grounds.

And in that instant, Jake realised what he had to do.

"Lisa's here?" he muttered, and then the question turned into an exclamation. "Lisa's here at the summer fair!"

"Well, yes of course she's here," Mrs Wishmore laughed. "How else do you think she delivered all those cakes she baked?"

But Jake wasn't listening anymore. His gaze was fixed on

Lisa as she hurried away from the coffee cart and towards the school exits.

"Sorry, Mrs Wishmore, I'll be right back," he muttered, and then broke into a run, Ruby barking in excitement as she barrelled along beside him.

Jake couldn't let Lisa disappear from his life, he knew that now. He had to find out if there might be a second chance for them and he had to tell her how he truly felt about her.

Even if it meant risking a broken heart, whether that broken heart happened now or later, it was a risk he had to take, or he'd regret it for the rest of his life.

LISA WAS MOVING past the picnic tables and chairs set up around the coffee cart when she heard excited barking and someone yelling her name. When she turned and saw Jake running towards her at full speed, with Ruby galloping at his heels, her eyes flew wide in alarmed astonishment.

She knew she shouldn't have stayed this long at the fair, because the longer she stayed, the more likely she was to bump into Jake. And now here he was, rushing towards her.

A strange thought seized her—was this what she'd wanted all along, to bump into Jake?

No, she didn't want to bump into him, or speak to him, or have anything to do with him whatsoever.

And yet, as she watched him draw closer, her heart clenched at the thrill of seeing him again.

She glanced at the school gates, which were only a few more steps away now. It wasn't too late to make good her escape. But her feet remained where they were, refusing to budge no matter how much she urged herself to keep walking.

"Lisa!" Jake said when he reached her, his voice breathless from running. "I didn't know you'd be here today."

"I was dropping off cakes for the baking stall," she replied in as icy a tone as she could muster. "I'm leaving now."

"No, wait! There's something I have to tell you."

Jake panted as he caught his breath and the determined look in his eyes kept Lisa standing where she was. Ruby pressed her little body against Lisa's legs in greeting and gazed up at her until she reached down and patted her scruffy head.

"I'm sorry for what I said on Friday night," Jake said. "I said you had emotional baggage, and that you didn't want to put it down. That isn't true and I wish I could take it back."

Lisa looked away, embarrassed at the reminder of their unhappy exchange of words. "Forget about it. It doesn't matter."

"It does matter. Lisa, you've survived a terrible loss and that fact that you're still standing, never mind getting on with living your life, is amazing. *You're* amazing."

A blush warmed her cheeks at his words. "Uh, look—"

"I hate myself for what I said," he interrupted. "And I only said it because…"

When he paused and looked at the ground, Lisa saw the tortured look on his face and wondered what he was about to say, and whether she wanted to hear it.

"I only said what I said because I wanted to push you away," Jake said and looked up to meet her gaze.

She wasn't sure what he might have been preparing to say, but it wasn't this. Lisa felt indignation rush over her like a crashing wave.

"Well, mission accomplished," she said with a confused head shake as she turned once more for the exit gates.

"I wanted to push you away because I'm falling in love with you, Lisa."

His words stopped her dead in her tracks. It took her a long moment to turn around. When she did, both Jake and Ruby were watching her wide-eyed.

"What did you just say?" she almost whispered.

"I said I'm falling in love with you," Jake said. "I'm crazy for you, Lisa. But I've had a lot of disappointment when it comes to relationships and I let it stop me from telling you the truth about how I felt. My relationships with women never last long before they decide I make a better friend than a partner, and I guessed that, at some point, you'd decide the same thing."

"So you decided for me?" Lisa frowned.

Jake sighed and waved a hand in the air, as if searching for the explanation he was seeking. "I could see with my own eyes how much you adored your fiancé, and I knew the chances of you falling for the first guy you started seeing after going through what you went through were non-existent. And because I didn't want to get hurt by falling for you, only for you to walk away some day and break my heart, I stupidly pushed you away first. That's why I said those terrible things I said on Friday. It made me sick to my stomach to say them, but I thought I was doing the right thing, not just for me, but for you. You deserve to be happy after what you've gone through, Lisa, and I wasn't sure I could give you that."

Lisa tried to absorb everything Jake had just said, but her head was spinning.

"You can't be falling in love with me," she murmured. "That's crazy. We only just met. We only just broke up!"

"But it's true, just the same." He closed the distance between them, making Lisa's heart hammer even harder in her chest. "I had to tell you how I feel. And I had to apologise for what I said." He raked a hand through his hair and looked off into the distance, his cheeks colouring. "Anyway, I don't expect you to say anything in return and I don't expect you to pretend you have feelings for me after what happened."

Lisa was too stunned by everything he'd said to speak. For a long beat they stood staring at one another. The soft and searching look in Jake's eyes held Lisa transfixed and the urge she'd felt to turn her back on this man and hope she never saw him again evaporated.

"Why are you carrying that milk jug around?" Lisa asked, pointing to the small jug Jake was holding. The soft pale yellow of the porcelain and the sweet painted daffodils around the rim had caught her eye and her interest, and although it was a ridiculous thing to fixate on right at this moment, she couldn't help wanting to know why he was carting it around.

Jake looked down at the item in his hand, as if surprised to find it there. His lips twitched. "It's a gift for you," he said, holding the porcelain jug towards her. "Although I just realised I may have stolen it."

Lisa peered at the pretty item. "You're giving me stolen goods?"

"Sort of," he said, letting out a low ripple of laughter. "If you'd like to have it, I'll make sure I return to the stall and pay for it."

Utterly confused by all this, Lisa could only accept the sweet milk jug Jake was offering. Admiring the gorgeous painted daffodils and the elegant handle and the delicate porcelain, she smiled. "Thank you."

"The daffodils made me think of you," Jake said. "And they made me think of new beginnings."

Lisa glanced up at Jake. There was a look in his eyes she couldn't resist.

"Anyway," Jake said, "I just wanted to say sorry, and—"

Before he could finish the sentence, Lisa stepped towards him and pulled him into a kiss. Her lips were already on his before she realised what she'd done. She sensed the surprised tension in his body at her unexpected move and then felt it drain away as his arms came around her waist and drew her closer.

When she came up for air, she looked into Jake's eyes and saw something there that looked an awful lot like the future she was waiting for.

"That's twice you've kissed me senseless here in the school grounds," Jake grinned. "Are you trying to get me fired?"

She laughed. "Did you mean what you said? About falling in love?"

"I meant it."

"It's a lot to take in."

"I know. And I don't want you to say it back just because you think I need to hear it. All I want is another chance."

Lisa blew out a breath. "That's what I want, too."

His gaze shifted down to her neck, and he lifted his fingers to the daffodil pendant that hung there. "You took off your engagement ring."

"It was time."

Jake gave her a soft smile. "Are you okay?"

"I'm more than okay," she said and kissed him again. "And it feels like everything is going to be okay now."

Jake looked deep into her eyes, making something shift inside her soul and filling her heart with longing for this man standing before her.

"Mr Reid!" came a voice behind them. "It's time for your scheduled soaking!"

Jake groaned and turned around. Lisa saw two young lads striding towards them, chortling to one another and waving a clipboard in their direction.

"If you don't get over to the water balloon stand, we'll end up running late," one of the boys said. "You can't let your fans down, Mr Reid."

"What's going on?" Lisa asked, amused at the pained expression now on Jake's face.

"I'm in the hot seat for the water balloon contest, as Bradley here has just reminded me," Jake told her. "I'd better get over there. Do you mind?"

Lisa grinned in delight. "Of course not. In fact, I insist on paying to throw the first balloon."

"What?" Jake cried.

"Too late!" one of the boys yelled.

Quick as a flash, Bradley pulled a water balloon from the pockets of his shorts and threw it at Jake's head. There was a dull thud followed by a splash as the balloon exploded on impact, drenching Jake in water that dripped from his hair and down his shirt.

As Jake stood stunned and wide-eyed at what had just happened while the two teenage schoolboys pranced around in delight at the trick they'd played and Ruby ran around in excited circles barking her scruffy little head off, Lisa felt a rumble of laughter roll through her.

"Laugh it up while you can," Jake told Lisa with a wry grin as he shook water from his drenched hair and shirt. "I'm putting your name down for the water balloon contest and we'll see how you like it."

"Don't you dare!" Lisa said, still laughing helplessly.

"Come on, sir," Bradley said. "You don't want to keep the customers waiting any longer."

Lisa watched as the two boys grabbed Jake's arms and hauled him off through the crowds with Ruby scampering along in their wake. She was about to follow behind them, not wanting to miss out on the sight of Jake being soaked with a torrent of water balloons thrown by his obviously adoring students, when she remembered the lovely little milk jug she was still holding. Glancing down at the item, she smiled and tucked it into her bag. She would cherish it, and this moment when Jake gave it to her, this moment that felt like the start of something wonderful.

As Lisa started walking, she caught sight of a figure over by the school gates. When she looked up, she saw Mrs Wishmore. The older lady smiled and raised her hand in a wave.

Lisa waved back, then watched as Mrs Wishmore walked through the school gates and disappeared off along the road.

A strange but certain thought struck her—that this was the last time she'd see Mrs Wishmore, and that the mysterious lady with the bright blue eyes and cloud of silvery hair had now gone from her life for good. Lisa knew she would miss her.

But she also knew that this was how it was supposed to be, although she couldn't have explained what she meant by that.

The sun shone down upon the perfect summer's day. With a smile, Lisa headed into the crowd and hurried to catch up with Jake. She didn't want to miss a single moment of what was coming next.

EPILOGUE

Mrs Wishmore walked along the pavement, leaving the summer fair and the school grounds behind.

Today had been a good day.

Things had worked out in the end between Lisa and Jake, and no one could have been more thrilled about that than Mrs Wishmore. The two young folk had taken a chance on themselves and on each other, and they both deserved the happiness she hoped they would now find. As the laughter and chatter from the fair faded into the distance, Mrs Wishmore thought about the sweet couple she'd left behind and wondered what lay in store for them.

In her mind, she saw a kindling romance and deep friendship and… yes, she saw love, too.

Jake was already in love, of course. He'd been falling for Lisa since the first moment they'd met. But soon, Lisa would fall in love, too, and when that happened, the young woman's heart would be healed and whole again.

Mrs Wishmore saw other glimpses of the young couple's future as she walked. She saw a wedding day with spring daffodils and blue skies, and a bride so beautiful that she glowed, and a groom struck speechless in adoration. She saw a cute little dog, Ruby, scampering around the feet of the happy couple and making them laugh on their happy day. She saw glimpses of the children Lisa and Jake would have one day, and the house in which they'd live together in Willowbridge, and all the wonderful years they'd spend there. Catching these glimpses, and feeling the love that filled them, made Mrs Wishmore very happy indeed.

No life ever avoided its share of heartbreak and grief and disappointment. But from now on, Lisa and Jake would find their way through those trials together.

Mrs Wishmore turned onto Willowbridge high street, which was quiet today on account of so many folk attending the summer fair at the high school. As she passed the Daffodil Café, she paused and looked inside, taking in the soft yellow walls and the daffodil paintings and the warm friendliness that imbued the place. She had enjoyed the time she'd spent there, helping Lisa navigate troubled waters, and she would cherish the memories she was now taking with her.

Mrs Wishmore knew it was important to keep those memories safe, because eventually she would be the only one who remembered them. Soon, Lisa would forget the face of the temporary waitress who'd once come to work at the Daffodil Café, and her memories of the older lady who'd helped her out of a tight spot would fade away. Lisa would move on and forget about the mysterious stranger who'd come into her life and helped her to transform it. Everyone else who Mrs Wishmore had met here would soon forget about her, too.

That was how it had always been where Mrs Wishmore's work was concerned and it was how it always would be.

But that didn't stop Mrs Wishmore from remembering

those she'd met and those she'd helped. She would remember Lisa and Jake, and of course sweet little Ruby, as she continued on her way.

Along the road from the Daffodil Café, a gentle breeze moved through the trees that lined the village green, rustling their leaves. It was time to move on. So many people in the world were lost and discouraged and wishing for a miracle… or at least for a helping hand from a kindly stranger. And when Mrs Wishmore heard those wishes, she would be ready.

Mrs Wishmore walked to the bus stop at the top of the high street. A bus arrived and its doors swung open. She took one last look around the pretty little town of Willowbridge before boarding the bus and paying the driver and finding a seat by the window.

The bus pulled away from the kerb and began its journey, carrying Mrs Wishmore off to her next destination. She smiled and wondered what adventure lay in store for her next.

A MESSAGE FROM ALIX

Dear Reader

I've always had a soft spot for angel stories, thanks to all the magical Christmas films I've loved ever since I was young. Park me in front of *It's A Wonderful Life* or *The Bishop's Wife* or *One Magic Christmas* and I'll savour every scene and then cry my eyes out at the end. There's something deeply comforting about the idea of a guardian angel appearing at our side just when we need it most and helping to show us the way.

I'm not religious in the conventional sense of the term, but I am spiritual and I believe that there are wonders out there in the universe we can't even begin to imagine, let alone understand. I also believe that love and hope always win, and that when we look for magic in our lives, we always find it. And the most magical thing about Mrs Wishmore is that she doesn't transform people into something they're not, or erase their troubles with one easy wave of a wand – instead, she simply reminds people to trust their hearts, find their courage, keep going even when it's hard, and have faith that there are better days to come. For me, those are the greatest miracles we can hope for in life.

Thank you for reading *A Wish At The Daffodil Cafe* and I hope you'll join Mrs Wishmore again soon. Until next time...

Alix Kelso
May 2022

Mrs Wishmore will return soon for a new adventure. While you're waiting for Book 2, you might enjoy the short stories I wrote featuring her. I recommend starting with her lovely tale in ***A Dog's Heart And Other Stories***.

Stay in touch
If you'd like to hear about new book news, then join my Reader's Club and I'll also send you an exclusive and heartwarming book to enjoy. Pop over to my website at www.alixkelso.com to sign up.

Please consider leaving a review
If you enjoyed this book, I'd be so grateful if you'd leave a review at the store where you bought it. Reviews are very helpful for readers searching for new books and for authors hoping for new readers. Thank you.

ABOUT THE AUTHOR

Alix Kelso writes warm-hearted stories about romance, friendship and family. She's happiest with her nose in a book and loves being whisked off to imaginary story worlds. Alix lives in Glasgow with her husband, where she enjoys pottering in the kitchen, exploring the great outdoors, and buying far too many Christmas decorations.

Alix loves to hear from her readers, and you can find her online on Facebook, Instagram and Twitter at @AlixKel-soAuthor.

Visit her website at www.alixkelso.com

ALSO BY ALIX KELSO

The Fairhill Series

The Perfect Moment (Book 1)

The Next Forever (Book 2)

The Magic Hour (Book 3)

A Little Romance (Novella)

The Story Collections

A Dog's Heart and Other Stories

The Food Of Love and Other Stories

A Dream Of Christmas and Other Stories

The Magic of Christmas and Other Stories

Home Sweet Home and Other Stories

Mrs Wishmore Series

A Wish At The Daffodil Cafe

Printed in Great Britain
by Amazon

19661611R00181